XENA
WARRIOR PRINCESS ™

THE THIEF OF HERMES

A novel by
Ru Emerson

based on the Universal television series
created by John Schulian and Robert Tapert

BOULEVARD BOOKS, NEW YORK

XENA: WARRIOR PRINCESS: THE THIEF OF HERMES

A novel by Ru Emerson. Based on the Universal television series *XENA:
WARRIOR PRINCESS*, created by John Schulian and Robert Tapert.

A Boulevard Book / published by arrangement with
MCA Publishing Rights, a Division of MCA, Inc.

PRINTING HISTORY
Boulevard edition / March 1997

The Putnam Berkley World Wide Web site address is
http://www.berkley.com/berkley

Make sure to check out *PB Plug*, the science fiction/fantasy newsletter, at
http://www.pbplug.com

ISBN: 1-57297-232-7

BOULEVARD
Boulevard Books are published by The Berkley Publishing Group,
200 Madison Avenue, New York, New York 10016.
BOULEVARD and its logo are trademarks
belonging to Berkley Publishing Corporation.

PRINTED IN THE UNITED STATES OF AMERICA

10 9 8 7 6 5 4 3 2 1

To Doug
of the rainbow-colored fiberglass leg,

to Roberta,
who still hopes I'll abandon that dratted computer
and hug with her full-time,

and to my invaluable editor,
Barry Neville,
for his support, great editing, and useful suggestions

Acknowledgments

Once again, I'd like to thank the fans of the show, especially the America Online fans. I have never met a more helpful, friendly, caring, and kind group of people, and I have greatly enjoyed our weekly chat sessions—this from a woman who long regarded on-line ''chats'' with a wary kind of horror, and feared ugly flame wars on all sides.

In particular, I would like to thank Lucia Correa, who did a splendid job of helping me the past several months, whether it was coordinating contests, interfacing with the fan groups I couldn't reach, or locating arcane bits of information about the show for me when I had no time to dig them out myself. Lucia, you've gone above and beyond, and become a good friend in the process.

Prologue

The wine market was even more crowded late than it had been early, three days before, Xena noted with sour displeasure. And just about as safe: purse snatchings or jewelry grabs seemed to run as counterpoint to the cries of the merchants seeking to pull in buyers. Even the addition of more guards stationed visibly around the market didn't seem to make much difference.

One notable change—and not a pleasant one. It was much louder than it had been, when she and Gabrielle had come looking for the women's foot races.

If I hadn't made that promise, we could have been long gone, she reminded herself. The mess with Atalanta had kept her from keeping her promise to the skinny little kid in the wine market who'd tried to steal her purse: *You don't try to steal from me and my companions, and I'll pay you two coppers.* The skinny, ragged little cutpurse hadn't touched her for the rest of that day, though—or Gabrielle, or Homer. He'd kept his word; she couldn't do any less, even if she kept it long after she'd said she would. And while the two coppers she'd promised him might not change his thieving ways, they might give him something to think about.

He'd been startled when she finally tracked him down, just at sunset. Then suspicious: "Why bother? No one honors their word anymore, do they?"

Her reply left him wide-eyed: "I do. And so do you. I'm only sorry I couldn't deliver when I said I would—"

He interrupted her. "I know why; everyone's talking about it. They said you're Xena." Not quite a question.

She nodded. "I'm Xena. Who're you?"

He gazed at her narrowly, and for a moment she thought he wouldn't answer. He finally shrugged. "I'm Kratos. But—I really want to know: Why? Why come back here to pay out two coppers? To me? I mean—" He stopped, then added carefully, explaining as much to himself as to her, "All you had to do was leave Athens; we'd never see each other again. But even if you stayed here forever, who'd *make* you pay someone like me? When it wasn't even for anything real?"

"It *was* real, Kratos. We made a bargain; you kept your end of it. And I don't do things that way. I swore an oath to you. Honorable people keep them. Like you did."

"Honorable," he spat; but a grin tugged at the corners of a ready mouth as he pocketed the two coppers. "You've fed my mother and me four nights to come with these coins, warrior. She'll thank you tonight, when she prays to Artemis."

"Tell her to pray her son becomes an honest man," the warrior replied sardonically. At that, Kratos's mouth had quirked in an amused, beyond-his-years grin and then he was gone.

Gabrielle was talking; Xena shook off the immediate past and tried to pay attention. "I said, when do you plan on

2

eating? Because that stand was so busy when I took Arachne for food, we had to go somewhere else, and it was okay but not really that great. And frankly, it's dark out, it's late, and I'm starved.''

''Told you,'' Xena said evenly. Furtive fingers slipped along her thigh; she slapped them away, hard enough to make their owner howl in agony. ''Your good-smelling stand poisoned everyone who ate there. And I don't want to spend another night in Athens, if I can help it.''

''I don't blame you, there,'' Gabrielle replied feelingly. ''I can't believe how big this city's gotten since I was here last! And some of the attitudes—really!'' She struck a pose, somehow managing to keep up with Argo and her mistress as she simpered: '' 'I'd like the best and the finest, I can pay for it, I've earned it and *you* haven't, and by the way, get out of the way between me and my home, I was due there an hour ago, and I'll run right over you to make up the time, if I have to. And *by* the way, don't touch the chariot, it was just repolished at the best shop in town.' ''

Xena laughed dryly, looking around at the oblivious bustle of commerce. ''Yeah. More I see of Athens, more I think poor little Lemnos was right: Spread the wealth.''

''Didn't spend any time with him,'' Gabrielle admitted. ''But from what you said of him, I'm glad he's there to both feed Queen Penelope and train her servants and herders in weaponry, so they can protect her if they have to. Until the King gets home, that is.''

''If he ever does,'' Xena replied.

''Oh—he will,'' Gabrielle replied cheerfully. ''I just have a feeling about it. In fact, I had a dream last night—can't remember much of it.'' She frowned. ''Just—Nausicaa standing in salt water to her ankles and a gray-haired man talking to her.''

"And you think it was a vision," Xena stated, her voice sardonic.

"Well—I get them, now and again, you know," Gabrielle replied seriously. "I mean, look at what happened in Ithaca . . . No, but my dream: it *had* to be him. Odysseus, I mean. Because, the sound of her voice—" She shrugged. "Anyway. Not half as important as *food* just now. Have I mentioned lately I ate my own stew, without complaint, for three days in a row?"

"Not in, oh, maybe an hour," Xena reminded her, with an upturn at the corners of her mouth. "It could have been worse, though—it could have been *me* doing the cooking." Gabrielle snorted; the warrior grinned. "But I know an inn near the western end of the city, good food, cheap." The grin became wry. "Lots of ambience, the way you like it."

"*No* fights," Gabrielle said firmly. "Last time we ate somewhere like *that,* some two-footed rat kicked my plate right off the table, and it took forever to get more food, *and* it was cold when I got it. And *I* know an inn near the western end of the city, too; and it better not be the same place! Even from the street, the smell would gag your friend the cyclops."

"He's not *my* friend. And what—you mean that place where those three men jumped you on our way to the races? That's not an inn," Xena replied. "That's a disaster. It's not that far, where we're going. If we keep moving that is," she added mildly as Gabrielle slowed to gaze in wide-eyed astonishment at some of the wares, most notably a hideous platter large enough to hold a roasted boar and garishly glazed in every color of the rainbow.

"Mmmmm?" She came back to the moment with a start as the warrior tapped her arm. "Oh—right. So. Where are we going next? *After* food, that is!"

"Don't know. Out of Athens first. Probably south after

4

that. I don't have any plans, though. Anything you'd like to see or do, Gabrielle?''

Gabrielle smiled ruefully and shook her head. "After the choice I made this time? Not a chance!"

Xena tugged on Argo's rein and edged them around a pudgy man in gold and blue stripes who was hawking a tray of small glazed clay ornaments, right in the midst of the walkway. "Don't take blame for things going wrong, Gabrielle. Not this time, at least."

Gabrielle sighed and shook her head. "Well, I don't, you know. It's just that—everything got so complicated!"

"The situation could've been tragic, if you hadn't insisted on coming to the races," Xena reminded her. "I'm not angry."

"Good. But—no, there's nothing special I want to see, or do." She drew a deep breath, then expelled it in a sigh. "Except eat."

Xena laughed. "Almost out of the market. It won't take long after that, I promise." But several moments later, she drew Argo to a halt, turned, and gazed out across the milling crowd, seaward, and when Gabrielle laughed and would have said something dryly witty, she held up a hand for silence. A deep, gruff male voice rose above the babble of excited shoppers, momentarily silencing it.

"I *told* you to put that coin where no one could get at it! Now look what's happened, you grubby little fool!" A hard crack followed, as an open palm cracked across flesh, then a boy's shrill cry of pain.

"I swear, I *did*! But he—" Another pained yelp, this one dissolving into sobs. People began moving away from the unpleasantness, a few casting disapproving looks at the maker of the scene, but most attempting to look as though they'd suddenly remembered something important they had to do, well away from here. All at once the warrior could

5

see a black-haired, scruffy brute of a man looming over a boy no larger than the little thief she'd just paid.

"Stop that whining," the man growled, "or I'll give you reason to whine!" The open hand clenched into a fist; the boy hiccuped and gulped, cowering back into a corner.

Xena swore under her breath, shoved the reins into Gabrielle's hands, closed Gabrielle's fingers around the leather strands, and leveled one of her own fingers at Gabrielle's nose. "Wait here, don't do *anything*. I'll be right back." She stalked across the now empty market grounds, came just up behind the man and boy, and tapped the larger of the two on the shoulder, hard. He turned, scowling furiously. Xena raised one eyebrow and gazed back at him, her face expressionless. Silence. He sneered and began turning back to the boy. Xena's mild voice stopped him. "I wouldn't do that, if I were you."

"Back off, you half-clad hussy," he snarled. "The boy's none of your business."

"I just made him my business," Xena replied flatly; her hands clamped on the man's arm and she spun him around. Two loud open-handed smacks followed, and then a blur of motion: the big man went flying, completed a full loop in midair, and landed flat on his back several paces away. He groaned once, then went limp. Xena's mouth twitched; she turned away and knelt before the still shivering child. "Boy," she said quietly. "That your father?"

The boy was sniffling quietly, staring in awe at the motionless brute. He started, then shook his head violently. "No. My papa was—he was nice. But he went to Troy and never came back. That's—" He licked his lips. "That's Olinus. He wants to marry my mama."

"He's hit you like this before?" The boy gave her a woebegone look and turned red, then nodded. She patted his head gently. "It's not your fault, all right? No kid could deserve getting hit that hard. He hit you when your mother's around?''

He shook his head. ''She wouldn't ever let him do that. My uncles—they live with mama and me—they wouldn't let him, either.''

''You didn't tell them he hit you, did you?'' The boy shook his head again; his eyes touched on the now moaning brute and flinched away. Xena's gaze narrowed. ''He scared you, so you wouldn't, that it?'' He bit his quivering lip, nodded. Better than it might be, she thought with relief, then gently shook him by one shoulder. ''All right. It's gonna be all right. You leave now, before he wakes up. Tell your mother *and* your uncles. I'll take care of Olinus.''

The boy nodded timidly. ''Thank you,'' he whispered, then turned and ducked back into the crowd that had gathered to stare at the fallen man, his attacker, and the boy. Xena closed her eyes briefly and sighed as she got to her feet. *Where were all of you when that child was being clobbered by someone three times his size?* She stalked over to stand, arms folded, above the groaning Olinus.

''I know you can hear me,'' she said finally. He opened one red-rimmed eye and glared up at her; the eye closed again when it found her looking back. ''Now, you listen to me. You're going to leave that boy alone. The boy *and* his mother.''

He tried to sit up; she shoved him flat with her boot and held him there. ''I don't take orders from no one,'' he spat.

''Oh, yes you do,'' Xena murmured. ''You won't like the alternative.''

''You got lucky,'' he growled.

''Fine.'' She stepped back a pace, flexed her hands, and grinned down at him, an expression that didn't reach her ice-cold eyes. ''Wanna try again?'' When he didn't move, her smile broadened, and she pitched her voice to reach the

7

murmuring crowd around them. "What I thought. You do just fine against children but anything bigger scares you, right? Like that boy's uncles? Me? Maybe the city guard?" She glanced over her shoulder. "Any of you! You see this brute hitting that boy—*any* child!—again, you report him *immediately* to one of the King's guards. That doesn't take anything but a mouth, and you've all got those." Silence. A middle-aged woman glared at her resentfully, mumbled something under her breath, and shuffled off. Xena glanced around her: people surrounded her and Olinus five deep. Gabrielle stood where she had been left, Argos's reins wound around her hand. Somewhere beyond her was the usual shouting; someone had just been robbed.

The commotion was heading their way, from the sound of things. Time to go. Xena brushed her hands together and gave Olinus one final hard look, then leveled a long finger at his nose. "I don't want to see you, or hear of you, again. Or there won't be enough left of you to fit in one of those wine cups over there. Got it?" Before he could answer, she turned to find a way through the crowd. Two women stopped her, a tall, pale girl and an older woman like enough to be her mother.

"Warrior, thank you," the older one murmured. "I've tried myself to protect the boy, but Olinus—" Her voice faded as someone nearby yelled, "Stop that boy! Thief!"

"Just remember what I said," Xena told her. Something was going on, up there: Gabrielle looked startled and Argo shied. The warrior patted the older woman's shoulder and eased around her.

Gabrielle had been standing on tiptoe, trying vainly to see what was going on, but as the crowd of silent onlookers grew, she couldn't even make out Xena, let alone the boy and the felled brute. She finally sighed and settled back on

8

her heels as the small boy, a red handprint clearly marking the entire right side of his face, ran past her. "Guess everything's settled," she murmured. Argo lipped her hair and she gave the mare a shove. "Poor little kid. I wonder what—" She broke off as shouts echoed from farther up the market, the way they'd just come. "Great. *Now* what?"

The crowd back that way was thinning rapidly, the reason for it suddenly apparent: sprinting toward her was the golden-haired boy who'd flashed past three days earlier, a couple of guards in hot pursuit but steadily losing ground. He ran with Atalanta's grace, that golden beauty. *Beautiful—and just as flawed, in his own way,* Gabrielle thought sadly.

A woman shrieked and leaped aside as the boy tore past. Gabrielle stared, mouth open; he was coming straight for her. Argo shifted, then began to back away from the oncoming source of the commotion, dragging her along. The boy shouted something at the guards trailing him—a taunt from the sound of his voice, though Gabrielle couldn't make out the words—then veered so he was on a collision course with her. Deeply amused, intensely aqua eyes met hers; a mobile and generous mouth quirked in a broad grin. "Catch!" he yelled cheerfully, then tossed a bag to her, shifted direction, and plunged into the crowd beyond her. Gabrielle automatically snatched at the small pouch, it was heavy. Blankly, she stared at the leather purse she'd just caught, then at the two enormous men in King's colors and tall, crested bronze helms who suddenly stood, grim-faced, before her. The bag fell from her hands with a loud *chink,* and she turned to point.

"He went that way," she began; two heavy hands fell on her shoulders, dragging her back around. "Hey!" she protested vigorously. "He went *that* way! Aren't you gonna go after him?"

"We know who he is," one of the guards said flatly. "And now we know why we never catch him with the goods; he's got an accomplice!"

"An a— An accomplice?" Gabrielle broke into nervous laughter. It faded as two grim-faced guards eyed her closely. "Look—you're kidding, right?" No reaction. "Ah—right. *Not* kidding, gotcha! But, look, I'm a stranger in Athens, just came to watch the women's races—"

"Women's races!" A familiar, whiny, reedy male voice came from behind her. Gabrielle glanced warily over her shoulder. Agrinon stood there, flexing his hands. "I might have known you'd be at the center of any trouble," he added flatly.

"Is there a problem here?" Xena's voice overrode whatever else he might have said.

"No problem!" Gabrielle replied brightly, then glanced at the fat purse lying at her feet and managed a rueful smile. "Well—maybe a *little* problem, but nothing we can't fix, okay?" Her mouth twitched nervously; Xena cast up her eyes, then turned to face the guards—now six in number.

"Look," she said persuasively, "I don't know what's happened here, but if it was illegal, I can assure you Gabrielle had no part in it. She's my companion, and—"

"Told you," Agrinon growled to his fellow guards. "No wonder we never catch the little creep, he's got *two* women to catch for him!" Xena started for him; someone whistled shrilly, and six swords were immediately out and at her throat, while ten more guards came pelting from half a dozen directions to join the six. The warrior glared around her, then transferred the dire gaze to Gabrielle, who looked as if she didn't know whether to smile or grimace as she gave the warrior a slightly dazed shrug. "Right," Agrinon said, his chest swelling with self-importance. "Guess the King'll be pleased to hear about *this* turn of events!"

10

"I'm sure," Xena murmured through clenched teeth. "Gabrielle?"

"I did nothing—I swear!" She threw her arms out in a broad shrug, then drew them hastily in as three swords shifted in her direction. "Sorry! Ah—if you wouldn't mind *not* poking me with those, I just washed this outfit and it's awfully hard to get blood out of this particular weave? Um—" She swallowed, and let her eyes flicker in Xena's direction. "Look, I know we can straighten this all out, really easily, it's just—it's a mistake, that's all! And—well, at least in prison we'll get fed, right?" She managed a faint smile as her companion cast up her eyes, spread her arms in surrender, and let the guards take her weaponry. Agrinon snatched the staff from Gabrielle's fingers. "Probably a lot sooner than if we'd walked across Athens to reach your inn."

"Probably," Xena murmured, and bit back a smile as Agrinon eagerly snatched the chakra from her belt and then swore as it cut his thumb. "So, how'd you acquire the purse?" she asked as the guards took both women by the arms and began to hustle them out of the silent, still-crowded market.

Gabrielle eyed her sidelong. "Purse—oh. *That* purse. Golden Boy—remember him? the thief?—tossed it right into my lap. You wait till I get my hands on him," she added angrily, "pulling a stunt like this! I'll pull every last hair out of his head—one at a time!" Agrinon snarled something inaudible, though Gabrielle caught the general meaning; she turned to glower at him. "Don't you try to make this personal," she said flatly. "I know about the rules the King's guard has to follow, and I'll report you if you even *think* about breaking them!"

"Leave be, Agrinon," another guardsman snapped—one

with a minor officer's badge. Agrinon's expression tightened but he backed away.

Gabrielle turned to look at Xena as they were pulled past wide-eyed, staring market patrons. The warrior's face was unreadable, but Gabrielle didn't think Agrinon had much of a chance, judging from the cold set of her eyes.

1

Things had changed, indeed, since the last time Xena had walked Athens: the wine market and surrounding area now had its own jail, a nearly new building walled all around, with a separate small stable for horses, a weapons room, a smithy, and a cook's building. The central structure was squat, built of enormous dressed stones impressively mortared together; beneath it was a large dungeon. The floor of the dungeon was comprised of massive blocks of granite, while the walls were the same heavily mortared stone of which the aboveground structure was made. The only place where light and air entered was one barred opening too narrow for even a woman Gabrielle's size to slide through. Outside the main cell room was a hallway, and though prisoners could hear the echoing footsteps of guards across its floor of polished blue marble, if they pressed their faces to the narrow opening in the heavily barred and braced cell door, they could also feel on their cheeks the open breeze from three tantalizingly unguarded windows.

Wind blew from the west at the moment, across the prison's walled grounds, invading the cell's sole window and

13

filling the chamber with dust and the smell of fresh horse manure. Argo was in that stable, Xena knew. The mare hadn't liked leaving her, and the guards hadn't liked letting her take the time to whisper against the golden ear, but that had saved the situation for everyone, in the long run. *They'd have been dead, or flattened, every single one of them,* Xena knew with grim certainty. *Argo would have attacked, and even twenty of them would have been no match for the pair of us—and Gabrielle, of course,* she reminded herself easily, with a sidelong glance at her very still companion. Gabrielle wasn't at all the liability she'd once been; at the moment, she was pale with fury and muttering something under her breath—a curse against that pale-haired market cutpurse, perhaps. Probably.

Yes. She and I could have fought, Xena thought, *both of us and Argo—the guard wouldn't have stood a chance.* But injuring or killing guards trying to do their duty wasn't what she did—not anymore. And there had been so many unarmed shoppers all around them; those people hadn't come to the market searching for a fight. Had it been only them against the stupid, stubborn, blind guards, the outcome might have been different. Xena took a deep breath, feeling the rage well up within her. *Those guards were only doing their job, and it isn't up to you to murder guardsmen for simple bad manners.* Though admittedly, one or two of them had pressed the boundaries as far as that was concerned. The one Gabrielle called Agrinon, for starters. "Agrinon," Xena murmured, with an unpleasant smile. "I'm going to remember that name."

No, she and Gabrielle certainly didn't have any responsibility to train King Theseus's guards in the niceties of courtesy. Then again, hanging out in a place like *this* wasn't a good compromise. *You could have beat in a few skulls, left behind a few headaches and a few choice words about jumping innocent strangers in the market: the smart ones would have learned something from the experience. And the rest—well, they won't last long in a city like this. Either someone with good fighting skills and Draco's temper will murder them, or the King will grow sense and send them out to herd goats. Skinny ones.*

If King Theseus hadn't changed from the man she'd once met, things would probably work out that way. She shook that off, flexed her hands with a deliberate motion, squared her shoulders, and carefully examined her surroundings. A dozen or more men—most grubby and very rough-looking, some drunk—occupied the one-room cell at present. Four who'd been sizing her up while she considered matters suddenly seemed to remember other things they needed to do—immediately. A fifth—notably staggering and reeking of bad drink—was persuaded by his two companions to find a bench on the far side of the cell, as quickly as they could get his feet moving.

The only other women besides Xena and Gabrielle circulated cheerfully among the men, inciting laughter and a few desperately rapt stares. The women's tight, brightly colored clothing, thickly applied makeup, and resolutely coarse style of speech and presentation served as a walking advertisement for *their* business, as well as their reason for being here. A gaunt man in some sort of priest's brown sackcloth glared at the women, until someone else—a much larger and visibly muscled someone—tapped him on the shoulder and shook his head briefly.

Far from all this, on a low, long bench in the corner, someone to all appearances seemed sound asleep. Xena peered curiously in that direction, then finally shrugged. The figure was so cloaked in shadow; Xena couldn't make out any detail at all. She wasn't even sure if it was a male or a female. Actually, she couldn't even really be sure if it was still alive.

Gabrielle eyed the chamber warily, then, following Xena's lead, squinted in the direction of the dark, seemingly un-inhabited corner. She couldn't make out anything worth-while. At least something in this cell was no threat, at the moment, she thought. She sighed very faintly, cast her companion a sidelong, abashed smile, then crossed to another, unoccupied wooden bench opposite the door, drew her legs up, crossed her ankles, braced her elbows on her knees, and settled her back against the wall. Xena said something under her breath, and then followed.

Gabrielle bit back another sigh and let her eyes close briefly. She allowed her head to rest against the cool, sub-terranean stone. *So how do I convince her the whole mess out there in the market really was not my fault? I mean—what was I supposed to do? I was staying out of trouble just fine, unlike Xena, I could add. Though I hardly blame her, if it had been up to me, I'd probably have clobbered that brute myself. But there I was, holding onto Argo, mind-ing my own business, and then—that lousy kid!* . . . Her thoughts took a dark—and momentarily—very pleasant—turn as she thought of several different endings to that scene in the market. Golden Boy flat on his back, eyes closed, her thick and ornate staff against his chin and the heavy coin purse sliding from his nerveless fingers just as the guard came up. Or herself throwing the bag back to Golden Boy, who caught it and stood there looking like a dummy as the guard came up. Or—*or anything but this,* she thought glumly. *Us here, a worried Argo in the stable, that stupid Agrinon out there somewhere, smugly aware he's caught us—and Xena next to me radiating pure fury.*

But when she opened her eyes and turned to her companion, Xena didn't look particularly furious. She was sitting next to Gabrielle, legs crossed on the bench the same way, eyes moving from clutch of men to single man, to men and women, never still as she evaluated those with whom they shared the cell.

Look around yourself, you. Do something right for a change, Gabrielle ordered herself. *She's always having to tell you to do that.*

From against this far wall, the chamber appeared much larger than it had; the floor was rough-dressed but dry, as were the walls. *Well, that's one good thing. There's nothing worse to my mind than a damp cell—unless it's a dry, web-filled one. Brrr! Wonder how poor little Arachne is doing, if that stupid Agrinon is still pestering her.* She dismissed the mental chatter, cast the motionless and intent Xena another sidelong glance, and went back to her study of the locked room and its inhabitants. Benches of the same rough stone had been placed throughout the cell, and in no particular pattern she could make out. No cushions, of course, though the stone under her wasn't that uncomfortable at the moment: neither overly rough, nor cold, nor damp. Thanks to the one small window high in the wall, and to those framing the long hallway that ran outside the far cell wall, the air was reasonably clean and fresh. Judging by the nearest men she could see—three brutes clad in greasy brown rags whose color surely owed more to history than to origin, and just beyond them, four drunkenly loud fellows who were arguing loudly over the merits of some alehouse and its nearest rival—the smell could have been much worse.

Several of the benches, like the one she and Xena had just taken over, were empty: there appeared to be enough of them for each to hold three occupants, seated. Sleeping would be another matter. *Maybe we'll get lucky, and we won't be here to find out about that,* she thought. *Right.*

Maybe this particular bench at the far wall of the cell wasn't a coveted perch. They'd be sleeping in turns tonight anyway, but it would be nice if they didn't have to fight for a bed. *This is where I can help,* Gabrielle decided, and leaned forward to study her fellow prisoners, the stone benches they occupied, and the empty benches.

Two benches near the entry were full; a third was apparently the object of a brief but fierce scuffle. The most popular of all was obviously the one with the window. Four grubby men had just begun fighting for possession of the view, but all activity ceased and the squabblers were suddenly quiet as someone in the hallway pounded on the bars. Outside the jail cell, two massive armor-clad and helmed men armed with javelins and drawn swords flanked a small, pale man who bore a long tray that had been heaped high with long, dark loaves and four teetering stacks of wooden bowls. Before him, two young boys staggered under the weight of a padded bar from which a heavy, fire-blackened pot hung from thick chains. They managed to get it down without incident, then each took a stack of bowls and, with a glance at the motionless and grim-faced guards, stood very still, waiting.

"All right!" one of the guards shouted. "You know the drill! Those of you too stupid or drunk to remember, or those of you who're new, I'll explain it just once, right now! You come over here one at a time! You keep your hands out, away from your bodies, you keep your fingers spread, and you move slowly! You do exactly what I say, when I say it, and you don't come forward to the bars until I tell you! You collect a bowl and a loaf, then you back away, slowly, carefully—and you go someplace *well* away from this front area entirely before you sit down to eat! Any argument with that procedure, we leave right now!

Anyone breaks the rules, we leave right now, and the rest of you go hungry the night!''

A bulky man in tattered gray rags detached himself from the window and grinned hugely, exposing dreadful teeth. ''Isn't none of us gonna go hungry here, Bernardius,'' he replied in a drink-hoarsened voice. We know the rules, and we'll hold to 'em.''

''See you do, Mondavius,'' the guard snapped back.

Mondavius glared impartially around him, and when one of the men who'd occupied the bench next to him snorted in contempt, the ragged man simply slammed a fist down onto the crown of his head. The man fell bonelessly to the floor. ''Happen I'll get his bowl and bread to *save* for him, of course,'' he added with another grin.

Bernardius cast up his eyes and his supple mouth curled humorlessly beneath his thick, black mustache. ''Usual payment, Mondavius,'' he snapped.

''Usual payment,'' Mondavius agreed, and scratched absentmindedly with ragged nails at a dirty pockmarked cheek.

''Ah—hey,'' Gabrielle murmured under her breath as she averted her eyes. ''The ambience is enough for the moment, right? And it looks like there's plenty of food, so I'm willing to wait, how about you?''

''The way that smells? I'll wait forever.'' Xena replied sotto voce. ''At least you've got your ambience; let's hope my nose isn't working right.''

Gabrielle smiled. ''Smells okay to me. And I'm hungry enough I could eat *anything*.''

Some time later, she set the rough-carved wooden bowl aside firmly and shook her head. ''I can't eat this.''

Xena gave her *that* look, then cast her eyes toward the ceiling. ''Then I think I'm in trouble.''

Gabrielle forced a laugh. "Well—but maybe the bread's all right." She picked up the loaf and eyed it dubiously, sniffed cautiously, then pulled a small chunk from one end and bit into it. Her face cleared; she took another bite— much larger, this—and nodded sharply. "Hey. Wow, amazing! The bread's absolutely *great*! Even better than that nuts-and-fruit stuff Isyphus made us, back in that village of the Trickster King's."

"Really," Xena murmured. She scooped up the heavy lump of bread, bit into it; her eyebrows went up and she tucked the bite into her cheek to mumble, "One for you, Gabrielle. This stuff's almost worth your fabled ambience—well, *almost*," she added sourly, as she looked around the cell and let her eyes rest on the large, ragged Mondavius, who growled at her, his own eyes all pupil and very black. Gabrielle, her cheekbones and the tip of her nose bright pink, glanced her companion's way, quirked her mouth in an apologetic grin, and went back to her bread.

Xena got to her feet, shoved the wooden bowl of stew well to the side, and strode to the window. Four different men occupied the bench at the moment. She tugged at the sandal strap of one then the ragged britches-leg of another. Two grubby, ugly-visaged men turned to glower down at her. She offered them a chill, faint smile, and a deprecating speech. "If you don't mind, I'd like to see what's out there myself." The sandal wearer squared his shoulders, then spat in her direction. Xena easily ducked, gave him a teeth-only grin, and tossed him head over heels across the cell, where he lay flat and unmoving and whimpering. The ragged man urgently nudged and elbowed his companions, tilted his head toward Xena, and then, even more frantically, toward their unconscious comrade. The three edged warily back from her, one slow pace at a time, then abruptly quit the bench. "Thanks," Xena murmured, leaping neatly onto the bench and gazing out the window, across the market guards' parade ground. There was activity everywhere: many wore the King's colors, while a few ragged ruffians or maybe impoverished fellows were dragged into the compound by the brightly clad guards—no way, at the moment, to simply slip away without causing havoc in some fashion. *The time'll come. Wait for it.*

Behind her, she could hear one of the men snarling something and she glanced over her shoulder. Gabrielle no longer occupied the bench; her bowl of inedible stew held pride of place; wisps of indubitably nasty steam rose from the rough wooden bowl. No clue as to who might be snarling at whom—but Gabrielle appeared to be no part of it. For once. Xena cast her eyes ceilingward and went back to her study of the parade ground.

Across the cell, Gabrielle gazed up at the bulky Mondavius, who bared his blackened, uneven teeth at her in what he might have thought was a grin; his left hand held his bread, while the right was an enormous claw, ready to snatch at her. "Think you didn't hear me right, little girl," he growled. "Said we'll trade for the stew."

Gabrielle sent her eyes right, left. The bench where her bowl sat was five long paces away—through Mondavius. *Could've traded him a face full of the hot stuff; that'd fix him.* At the moment, though—well, there wasn't much of a way out at the moment. *Right. He's got you backed into a corner, Gabrielle. Where's Xena the one time you could use her?* She smiled brightly then. Mondavius's scowl turned wary; his grip tightened on the bread, nearly halving it. "Trade—oh! Great! You know, I was really hoping that bowl of—stew, is it?—well I was hoping it wouldn't go to waste. You see, I'm trying to watch my weight, and—"

21

"Don't be more of an idiot than you can help!" the brute snapped; his breath was ghastly. Her nose wrinkled. *Wonder how long I can keep from inhaling,* Gabrielle thought. Mondavius snatched at the bread in her hand and tightened his grasp on his own mostly flattened loaf. "You don't get it, do you, little girl? All right—give me your bread, you get to keep your stew. *And* your life!"

"My—oh—you want my bread?" Gabrielle glanced at her half-eaten loaf, tore a huge chunk from it, and stuffed it hurriedly in her mouth. "Don't think so," she mumbled indistinctly around the bite. Mondavius roared and snatched for her, but she wasn't where he expected; crouching, she slammed her heel into his right kneecap, sending him forward, hands-first into the wall. Gabrielle whirled to one side, ducked hurriedly under his arm as he began to sag, then spun back to face him, left hand still clinging to her half-eaten loaf.

But he wasn't there anymore. Gabrielle blinked, then stared at her would-be assailant. The blank-eyed, grubby brute was splayed half sideways along the back wall, a good five paces from the corner where he'd accosted her. His eyes slowly closed and he slid limply to the floor. Xena brushed her hands together, snatched the uneaten loaf from his nerveless fingers, then tugged at her companion's shirt and muttered, "Better finish that now, don't you think?"

"Ahhhh—Oh! The bread! Right!" Gabrielle swallowed, divided the rest of the bread into two bites, tucked the first one in her cheek, and balled the second in her left fist. "Good idea. And thanks!"

Xena rolled a quarter of the loaf into a large pellet, tossed it high, caught it between her teeth, chewed briefly, then pressed the rest into her cheek and nodded. "Anytime. I'm gonna go claim the window again. Air's better up there, and besides, I might see some way to get us out of here. Stay out of trouble, okay?"

Gabrielle gestured broadly with both arms. "Hey," she replied dryly. "What trouble can I get into in here?" Xena uttered a snort that might have been laughter, and went back to the window. In her absence, three more men had taken up occupation of the window bench; as Gabrielle regained her own seat and set the rapidly cooling—and congealing—bowl of stew on the floor, she noticed with amusement that the warrior had only to clear her throat, and all three brutes scattered.

Noise in the hallway momentarily silenced the cell's inhabitants, and brought men and women alike forward to stare toward the outer world. Gabrielle stood on her bench and gazed over their heads as two guards dragged a tall, pale-haired, manacled prisoner between them. *Familiar— do I know him?* she wondered. *But this is Athens, who do I know in Athens? Well, Homer and some of the apprentices at the Academy. But this—he isn't a bard—or is he?*

Her musings were interrupted by a harsh, echoing voice. One of the two guards was snarling something at the prisoner, whose mouth quickened in amusement; he shrugged, then said something only the nearest guard could hear. The guard didn't seem at all amused. He gestured for his fellow to open the cell door, then motioned angrily and snarled something. The pale-haired man spread his arms as wide as the chain would allow as he was thrust, pell-mell, into the cell. Somehow he kept his feet under him; at another furious order from the now openly armed guard, he staggered back to the cell door and held out his arms so the manacles could be removed. The key holder grinned broadly and maliciously; his companion said something visibly sarcastic—but between the noise in the cell and the distance, Gabrielle couldn't make out what he said. The heavy door swung shut. The prisoner clutched the bars in his hard fists and tried to shake them. In vain. The two guards laughed raucously, and strolled away.

Those inside the cell were laughing, too, though Gabrielle doubted any but those nearest the entry could have heard the exchange. Most had already lost interest and were wandering away.

"It isn't fair!" the latest prisoner shouted; he was now pounding on the bars. "I have friends out there—friends at the Bards' Academy *and* at court! I can see you sent to the wrong side of your Hades!" His words were mildly accented, and suddenly he didn't sound so furious anymore, just amused. "I can see you—*each* of you!—honored with an ode that will haunt you with the market's laughter for the remainder of your days!"

I knew I recognized that form, that hair . . . "Peder!" Gabrielle exclaimed in delight, and jumped to her feet. "It just has to be you!"

"It doesn't *have* to be me," Peder informed her evenly, but a wide smile turned the corners of his lips, and his pale blue eyes were lively. "Actually, at the moment, I rather wish it weren't me. Ah, well. Do we know each other, you and I?" But as Gabrielle was about to speak, he held up a hand and said, "Wait. You're the little girl—sorry, I remember, you're the young bard who took the Academy's tests and won, but decided not to remain in Athens. You see? I do remember you. Ah . . . ah . . ."

"Gabrielle," she inserted as he paused.

"Gabrielle. I knew that." He eyed her cannily. "But last I heard from one of the students, you were going back to join the warrior princess. Tell me you haven't been in *here* all this time!"

"Got here just before you," she said. "But—Peder, you're a scroll merchant! What could you possibly have done to get thrown in *here*?"

He smiled. "Where I come from, nice young ladies don't ask such a question." Gabrielle considered this, then blushed; Peder laughed. "No, no. Nothing—well, whatever you're imagining, it couldn't possibly be that! No—it was a—well, ahem." He cleared his throat, stared across the cell. "One of the wine merchant's wives made a complaint, that I'd set her to laughing so hard, she'd been unable to keep her feet." His smile widened and his eyes fixed on a spot somewhere beyond the stone wall. "You can't imagine how funny it was," he said dreamily, "a woman of that financial class—I say nothing of any other sort of class, mind you!—sitting on her wealthy backside in the very midst of the market, her back against my stand, tears of laughter rolling down her cheeks." He shook himself; his glance touched Gabrielle's face and he laughed. "Of course, each time the woman seemed likely to regain her composure, however briefly—" The smile was absolutely malicious, his eyes wicked, as he brought his hands together ringingly. "I was only amusing the lady, you understand. And the lady *was* amused, but her politically ambitious mate apparently was not." He spread his hands wide once more. Gabrielle couldn't help but smile; Peder hadn't changed a bit. Steadfastly ignoring her rueful expression, he continued. "And so, here I am," he said with a flourish. Gabrielle drew a deep breath.

"Peder, you're mad! Not—not *that* scroll?"

"What can a poor scroll merchant do?" he countered smoothly. "The woman hears about this particular illustrated tale, she demands to see it, she—"

"She laughs herself sick," Gabrielle inserted flatly, then moments later spoiled it by giggling herself. "But—wait a minute. The guard threw you in *here*? For *that*?"

"A year ago, they wouldn't have, probably." Peder shrugged. "The new guards' captain isn't as easygoing as the last, I fear. But it's just as likely the guards who arrested me hoped for a bribe of some sort, in exchange for my immediate freedom.''

''I don't know about the last guards' captain,'' Gabrielle said darkly. ''But I can tell you the current one isn't high on my list of nice guys.'' She briefly explained the events of the past several hours; the tall scroll merchant shook his head.

''They certainly should have known better; that's just the sort of thing that's happening in this end of the city these days.'' His eyes went up and beyond her; they widened. Gabrielle glanced nervously over her shoulder, then sighed faintly.

''Knew it was you,'' she mumbled as Xena joined her. ''Anything new and exciting out there?''

The warrior shrugged. ''Not really. The air's better, though, even with the smell of stable blowing this way. Who's your friend?''

''Oh—right! I forgot you weren't with me last time. This is—Let me see if I can do this right,'' she muttered and frowned in concentration. ''This is Peder, son of Wagt, from the city of Skjold, *very* far to the north.'' Peder gave her a surprised look and quiet applause; Gabrielle bowed. ''You'll have to admit, it's not an easy name to forget once you get it straight,'' she said. ''Unusual. He came south with the tin traders,'' she added in explanation.

''It's warmer here,'' Peder said, and held out his hand. ''Less snow. More customers.''

''He's a scroll merchant; came to the Academy selling scrolls—blank ones and some with stories and pictures already on them.''

Xena met the long-fingered hand halfway and eyed the lanky merchant. ''So, what's a scroll merchant doing in a prison cell?'' she asked.

"I wish I could say mistaken identity," he replied gloomily.

Gabrielle clapped a hand over her mouth to stifle laughter. "It's *that* scroll," she said finally. "Remember—the one I told you about, and you said—"

"That? Oh. *That* scroll. I remember. I said, 'That's sick,' " Xena finished for her. She eyed the merchant more closely; he took one step back against the bars of the cell door and smiled weakly. "I still say it's sick."

Gabrielle patted his arm. "Different sense of humor, that's all." She turned back to Xena. "Honestly, it's not like they were *real* little flying creatures, or anything. It's a copy of a scroll, a story from Peder's homeland, about a girl who is supposed to preserve flowers, flatten them, but she finds these little mythical beings and—I mean, they aren't real, you know? It's a *story*!"

"Yeah. Drawings of little flattened winged creatures making faces," Xena said evenly. "I remember."

We aren't going to resolve this *one tonight, either,* Gabrielle realized. She bit the corner of her mouth to keep from giggling as she recalled one of the sillier images from Peder's scroll. "Ah—well, right," she said brightly. "Guess we can agree to disagree on this one, can't we?" She glanced over her shoulder at Peder, who smirked and brought his hands softly together, squashing imaginary little flying creatures. "Cut it out," she hissed and urgently eyed her very unamused companion. The scroll merchant's smile vanished; he glanced at the still, expressionless warrior and shrugged broadly. Gabrielle sighed. "I—Hey!" Something tugged, hard, at the hem of her skirt; she jumped back in surprise.

Xena had seen the boy's mesmerizingly fine hand snake out to grab hold of Gabrielle's skirt; her friend's yelp of surprise barely registered as she started forward for a closer look.

"Shhhhh!" The very faint, urgent whisper barely reached Xena, who pressed merchant and companion aside and knelt where Gabrielle had been standing. Thin, ragged little Kratos was a mere shadow against the bars. He beckoned; Xena leaned forward so he could whisper against her ear. "I just heard they put you in here. I'll get you and her out, just before the guard change at midnight."

"Bad idea," Xena whispered in reply. "You'll get caught. We'll be out of here in the morning anyway—" But he was already shaking his head.

"Maybe not. There's a guard—Agrinon—who really doesn't like *her*." His eyes moved in Gabrielle's direction. "But I never get caught, and I do this all the time."

I knew Athens was a mistake, right from the start, Xena thought grimly. She kept her whisper low and soft, no trace of the anger there for the boy to hear: he might think she was angry with him. "All right. We'll pay you—"

He shook his head once again. "No, not for that. But— there's a woman in here, littler than *her*," a swift gesture indicated Gabrielle, "and dark; she's got hair almost as dark as yours and she's wearing brown stuff, pretty ragged."

"I haven't— Wait." The sleeper against the back wall. "I think I saw her."

"Good. That's—that's my mother." He froze, then glanced all around; Xena came partway to her feet, hand grasping for her dagger. She swore silently as her fingers snatched air—the weapon, like all the others, had been taken from her—then knelt again as the boy beckoned. "Her name's Elyseba. Tell her I'll get her out, tonight, and Netteron will get her to safety. I mean—will you? P-please?" For answer, Xena nodded. The boy touched her hand and managed what was probably meant as a reassuring smile before he faded into shadows and was gone.

Xena got to her feet and, when Gabrielle was about to say something, held up a hand for silence. She turned to study the cell and its inhabitants. Two benches nearby were occupied by sleeping men and the only others who might have seen or heard the boy were the brightly-clad women who were arguing with one of the drunkards. The warrior gestured; Gabrielle leaned close to her. "That was the cut-purse I paid this afternoon; he's getting us out tonight. Go find a woman smaller and darker than you are, wearing brown rags. I think she's the one sleeping on that bench against the far wall. Her name's Elyseba. Tell her that her son's coming to get her out at midnight and someone called Netteron has a refuge for her. Got that?" Gabrielle nodded. "Good. Keep it *quiet*. We'll have a riot on our hands if anyone else hears about this." Her gaze continued around the cell, fixed briefly on the enormous Mondavius, who leaned against the wall just short of the bench beneath the window; he was arguing with a much smaller man who now began to shout at him. The larger brute laughed sourly and swung a huge fist overhand, slamming it down hard on the other man's head. "And there's some who don't belong any place but here," Xena added softly.

Gabrielle nodded once, sharply. "Got it. Um—Peder?" She looked inquiringly at the scroll merchant, who hadn't moved since the boy first appeared. "*You* don't belong in here either. Um—I think we could probably—" Her eyes flickered toward Xena, back to him.

He shook his head. "Wager you anything I'll be out of here at first light if not sooner. Once that man gains his senses and realizes it's not good politics to lock up honest businessmen. And I do have a flourishing business to run; I can't do that if I'm running from the guard, can I?"

Gabrielle patted his arm sympathetically. "Ah—if you have the opportunity, however," he continued. "Or if the boy does. If someone could go to my shop tomorrow and remind my assistant where I went? In case the guard forgets I'm here?"

"Someone will, Peder," Gabrielle said and nodded. Then she turned to begin making her way through the cell. At least half of the occupants were asleep or dozing; the drunker of them had probably passed out. Several others were talking in small groups of three or four; all of them ignored the slight blond woman easing her way past them. She avoided the window, its bench and the enormous—and still argumentative, from the sounds of things over there—Mondavius.

There was a long, thoughtful silence behind Xena as she watched her friend move off through the dungeon's gathering gloom. Peder leaned against the prison door, folded his arms over his chest, and gazed at the warrior thoughtfully. Xena slouched one shoulder into the door's bars a foot or so away, and waited. "I've heard a lot about you," he said finally. "The warlord who used to kill and destroy, and who's decided to help people, instead. Makes quite a story."

"I never killed innocent people—not deliberately," Xena replied. "But the story—that's one of the things Gabrielle does."

"Oh, I wasn't asking for the right to tell it. Not my sort of tale."

"I gathered." She smiled meaningfully as she brought her hands together in a quiet parody of Peder's previous gesture. The merchant gave her an abashed grin.

"Not your sort of humor. I know. And I know about Gabrielle—I heard the end of one of her stories when I made a delivery to the Academy. That wasn't what I wanted to say to you, though. Athens could use the kind of help you've given some of those outside villages. Particularly the market—'' He hesitated; Xena was already shaking her head.

''I don't work that way,'' she said flatly. ''Athens has a king, a company of guards— I know, you said some of the guard is corrupt. They can't all be. Clever man like you should have an idea who can be trusted. Or get word to King Theseus, if you have a problem.''

''That's part of the problem,'' Peder replied. ''No one can get to the King—no one of my class, at least. If I had money or influence—but I don't. You saw that boy, just now? His name's Kratos, and he—''

''I know who he is, and what he is. He's going to have to decide for himself whether he wants to grow up honest or grow up without a hand, I can't change him if he doesn't want to change.''

''But that's—''

''I'm a warrior, a fighter,'' Xena broke in firmly. ''Not a politician or a city guard.'' She looked at his worried expression and sighed faintly. When she spoke again, her voice was less harsh but no less firm. ''Look, I'm sorry if you're having troubles, but there's nothing I can do to help you. Find someone with money or influence to get word to the King, if that's what it takes. Send word there's too much poverty and his guards aren't doing their job. Last I heard, King Theseus was an honest and caring man, and good at making things work. And that's his job. I don't work for money, or for cities.'' Before he could say anything else, she turned and left him.

2

It was much darker back here; Gabrielle had to feel along cautiously to keep from stepping on any of the men sprawled on the stone floor, and almost ran into a long leg jutting from one of the benches. Fortunately a sharp, sudden snore from the sleeper there warned her in time.

The small figure on the back bench hadn't moved, that she could tell. The light was dim here, but a faint beam of wavery torchlight from beyond the barred window let her pick her way, and when she squatted down, she could make out features: a narrow face, young but careworn, surrounded by dark hair and a tattered shawl. As she knelt, the woman started; Gabrielle smiled reassuringly and laid a finger against her lips. The woman nodded, sat up, and eyed her, but when Gabrielle leaned curiously close to whisper against her ear, the woman shook her head again, shoved the scarf back so she could touch one small ear, and shook her head yet again.

It took a moment, after everything else that had happened in such a short period of time. *She's deaf,* Gabrielle suddenly realized. *Great. The boy didn't mention that. How to*

32

get across what she needed to say? There were hand signs, she was aware of that much—but she didn't know any of them, and this dark corner was scarcely the place to try to convey a message with gestures. But—there'd been a boy, the village beyond hers, she remembered. A boy who'd been born without hearing. So long as he could see the speaker's lips, he could understand what was being said. She touched the woman's arm to get her attention, touched her own lips, looked at her questioningly, and when it seemed it must be too dark for the woman to understand, leaned closer and shifted so what little light there was was on her face. She broadly mouthed, "Can you understand this?" The woman nodded at once and her face cleared; she looked around them, then pointed toward the outer wall of the cell, where Xena and Peder stood talking, and where there was—perhaps—a little more light. Gabrielle nodded emphatically and got up to lead the way.

The light still wasn't good by the door and it took time. At least, Gabrielle thought as she glanced nervously over her shoulder at the empty hallway once again, she didn't have to shout, or even to speak aloud and risk anyone else hearing. At the moment, Xena was off, probably just being generally intimidating, while Peder had gone to see if he couldn't find a quiet corner to get some sleep, and even Mondavius and his two grubby companions seemed to be dozing over by the window. The cell was very quiet. Not that she could see much from where she and Elyseba sat on the stone floor, next to the bars.

"Kratos was here just now," she mouthed. "He is coming back for us—me, you, and *her*." A gesture took in Xena, who was across the room, moving toward them.

Elyseba bit her lip and one nervous hand plucked at her skirts. "He cannot," she murmured finally. Gabrielle had to lean very close both to hear and to understand her words. "He must not dare! It—it is dangerous."

"I know," she agreed softly. "We tried to tell him, but he would not listen."

"That is my son," Elyseba agreed, and her mouth drooped. "He also does not listen to me."

Gabrielle patted her arm gently. "So we must be ready. Can you run?" The woman sighed in resignation, but after a moment nodded. "I'm—I am sorry," Gabrielle added helplessly. The woman managed a faint smile, then settled her shoulders in the corner where the bars and the wall came together, pulled the scarf over her hair once more, and closed her eyes.

Practical, Gabrielle thought; *she can't hear any of the lowlifes in this place sneaking up on her, so she puts herself where they can't get behind her.*

A light touch on Gabrielle's shoulder roused her; she used the bars to pull herself to her feet and stretched hard. Xena sent her eyes toward the window, held a finger to her lips, then leaned close to her companion's ear. "There was a bit of a fuss out there, just now; quiet again, though. She all right?"

"Under the circumstances," Gabrielle whispered in reply. "She doesn't hear."

"Oh." Xena frowned, and stared into the distance. "What's a woman like that doing in here? I mean, what possible trouble could she have caused?" Gabrielle shrugged; the warrior didn't see her. "Guess we'll find out when the boy gets back."

"The boy—" Gabrielle caught hold of Xena's wrist. "You don't think that noise out there just now was *him,* do you?" Xena frowned, shook her head. "I mean—the boy getting caught?"

"Don't know—didn't sound like that, though. More like change of guards, or a couple men gambling or something." She shrugged. "Wager we'd have heard the boy; he'd make enough noise to let us know he wasn't coming back the way he'd planned."

"Mmmm. Good point," Gabrielle conceded softly. "Besides, he's not down here yet, being carried by a couple of guards." She glanced up at her companion; Xena was straining to get a clear view of the hall through the door's narrow gaps, but after a moment she shrugged, turned, and sat with her back to the bars. Gabrielle joined her. "Um—what were you and Peder talking about?"

"Nothing important. Especially since we're leaving Athens as soon as you, I, and Argo get out of here," she added firmly. She was aware of Gabrielle's curious gaze as she closed her eyes and settled her shoulders as comfortably as possible against the uneven surface. With a faint sigh, Gabrielle eased down next to her.

"Well, I'd give a lot for one clear swing at Golden Boy," she grumbled. "The nerve of him, tossing me that purse!"

Xena bit back what sounded like laughter. "Give it up, Gabrielle," she murmured. "This time tomorrow, I'll wager anything you like there'll be another gadfly to take his place."

Gabrielle cast her a sidelong look; her mouth twisted in a sour grin. "Yeah, right. He'd have to be working at it *awfully* hard, to beat Golden Boy." Xena patted her shoulder, then resettled herself, seeking a last measure of comfort, and resolutely closed her eyes. She seemed to be asleep within moments.

Gabrielle tried, but it wasn't working. *Nervous,* she finally realized, and with a near-silent sigh, she sat up a little straighter and opened her eyes. *All right, there's nothing wrong with being nervous in a cell full of drunks, cutpurses, and—and whatever else there is here,* she finished lamely. That brute Mondavius was enough all by himself to make a sensible person wary. Though from the sounds of things over by the window, he and his companions were deeply asleep. Gabrielle sighed again and rolled her eyes as a louder than usual gurgling snort briefly woke someone on one of the nearest benches. After a string of curses too low for her to catch—no doubt to keep any of the brutes surrounding Mondavius from hearing—the wakened man subsided. She glanced at the boy's mother, who had slid down in her corner a little, with only the rhythmic rise and fall of her head to show she was not a statue. Next to her slept Xena, her head rolled against one of the bars, arms folded across her chest. *Well, at least two of us are gonna be rested when the boy comes.*

If he did. Gabrielle swallowed. What if it was someone's idea of a joke? Golden Boy would probably find a trick like that hilarious. Her eyes narrowed, briefly. *One good crack at him, just one.*

Of course, she had no proof the two boys were working together out there—let alone that the golden-haired cutpurse would bother to think up such an elaborate plan. And while *he* seemed to bounce around the market wreaking as much havoc as he could—and drawing as much attention to himself—the smaller boy didn't strike her as the same type at all. *Unless I'm really wrong about him, he's lifting coins in order to feed himself and his mother.* Didn't make it any more honest—just more understandable.

But why in a city like Athens should a boy that age have to support his mother by theft? Not that Gabrielle had spent much time in any city, let alone this one—and her first and only stay in the city had been in the almost cloisterlike conditions of the Academy. But Athens had a reputation, thanks to King Theseus: the city was known as a place where those who were able cared for themselves and their own; where those men who weren't able—because of injury suffered in the war against Troy, or illness—were cared for; where no woman widowed by that war in Troy went hungry; where the poor and weak were given a voice, and that voice was heard by the King.

It was an amazing style of governing. And a complete change in the city's King in only a very few years. The young Theseus had made a name for himself among the bards as a swaggerer and a self-proclaiming hero—a lad constantly in search of the next brash venture. *Maybe. Maybe he just did what he had to,* Gabrielle thought. The tales simplified people's lives, as she well knew—and in the doing, left out a lot.

He'd married an Amazon—that much *was* true, of course. But perhaps the younger Theseus hadn't been such a wild kid as was said of him: certainly, when he'd assumed the throne, he proved himself to be a sensible and thoughtful man. The city ruled directly by his father for so many years—justly, they said, but with a firm hand—was now divided into sectors, each sector controlled by an administrator who dealt directly with the people—rich and poor, those who could afford to bribe their way in to see royalty and those who ordinarily had no voice loud enough to reach the King's ear. But Theseus not only heard, he acted when there was need.

Or so they'd said at the Academy. Something had changed since her last visit to Athens. Children sneaking about the market, stealing—women like Elyseba in a prison cell—it didn't make sense.

Gabrielle frowned at her fingers; one of the torches beyond the window had either guttered out in the past moments or been moved, and she could barely make out the pale digits when she held them close to her chin and wiggled them. *Make it easier for the boy to sneak in and get us out, unseen,* she decided. If the boy was really coming. She drew a deep breath, then let it out slowly and quietly. Full circle in a round of gloomy thought. Maybe if she simply closed her eyes again, she'd be able to at least rest, if not actually sleep.

But she must have slept, she realized dazedly some time later: there was a guttering torch not far from the window, just out of sight, where it cast weird shadows across the cell—and Xena tugging urgently at her sleeve, her free hand resting lightly on Gabrielle's mouth. Gabrielle looked up, understanding, and cautiously nodded. Xena squatted down to murmur against her ear: "I just heard someone coming down the steps from outside, very quietly. Wake the boy's mother." Gabrielle nodded once more, eased carefully onto her knees, and closed the slight distance between them.

Elyseba was awake, but nothing was moving but her eyes. Gabrielle gave her a reassuring smile, glanced warily to both sides—no one nearby *or* awake, that she could tell—and pointed toward the entry. Elyseba caught her lower lip in her teeth, looked in that direction, and briefly let her eyes close. Gabrielle followed her gaze: beyond the bars, the darker shadow among shadows was surely the woman's son.

Xena slipped a hand between the bars and gestured sharply. The boy crossed the open floor and knelt next to her. He said nothing, merely held up a long, narrow key. Xena nodded and held out her hand, and the boy edged the key just out of reach, until his nervous gaze found his mother. He held a hand to his lips—unnecessarily, Gabrielle thought tiredly, but then, he was being cautious. And dealing with women, he didn't know. And there was more than his own freedom riding on the moment, she reminded herself as she got to her feet and held out a hand for Elyseba.

Kratos gestured again, urgently; Xena cast Gabrielle a quick look and motioned for her to go back to her knees. The boy waited until all three women were close enough to touch, then breathed, "Wait. A moment only." He sped back toward the entry, his steps utterly silent, and returned almost before Gabrielle had the chance to draw a breath, and fitted the key into the lock.

It wouldn't turn for him. He looked at Xena questioningly; she took hold of it, thought, then snagged Elyseba's scarf to wrap around it. There followed a very faint sound of metal gritting against metal—then silence again. The warrior shook out the scarf and tossed it back to its owner, set both hands cautiously on the cell door, and eased it open, very slowly. Gabrielle found she was holding her breath, and let it out. Her mouth was dry. Xena edged through the opening and melted into shadow; Gabrielle glanced around, put the boy's mother before her, and eased the cell door closed behind her. The boy tugged at Gabrielle's skirt, and pointed to her ear; she went halfway to one knee so he could whisper. "Leave the key there, the door as it is. More confusion."

She nodded, got back to her feet, and hurried past Elyseba, across the open hallway; Xena's hand came out of a particularly dark corner and hauled her out of sight. Kratos gripped his mother's hand and pulled her after.

"Now what?" Gabrielle asked. Kratos pointed toward the stairs and held a finger to his lips. He would have led the way, but Xena caught hold of his shoulder and bent over to murmur, "My horse. The weapons. Where?"

For a moment, she thought he was going to refuse; he patted his mother's arm awkwardly. "We get her to safety—*her* to stay with my mother," he singled out Gabrielle with an inclination of his head. "I take you then."

"Fine," Xena breathed. "Let's go."

Behind them in the cell, someone let out a sudden, raucous snort, and someone else yelped in surprise; Gabrielle could feel her heart thudding as one of the other men snarled something at the snorer and a high-pitched voice snapped back. Kratos stood motionless, his mother's hand in his, ready to bolt. Half a dozen sleepy, angry voices murmured and muttered, too quiet or too slurred to understand—the argument faded quickly, leaving only silence, and the sound of someone far down the courtyard calling out the hour. Kratos nodded sharply, tugged at Gabrielle's skirt to get her attention, and led his mother out of the subterranian chamber. Gabrielle followed; Xena brought up the rear.

The courtyard was mostly dark, deserted except for a lone, helmeted, and cloaked figure pacing the wall some distance away. "Main gate," Kratos whispered, then led the women quickly in the other direction. A small gate made of wooden slats stood ajar; he eased through, bringing Elyseba with him, and then gestured urgently for Gabrielle to join them. Gabrielle hesitated; suddenly, Xena was beside her, whispering.

"Stay with her, keep her safe. The boy won't cooperate otherwise, and I need him to get me to Argo."

"Ah—don't get caught again, okay?" Gabrielle whispered; she was smiling, but her eyes remained anxious.

"You know me better than that," Xena replied easily, and in a voice that wouldn't carry four paces. "Boy— where you want them to hide? So we can find them again when we get out of here?"

For an answer, he moved up next to Gabrielle, turned, and pointed down a long, narrow, and very dark alley. "Fourteen paces after you reach the first house, turn to face the right wall, take two paces. You'll see an upended merchant's cart, and behind that, a tall bush. Behind the bush, there's a space big enough to hold both of you. Don't come out unless you know it's us."

"Yeah," Gabrielle whispered doubtfully. "How d'we know? It's *dark* down there."

"Nightjar," Xena replied tersely. She patted Elyseba on the shoulder, set her hand in Gabrielle's, and gave her companion a little shove. *I hope I can remember what a nightjar sounds like,* Gabrielle thought nervously as she and the other woman hurried away from the wall and down the alley. Her back prickled eerily and it took a strong effort not to turn and look over her shoulder. At any moment she expected to hear someone shouting the alarm—from the vicinity of the cell, as their absence was discovered or, worse yet, from the wall, as that guard spotted them running away.

But there was no outcry, no threat of any kind. The street, the nearby houses, and all Athens seemed utterly silent as they moved as quickly and quietly as possible into darker shadow. When Gabrielle slowed and turned to look the way they'd come, there was no sign of anyone on the walls, or outlined by distant torchlight before the small gate: no guard, no Kratos. No Xena.

Next to her was Elyseba, who stared at the gate for a very long moment before she sighed quietly and shook her head. When Gabrielle finally tugged at her fingers she came readily. Starting forward, Gabrielle was shocked by the lack of torchlight and the almost impenetrable darkness. *Count,* she reminded herself as the way narrowed precipitously: tall, dark houses suddenly loomed blackly on both sides of the dressed stone street. Fourteen paces—she could only

41

hope the boy meant adult-sized steps. The footing was smooth but slick—water coming from somewhere. She sniffed cautiously, then sighed with relief. It *was* water— not one of the dozen other, and much less pleasant, things it could have been.

She'd reached a count of seventeen when the cart loomed up as an awkward, high-rearing shape against lesser darkness. Almost where the boy had said. Someone still used it to transport melons, by the smell of things—the lush odor was nearly overwhelming in the narrow alley. But once they'd edged around it, mostly by feel, the scent of the bush became apparent. *Rosemary,* Gabrielle thought glumly. *Dust-covered rosemary, in full bloom.* She stifled a sneeze as she and Elyseba worked their way behind it, and careful as she was to avoid the plant, her hands and her skirts reeked of rosemary by the time she found the back wall, and a low, rough bench hidden there. The other woman leaned back against the wall, drew a deep breath, and let it out gustily.

It was too dark even to make out her features, let alone attempt communication. Gabrielle squeezed the woman's shoulder sympathetically, and settled her shoulders against the cool whitewashed wall.

She would never have discovered the hiding place on her own—from the size and shape of the opening behind that pungent rosemary bush, she figured she might not have found it during the day, either. *Let's hope the guard doesn't know about it,* she thought. *Just—just in case.* She cast her companion a sidelong glance: Elyseba seemed to have settled in to their new accommodation with a minimum of fuss. *Good. One of us seems to be taking things calmly. I wonder what Xena's up to, back there. I wonder how she plans on getting Argo and that boy across that courtyard, under the guard's nose, and out here to find us.*

Xena could take care of herself, of course. Even the entire company that operated out of this compound wouldn't be a match for her, even if she hadn't a chance to arm herself. But it would give the alarm ... *I'd really just as soon be gone without all the fanfare. And this poor woman—* She darted a glance across the small cubby, but her companion was lost in shadow, utterly still and completely silent. *Bet she'd like to have her boy back, be gone and not have the guard on her heels.* Something about someone—the boy had given them a name, someone who'd hide his mother.

Gabrielle frowned and plaited her fingers together, untangled them, put them down. She was no closer to an answer than she had been, and no happier with the situation: Who needed to be hidden—to be protected from city guards? In Athens, of all places?

Xena watched Gabrielle hurry away from the guards' compound, the boy's mother at her side, then her eyes shifted to the still, silent boy next to her. He was gazing after his mother, his lip caught between his teeth, but at that slight movement on the warrior's part, he looked up at her, eyes wide and candid. *Candid seeming,* Xena reminded herself sharply. *Remember what he does for a living; I'll bet a look like that gets him close to a lot of marks and out of a lot of trouble.* She glanced back at the narrow street; the women were gone. She mumbled a curse under her breath at the entire situation, then touched the boy's shoulder lightly. "All right," she murmured. "She's safe for the moment. Where's my horse?"

For answer he turned, eased into the deeper shadow left of the gate, knelt, and pointed. Xena dropped down next to him. "That's the stables," he whispered. She noted with approval that he lisped his *s* sounds: like the rest of his speech the silibants were understandable but did not carry beyond his companion. "Mount is there, everything else kept there, too."

A brief fury washed through her. A boy this one's age shouldn't have to know such tricks: not thieving, not this kind of type of sneaking about. Not in a place like Athens, which was supposedly under King Theseus's benevolent leadership. She shook such thoughts from her mind: later, when she and Gabrielle were on the road once more. If she felt like worrying about it, which wasn't likely. *For some boys, things like this are a game. Like playing cutpurse. Some boys are overly thin at that age, no matter how much you feed them.* "Everything?" she asked finally. He nodded. "Weapons? Bags?" He nodded again. "Good. Let's go."

For a moment, she thought he figured he'd stay put—or vanish the moment she stepped away from him. A hard look from her quelled that thought at once. He offered her a faint, weak smile, and gestured again toward the stables— a dark blot against the far wall, perhaps twenty paces from the entry to the underground cell, with an even darker slot that must be the partly open door. At her ironic smile and gesture, he sighed very faintly and preceded her.

The dark spot was the doorway—the structure was so new the smell of fresh wood was even more noticeable than the odor of straw, hay, and grain. She and the boy slid into warmth and a darkness so complete she couldn't see anything for a long moment. The odor of new-cut wood receded, was gradually covered by sweet grain, horses, well-polished leather, and—only just—horse droppings. *Clean stable. Nice,* Xena thought approvingly. There was a little more light, all at once—that guttering torch outside the cell window, she thought, its light making its way in through openings near the eaves. It was still too dark to

44

make out more than the occasional shape of a neck, the point of ears—but Argo whickered softly as she moved down the dry, well-swept aisle between the stalls. The boy eased away from her; she caught hold of his thin jerkin and drew him back. "You stay here with me," she ordered softly. "Sooner we find my saddle, my gear, my weapons, the sooner you join your mother, and I get Gabrielle back. Got it?"

"I swore," he mumbled resentfully. "Won't leave. Was just going for your weapons." Beyond him, perhaps ten paces away, Argo stamped her feet and shifted in her stall.

"All right," Xena murmured. "Be careful; everything's *real* sharp."

"I know," he replied, and slipped away. By now her eyes had adjusted to the dark as much as possible, but it was still impossible to make out much in the way of shapes—and possible impediments. Though, in all justice to whoever kept the stables clean, she had to admit there didn't seem to be anything larger than a stray bit of straw underfoot. Which would make it all the more stupid to fall and cause a racket at this point. She caught hold of a stall divider, eased past an empty box, then two occupied ones, another empty . . . Argo whickered very softly as she slid a hand over the mare's firm, golden rump, up her flank to her neck, and then along the underside of her throat and jaw. The bridle was still there, used to tie her in place; someone had removed the gear and saddle, rubbed her down, and smoothed a lightweight blanket across her back. *I owe someone,* Xena thought gratefully. *For someone to show that much care for a prisoner's mount—someone in this compound loves horses.*

It took her a moment to find the unfamiliar knot at the end of the bridle that secured Argo to the wall, then several long and anxious moments to figure how it worked and to undo it. By the time she was done, Aryo was shifting impatiently, eager to be gone, and Kratos had come back with one load of her weaponry.

The warrior knelt, locating things by touch, and restoring them to their proper sheaths: the chakra to its place at her left side, the daggers to their individual homes, the sword at the back of her neck, another dagger down the right boot. The boy was back again, a pile of bags nearly his own size weighing him down.

"Saddle: where?" Xena demanded. The boy nodded, caught his breath quickly, and took a few steps down the open aisle between stalls, returning with the blanket and saddle. "Thanks," Xena said.

"Hurry!" he demanded softly, and she gazed down at him, saddle in her hands. He was clasping and unclasping his hands, watching the way they'd come into the stables, the various window openings, and the far end of the aisle. Nervous.

"I *am* hurrying," she whispered. "Either I carry all this, or *she* does. I fight better with my hands free, and she doesn't care how many packs she's wearing if *she* has to fight."

To his credit, the boy was still a long moment, then finally nodded.

"Keep watch," Xena ordered softly. "I'm wasting no time, trust me."

It wasn't that much longer; the boy was growing restive again, but then, he wasn't old enough to be that good at patience, Xena reminded herself. She slipped the last pack—Gabrielle's cooking pot, which held the bag of dry soup makings—into its usual spot on Argo's backside, tied leather pack thongs to her saddle thongs, and slipped a hand under the horse's jaw, whispering against her ear. Argo backed obediently and quietly from the stall, settled her chin on the warrior's near shoulder, and walked quietly down the main aisle with her.

"Hey!" A sudden, sharp voice from the main entry caught her by surprise. Kratos gasped, but bit back further sound as Xena's free hand clamped down on his shoulder; she shook her head. He nodded, took the reins she stuffed into his fingers, and stayed where he was as the warrior melted into the shadows. "Hey, you!" the voice added; it echoed through the stable, and other horses shifted nervously up and down the straw-laden aisle. "There's no one allowed to be in the stables at *this* hour but me! Who're you, and why're you here?"

"Um. Sorry, sir. Captain sent me to ready his mount, so's he could leave early. Sir." Kratos's voice quavered; his accent was no longer the young thief's usual—and memorable—Athens Street, Xena realized. *Thinks on his feet; I like that.* The guardsman would be forever trying to sort out where that accent came from. *If he lives beyond the hour,* she thought coldly. Sliding from behind the divider nearest the man, with one sharp fist to the throat she left him flattened and silent. A second jab—this to the back of the neck—made certain he'd remain both silent *and* flattened for some time to come.

Kratos came up as she was dragging the man into the nearest empty stall; he watched silently as she tossed two double armfuls of straw over the guard. She paused with a last load of straw, knelt, and fumbled to release the helm straps. Then, shoving long hair behind her ears, she tugged the high-peaked bronze helmet snugly down onto her head. "Stay right with me," she ordered softly. "And between me and Argo. She won't hurt you," she added as the boy eyed the enormous, golden beast warily. "She pays attention to what I tell her and she doesn't like stepping on

47

people. Stay right here,'' she positioned him between her and Argo, ''and do what I say.''

''I can get back out unseen—'' he began. Her hand tightened on his arm.

''I know. But someone just might see you, even if they don't catch you. This way, someone on the wall looks over at the wrong moment, all they see is the horse and the guard's helm. Your mother would like that, don't you think?''

The boy bit his lip, and in the faint, guttering light of a distant torch, his eyes were very bright. ''My mother,'' he whispered. ''Warrior. I'll do whatever you say. Help me get her to safely.''

''Good boy,'' Xena murmured, and cast him a smile. A very faint answering flash of teeth was her only reply. Kratos took hold of the near stirrup as Xena whispered against Argo's ear and the horse headed slowly and easily out of the stable and across the courtyard.

None of it was well lit—fortunately. A compound guard taking a horse out wouldn't be sneaking from the stable through the deepest shadows. At this point, none of that mattered, Xena thought. The gate was still open and near enough that there'd be no one to catch them. Ten paces— seven. Five. Another two steps and she could catch hold of the gate, ease it the rest of the way open. Behind them, high on the wall, someone shouted, and she swore under her breath. The boy gave her an astonished look.

''Hey! You there! Apolodiun! What're you doing with that beast? I said—'' Whatever else he was saying, Xena didn't hear. She tore at the gate, then scooped up the boy, threw herself into the saddle, and hauled the boy across her legs. Argo needed no further invitation than the dark street stretching before her; she took off at a dead run, and the guard's furious shouts faded. The clatter of shod hooves on

48

stone paving echoed off the surrounding buildings. At the first broadening of the way, Xena reined in before an arbor with a small fountain underneath it and a small oil lamp reflecting off the still water and setting leaf shadows dancing on the street and houses.

The warrior drew Argo in, let the boy down, and jumped down next to him. He took her free hand and tugged urgently; she followed, Argo trailing after her—around the fountain, between two flat-roofed houses, then behind one of them, where another arbor held up grapevines. Xena stood very still, aware of small rustlings in the vines— mice, perhaps—and the low murmur of voices in one of the houses. From the street there was nothing. She could feel the boy practically vibrating at her elbow, turning down fingers one after the other as he counted. Finally, his shoulders sagged, and he tugged at her arm to get her attention. "They aren't following," he whispered. "Let's go back to your friend, and my mother."

"Fine with me," Xena whispered back. She was certainly seeing all the best of Athens, this trip. A dry smile quirked the corners of her mouth as she followed the boy back to the fountain, and then back up the street.

Gabrielle started as the sounds of a running horse filled the small shelter, then faded. Elyseba hadn't heard that, but she'd felt the vibration—she eased over next to Gabrielle, who shrugged. She didn't feel safe talking in here; neither, apparently, did Elyseba. *I hope that was Xena. But if it was, I hope that boy remembers where he told us to come. Or that she can find us. Or that—* She bit the corner of her mouth and tried to force the gloomy thoughts away. *Think of something pleasant, why don't you?* At the moment, nothing would come.

3

Argo hadn't particularly wanted to leave the shelter of the arbor—the mare had found something pleasant to eat back there, Xena wasn't certain what. But at the second, barely patient tug on the rein, she shook herself, turned, and quietly followed Xena from the dark, leafy sanctuary back into the square. The boy was a small, narrow shadow against the fountain for one brief moment, then nowhere in sight. The warrior cursed as she went into a crouch, hands quivering above chakra and daggers, but he reappeared at her side a moment later.

"I had to be certain of a place over there," he whispered. He was pointing, she thought; she couldn't discern what direction, or what thing he pointed out to her. "Guards know of it."

It's dark here; I can't make out anything and I don't know his signals. Not a safe combination. She bit back a curse and mildly said, "Oh. Fine. Let's go."

She let him take the lead, then watched as he flitted from one side of the narrow alley to the other, checking various places to make certain there was no ambush awaiting them.

For all the world like a small boy playing an elaborate hiding game, or playing the war game children always play, she thought with amusement. That faded. He wasn't playing—whether the threat was real or not, the boy perceived danger, and had learned to act accordingly. *Boys that age shouldn't need to know such things.*

A blocky shadow loomed to her left, just as the alley opened up and the compound wall loomed ahead: it took her a moment to recognize the merchant's upended cart from this side. The boy tugged at her near arm, held up one hand against her chest, then indicated the compound itself with an outstretched arm and darted away before she could say anything. She swore under her breath, then shrugged. He was fast and cautious: he'd already proven he could stay uncaught. She'd just have to trust that her escape hadn't yet been discovered for what it really was, and that the guards in the compound weren't any more alert than they had been all night.

The boy, his mother—all Athens!—such things weren't her concern anyway. In another hour, they'd be beyond worrying about such things entirely.

Get the boy and his mother on their way, get me and Gabrielle out of this city before something else goes wrong. She puckered her lips and uttered a trilling birdcall. There was no chance any sensible nightjar would be found in a man-made stone canyon like this one, but which of its city-bred inhabitants would know that? Besides, this way Gabrielle wouldn't be wondering which bird was a real one, which a warrior.

No response. Xena sighed faintly, then edged over past the cart, eyes still studying the compound wall as she whistled again.

No sign of the boy up there; she could see one guard pacing the wall—stopping every few paces to gaze all around him. A flickering light showed just on the other side of the gate. Another light—lantern, candle, or lamp, who could tell at this distance?—crossed from the stable area toward the cell, as one of the guards came from a check of the stables or its environs to make his report to the jail captain: she'd watched too many such movements of guards this evening from that inside bench to doubt that was exactly what was going on in there. Still—no outcry, no excitement. *We can't have gotten away that easily. Can we?*

Then again, most companies didn't pay low-ranked guards to do anything but follow orders. Maybe the fool on the outer walls really had thought she was his fellow—the man she'd flattened in the stables, no doubt—and after his initial surprise at seeing Argo led out and ridden off at speed, he'd assumed the man had urgent orders to be elsewhere, and that none of it was his concern. *Stranger things happen among guard companies, after all.*

The boy was back at her side, not even noticeably winded, as Gabrielle emerged from the darkness beyond the cart, brushed at her skirts, then turned back to make certain the boy's mother was all right. Elyseba came into the open on all fours, then stood cautiously; the boy darted to her side and hugged her fiercely, then drew her into the alley and back the way he and Xena had just come. He tugged at her hand, the woman nodded, drew a deep breath, and set off at a decent pace.

Xena glanced over her shoulder: still quiet in the compound. She sighed. ''All right. Gabrielle, I've had enough fun for one day, let's—'' She turned. Gabrielle wasn't at her side any longer; she was running to keep up with the boy and his mother. The warrior cast up her eyes, shook her head, and followed.

●　　●　　●

She lost track of where they were all too quickly, lost track of direction not long after. Kratos led them through narrow walkways separating tumbledown shops, past piles of rubble that had been impoverished shops or homes, across a small square—at first she thought it the square where they'd hidden, but this one's pool was different, more circular. They dashed beneath an area shielded by awnings, where covered individual stands reeked of overripe fruit. He barely slowed at any point and for most of the distance kept up that same ground-eating, loping pace.

To the warrior's surprise, Kratos's mother held up as well as any of them. *Athlete. Or at least one who's strong in need.* The woman was breathing more quietly than Gabrielle when the boy finally slowed them to a walk leading them through a rubble-strewn passageway, across a deserted courtyard festooned with thistles, and through a thick door. He stepped to one side to let his companions—female and equine—pass through before he dragged it into place behind them.

It was extremely dark and close, wherever this place was. The boy murmured, "Wait here," and Xena could just make out the sound of his feet moving away. The very faint noise of flint and tinder followed, and then a ruddy light shone from behind a crumbling wall. Kratos reappeared, one hand clutching a plain clay oil lamp, the other sheltering the tiny flame.

"That a good idea?" Xena asked quietly, gesturing toward the lamp as she glanced at the rough-looking walls all around her.

"You can't see light from outside this place," he replied, his voice calm though his eyes looked resentful. "I know, I've tested it myself. And if my mother can't see your face, and your mouth, she can't understand you."

"Understand—got it," Gabrielle replied breathily. She drew a deep breath, coughed faintly as she looked around, then found a low, flat stone that didn't seem too filthy, brushed it off, and sat back against the wall. She shifted slightly. Elyseba sat on a low stool next to a rickety table; the boy deposited the lamp there, then laid a tender hand on his mother's cheek. She smiled up at him, and covered the hand briefly with her own. He drew away after a moment, and wove a series of complicated-looking hand-signals. She replied the same way, though more briefly. The boy glanced at their companions, back at his mother, then said, "I was telling her that I'll go fetch Netteron for her, now, so she can be safely hidden from the guards before the sun rises. I'll have food and water brought for you."

"You don't need to," Xena said evenly. "Thanks for getting us out of that cell. We'll be going now."

"No—no, please." The boy crossed to her and stared deep into her eyes, then shook his head, hard. "I—In the market, I did you a favor and you paid me. Now I've done you another favor."

"And I owe you, that about it?" Xena asked. He eyed her warily, but his mouth was stubborn as he nodded. "Fine. I have coin."

"Coin," the boy said dismissively. "I can get coin anytime."

"What—by stealing? Anyone ever tell you that's dishonest, boy?"

His mouth twisted. "I should have known you'd be one of *those*."

"One of what?" Gabrielle asked as Xena folded her arms and gazed down at him. "I mean—honestly, lad, she's right, you know. There are other ways to get coin, even if you live some place like *this*. Stealing's no answer—"

"You don't have all the answers," he broke in flatly, angrily. "You don't know anything!" Elyseba stirred and made an unhappy little sound at the look on his face, and held out a hand to him. His mouth softened. "I'm sorry, Mother." He turned back to Xena; his eyes caught Gabrielle's briefly and he moved so Elyseba could no longer see his face. "Stay with her, please, warrior. She can't hear, you know that. So, if someone *did* find this place, she'd never know they were there. She'll be frightened if she's here alone. I won't ask anything else, not a single copper, nothing. And—and by the honor code of warriors the scroll merchant told me about—well, we'll no longer be in each other's debt, will we?"

"I—" Xena sighed tiredly. "All right. Don't take the rest of the night; I want to be *gone* before full light."

"Wait." Gabrielle held up a hand as the boy was about to turn and leave them. "Who's Golden Boy? The cute guy with the stolen purse who got us tossed in there in the first place?"

"I—" For a moment she thought the boy wasn't going to answer her.

So did the boy. But his mother had been watching the exchange; she sighed faintly and said, "He's Helarion. Son of my older sister, Kratos's cousin. He— My son isn't like Helarion," she added angrily.

Sure, Xena thought tiredly. *Your son just got in with the wrong boys, did the wrong things because they egged him on, or told him to—was stupid because someone said be stupid.* But, from the sound of the conversation out there, maybe it wasn't—precisely—that. Not the ordinary mother's plaint when a son turned out bad.

"I can tell as much," Gabrielle told her softly. "Helarion," she added in a musing tone, then turned to eye the boy once more. "All right. So, why'd he pick on *me*?"

"You were there, why not hand off to you?" Kratos replied with a shrug. "He doesn't worry about things like that; he doesn't have to. The laws of Athens don't apply to him, you know; after all, his father—"

"Son!" Elyseba said sharply.

"It's true, Mother," Kratos insisted. "He's told me the story over and over, and my aunt Sybella doesn't deny it, does she? He's the son of Hermes; the god protects him."

Elyseba merely shook her head; Gabrielle thought the woman was embarrassed by the whole story. Xena stared at the boy.

"A god who takes care of thieves?"

"Not—really," Gabrielle replied, promptly interrupting. "Hermes is the messenger for the other gods; he's quick and deft and he's a trickster—but he's more likely to care for someone like King Odysseus than a common cutpurse." Kratos glowered at her; she ignored him. "Trickery isn't necessarily dishonest, you know. Stealing purses is—and tossing blame onto someone else who's merely minding her own business—well, he won't have any protection against *me,* if I get my fingers on him! Personally, I don't care if his papa is Zeus, or the really nasty cold-climate gods my friend Peder told me about, that arrogant little thief is *not* going to be in good shape, if I can get even one hand around his throat!"

Silence. Xena raised one eyebrow and Gabrielle shook her head; her color was rather high. "You want to talk to him?" Kratos suddenly demanded. "I can bring him here."

"Never mind," Xena began hastily, but Gabrielle was already nodding.

"Do it," she said flatly.

"Gabrielle," Xena warned. "We're leaving here the first moment we can—"

"No! *You* can leave," Gabrielle replied, even more flatly, and her eyes were stormy. "I'm going nowhere until

56

I give that spoiled little monster a piece of my mind. Or a couple of bruises he won't forget in a hurry, and let's see if his wing-footed father protects him from *that*." She met her companion's eyes. "You can leave if you want to," she went on flatly, and there was no give in her voice. "Tell me where you want to meet, and when, and I'll—"

Xena's mouth gave in to an involuntary grin. "What— all the trouble you've gotten into in Athens, and you think I'm going to leave you here alone?" Her eyes fixed on Kratos. "Get going," she said flatly. "I still don't want to stay in Athens any longer than I have to. Sooner you get back here, sooner we're gone."

He merely nodded, then moved into the open and pressed one hand against his breast, lay the other fist over it. His mother smiled and whispered, "Yes, I know. Go, my son." Kratos hesitated only a moment, his thin young face bleak, then turned and hurried into the side room once again. Xena heard a faint scrape of stone, then an even fainter clatter of small rocks—a distant, muted grating. Nothing else.

"Must be a back way out," she said as Gabrielle got to her feet and stretched cautiously. Elyseba, who had kept her eyes on the warrior's face, nodded.

"Only a small boy can fit through it. We're . . . as safe here as anywhere." She shuddered. "Safer than in that cell."

"You're not wrong about that," Gabrielle mumbled. "What . . . was that your son did? That movement with his hands?" She copied his gesture, hand over heart, fist over hand. Elyseba smiled. *She's not nearly as old as I thought,* Xena realized with a start. *Barely old enough to have a boy of nine or so years. And not just emotionally, but physically, stronger than I'd have thought.* Her arms—bared nearly to the shoulder, now that she'd shed that tattered long scarf— were well muscled. Not a sword wielder's muscles, but beyond the kind of strength one would expect of even a village woman used to hauling loads of grain or heavy buckets of water. Her face was too thin, careworn.

Elyseba smiled; dark blue eyes kindled. "That's our own personal sign—we have a lot of them, just between the two of us. That one, I made up for him when he was much younger. It means, 'I love you, take care of yourself.' "

"Oh." Gabrielle smiled. "That's really sweet."

The other woman's smile slipped. "In the past year or so, he's needed it—in ways I'd never have thought when I first made it up." She sighed, let her eyes close and braced her elbows on the table so she could rest her cheek on one hand. Gabrielle's light touch roused her once more.

"I'm very confused," she said. "Why would they put a woman like you in a place like *that*? I mean—well, okay, it isn't my business, I know that! But still, you don't look like a thief, or a—"

"Gabrielle," Xena put in softly, and the girl went red to her hairline.

"I didn't mean *that*," she whispered to her companion, then turned back to the boy's mother.

Elyseba sagged even further and fetched a tired-sounding breath. "It was because of my son," she murmured. "They were so angry three nights ago, when he brought them no purses, no coin, no gems or rings, and he told them that a woman warrior had warned him not to steal, threatened him, so he didn't—"

"She didn't threaten him, honestly. Xena would never threaten a boy, especially one like your son," Gabrielle put in as the woman paused.

"I know. He told me about it, just before they came. Thank you, warrior," she added, then shook her head. "I am sorry. I was there two nights and I didn't dare sleep much. I . . . don't think I can stay awake any longer." She let her eyes close, dropped her head down on folded arms, and tried to settle. Gabrielle touched her arm to get her attention and patted her lap.

"Here," she said. "More comfortable. We two will watch." The woman considered this, smiled faintly, and eased onto the floor, cushioning her head on Gabrielle's thigh. She seemed to sleep almost at once.

There was a long silence, broken only by the occasional snap of the lamp flame and the soft, steady breathing of the boy's mother. Xena stirred, got to her feet, and began pacing the hovel: four steps one way, five the other. "Gabrielle," she said finally.

But Gabrielle was already shaking her head. "No. I know what you're gonna say, and I don't care. It's— If it had been an accident or something like that, fine. If— He ran straight for me, and he was *laughing* as he tossed me that bag."

"Gabrielle. Think about it. Someone like that has *no* moral sense. You can't beat something into him that he doesn't possess. And besides, Athens has been a jinx for us: every time, something bad happens. If we just leave, now—all right, as soon as the boy returns for his mother; I agree we can't leave her here alone. But—"

"No," Gabrielle said as her companion hesitated. The woman resting on her thigh stirred; Gabrielle smiled down at her, stroked dark brown hair, and waited until the woman's deep, steady breathing assured her Elyseba was asleep again—or at least still. "You want to leave, I don't blame you. I know how much fun Athens has been for both of us. And I know what you're telling me about that boy. I don't care. I don't want to rehabilitate him, I want to flatten him. Maybe he won't be a finer young man because I talked him into leading a life for good, but he'll remember the headache he got when I whacked him one for setting me up with those guards.'' Her eyes were dark, sea-storm blue, her mouth angry. ''Did I mention he was not only laughing at me, but he put me into Agrinon's hands? After I flattened the stupid man out there on the sand for harassing his girl-friend?''

''I met the girlfriend, remember? The weaver, see?'' Xena smiled faintly; Gabrielle's mouth softened and she rolled her eyes, but the atmosphere in the small chamber was much less tense, all at once. ''You can't change men like that, Gabrielle; you won't make any impression on that boy. Not one.''

''I might. Not the way you mean.''

''It doesn't matter. He won't change. You'll frustrate yourself for no purpose, trying to argue with him; you hit him, it won't matter to him. Probably everyone in his whole life except his mother and his *supposed* father have done that. Maybe them, too.'' Silence. ''Gabrielle, you can't change everything.''

''I don't care.''

''You do care. I don't want to see you even more upset from confronting this boy and realizing it didn't make any difference to him, no matter what you said *or* did.''

''We'll just see,'' Gabrielle said flatly. She stirred, then subsided, shaking her head. ''Thought I heard—but I didn't. And before we leave Athens, I need to visit Peder's scroll shop, make certain his assistant knows where he went.''

''Peder,'' Xena growled. Gabrielle gave her an amused glance, then bit back what sounded suspiciously like a gig-gle.

''You don't need to go, or anything like that. I could see you didn't like him.''

''He's mad. *And* sick.''

"Oh—but listen, those little winged creatures aren't even *real*! They're like dryads or harpies or something. Well, okay, I'll agree there might be dryads, that friend of Homer's and all. But these," she snapped her fingers, "fairies! They aren't real, any more than harpies are. It isn't like they killed any to make the scroll . . ." Her voice trailed away as Xena shook her head grimly. "Well, okay, but he doesn't belong in prison for bringing out the scroll for some wealthy woman who wanted to see it—I mean, what if he hadn't and she got stuffy about that?"

"Either way, he's in the cell," Xena said. "All right, point taken. It's not the real or not real, you know, it's the laughter. Little mangled bodies. Sick," she added firmly. *Not real like harpies?* she asked herself, and a wry smile appeared. She and Marcus—*gods protect you, my beloved*—could tell Gabrielle a thing or two about harpies.

"Well, I don't think about that part," Gabrielle admitted. It was as close to a truce as they'd get on this matter. "Just the faces." She made one—a hideous, cross-eyed distortion—and Xena bit back an involuntary grin. "But they might decide to keep him there—maybe not enough coin for bribes, or the woman gets stuffy or her husband stays stuffy—did I tell you Peder says he's a politician?—and no one knows where he's gone? The Academy really needs someone like Peder, he supplies them with blank scrolls, with supplies for making scrolls, with ready-created tales printed on scrolls so those who need help with their declaiming can have that, without having to remember a story at the same time as they're trying to remember how to *deliver* the story. It's such a new thing, no one in Athens has done that much with it." Xena shook her head as Gabrielle paused. Gabrielle considered for a moment, then said, "All right. Think about this: I tell a tale about—okay, say about you beating the Titans. And others listen. And maybe another would-be bard or so picks up the story, changes a thing or two, tells the stories again. And that goes on, and on—and after a while, I hear the story from someone, and I think, *Wow, that sounds kinda familiar— but not really . . .''*

"All right," Xena replied steadily. "I can understand that. But why—"

"Because, with Peder's scrolls—anyone's, but he's the only merchant in Athens who bothers to sell scrolls with the stories he's heard already printed upon them—the story that's on the scroll, if it's mine, it stays mine. If it's about you taking on the Titans, it doesn't become—oh, Hercules and Iolaus fighting them."

"Hercules wouldn't care," Xena said. "Why should I?"

"Well—I care," Gabrielle retorted quietly. "It takes a little work to come up with the rhymes and the right meter and all that; I would just as soon someone else didn't claim *all* my work." She shifted, and gazed toward the door the boy'd brought them through. "Did I just hear something?"

"Argo'd let you know, if you did. There's nothing," Xena said. She came over to clasp her companion's shoulder. Gabrielle smiled and laid her hand over Xena's. "Why don't you sleep? You could probably use the rest as much as she could, and I'm not tired, I'll keep watch with Argo. Besides," she added with a wry smile, "you're gonna flatten Golden Boy, you'd better be ready, hadn't you?"

"Flatten him like one of Peder's—whadiyacallems. Fairies," Gabrielle mumbled sourly, but she settled her shoulders against the wall, shifted carefully so Elyseba wouldn't be disturbed and let her eyes close. Xena's eyes lost their angry edge, and her mouth softened as her companion's breathing slowed and eased into deeper sleep. *Flatten him like—that's sick,* she thought, but a faint smile quivered at the corners of her mouth. Maybe Gabrielle had something; not everything was as literal as most people—including her—made it.

She shifted cautiously and quietly, got to her feet, and went to inspect the next chamber. It was even less habitable than the main room: stone lay everywhere, as did trash, bits of cloth, remnants of meals, broken pottery, and rusted blades. The smell wasn't too wonderful, either; her nose wrinkled involuntarily. She made certain Elyseba had been right about the size of the boy's bolt hole, then retreated swiftly, holding her breath until she gained the relative pleasure dome of the main room in the tumbledown building.

How did such places occur in a city supposedly under the aegis of an enlightened prince—a commander in chief, your pardon, sir, she thought sourly—as Theseus. The Theseus she remembered hadn't liked being addressed as Prince or King, at least; he'd let it be known he preferred to be thought of as a man whose word could be questioned, and whose decisions—if wrongly made—could be righted.

And Hippolyta. She'd been defeated in battle by Theseus but everyone knew the relationship between them wasn't the usual result of such a meeting.

It was all supposed to have made a difference. And the last time she had been in Athens, the difference had been clear.

And now—it was just like Sparta, or any of the other major cities: poverty, hungry children, cutpurses everywhere, and indifferent guards, or guards who were no better than the thieves they supposedly controlled.

A city where a woman of Elyseba's kind—impoverished and powerless—could be thrown into prison among rough and drunken men, and brutes like that monster—Mondavius, wasn't it?—him or any other such brute, and for no cause at all, that she could see. Surely the woman hadn't been trying to say she'd been imprisoned because her son wouldn't steal for someone!

You're becoming involved in all this. Don't, Xena ordered herself flatly, but the matter returned in different guise.

See yourself back then—a village girl, strong but not that kind of strong. If someone had gotten the plea of your people to the King and the King responded immediately, what would that have done to your life?

Enough. She shook the matter aside, though it wasn't easy. "What was, has already happened," Xena whispered. "What is, is. What might be, or might have been, is a lie." Besides, she'd become what too many people needed: her hard-won strength was needed against their adversities. However long and complicated a road it had taken to get her to this point.

Her thoughts resulted in a dry grin. *Remind yourself of that often enough, it might even sound like you meant it all along.* At the sight of her companions the smile softened: Gabrielle sprawled against the rough wall of the deserted hut, her head nestled against a protruding beam, a protective hand on Elyseba's shoulder. The other woman was a dark, curled-up shadow against her left leg, but a very faint smile briefly turned the corner of the woman's mouth, and for that moment, she looked as young as Gabrielle.

Don't get involved in this, Xena reminded herself, and turned away to stare at the patterns the oil lamp made on the far wall. *You don't belong in Athens, and neither does Gabrielle.*

• • •

The boy returned an hour later, dust-streaked and out of breath. Elyseba was still asleep, though Gabrielle came partly awake as the boy leaned against the wall to catch his breath. Xena murmured, "It's all right, just the boy. Get some more sleep."

"Mmmm—right." Gabrielle drew a deep breath, and let it out as a sigh as her eyelids sagged shut. Kratos held his breath as Elyseba shifted, but the woman merely eased the angle of her neck and was still once more.

"What news?" Xena whispered. Kratos nodded sharply, then moved away from the wall. He was still short of breath and his color was high, as though he'd run the entire distance.

"Netteron will be here—he had to—he's on his way. I came ahead, so you'd know it was him. He's telling his brother, so his brother can come and tell you—talk to you. And he said—said he'd tell Helarion that *she* wants to see him."

"You think he'll bother?"

"Bother? Oh." The boy considered this gravely, then grinned; for the first time, Xena thought, he looked like what he should be—a carefree, mischievious young boy. "He'll think it's funny. So he'll come." Catching sight of her frown, he shook his head and tried to explain. "He's— It's not just who his father is, you know. It's . . . He doesn't know . . . I mean . . ." He shook his head, hard, in obvious frustration. Xena waited; he tried again. "I know it's wrong to steal, but if I don't, my mother doesn't have anything to eat—and if I don't—well, you saw where she was. But Helarion: it's all a joke to him, it's like, nothing really *belongs* to anybody, so it's all right if he takes whatever he wants, or does whatever he wants. It doesn't matter to him."

"He doesn't have any sense of right or wrong, that it?" Xena asked softly. Behind her, Gabrielle shifted slightly, and one of the women moaned, but when she glanced over her shoulder, both were still and silent. Kratos nodded.

"And it's not because of my aunt, she's—she's like my mother, she's—she's honest."

"Silly, though," Xena said, "if she filled his head with all those stories about Hermes."

The boy frowned. "But *that's* true. I mean, if you *saw* him, you would know."

"I've seen him," Xena replied neutrally. "Let it go, okay? And listen, you've really picked the wrong people to help you. I don't know this city, I don't know the people. I can't help you."

"*She* said—" Kratos began, his eyes fixed on Gabrielle.

"Oh, I know what she said. She's got a soft heart and sometimes it gets in the way of sense. Sensibly, you need to find men here in the city who can help you." She looked at him; his mouth was set in a stubborn line. The warrior sighed heavily. "Look, I told her I'd stay while she talks things over with your cousin; I won't go back on that. For the rest—just don't let yourself hope, all right? Because we aren't staying here to do your king's job for him, and even if we did, we wouldn't know where to start." She half expected an argument, but the boy merely turned away from her. "I'm sorry if that isn't the answer you wanted to hear, but things are like that."

"I know," he mumbled. She debated saying something else, and decided to let it go. *Let Gabrielle talk to him, if words are going to make a difference.* A moment later, she turned sharply and came to her feet, one hand on the chakra. Kratos pressed past her and laid his ear against the door they'd come through earlier. There was faint scratching on the other side; he tapped lightly against the door with one grubby knuckle, listened, then nodded. "It's Netteron," he whispered.

"Sure?"

"Certain," he replied, and set his shoulder against the end of the sagging door. Xena resettled the chakra and moved to help him.

The man who slipped through the narrow opening was a little taller than Xena and much thinner, a long, dark bone of a man with curling blue-black hair that fell over his eyes. He shoved it impatiently back, and laid a long-fingered hand on the boy's shoulder. At his feet, Gabrielle shifted, stretched, and woke with a start. Kratos knelt at his mother's side as the sudden movement on her companion's part brought her muzzily awake. He patted her cheek gently, smiled as she looked up at him, then indicated Netteron with a brief nod. The woman's smile slipped; she sat up and took the boy's hands between her own. He freed them and began signing rapidly. Xena turned back to the tall man.

"You're Netteron?" He nodded. "Certain you can keep her out of that cell?"

"She'll be safe," he replied neutrally; he studied Xena warily, finally held out a hand. "You're the warrior princess. We'd heard of you before this—but those children, the races—"

"That was Atalanta," Xena put in smoothly as he searched for words. "I was just along to help out. What's the hour, out there?"

"Nearly daybreak," he said. Kratos's shoulders slumped; he stood, helped his mother up, and let himself be hugged.

"Remember." Elyseba leaned away from him and cupped his chin with her hand. "You don't have to do

67

bad things to keep me safe for now. So don't do them. Swear?'' He nodded reluctantly. "And I will miss you terribly, but you must not come see me too often—you'll be caught.''

He spoke aloud, moving his hands at the same time—letting his companions in on the conversation as well, Gabrielle thought as she got to her feet and rubbed her eyes. "I won't do that, Mother—they'd catch you again, and I won't let that happen. I'll miss you, too,'' he finished, and he sounded very young. Elyseba gave him one last hug, then held out a hand to Netteron, who drew her from the small room and into the deserted, weed-strewn courtyard. Xena watched them go, then eased the door closed behind them.

4

Gabrielle yawned cavernously, stretched hard, and blinked as she got partway to her feet. "Any idea what time it is?" she mumbled.

"Early," Xena assured her. "*Very* early."

"Mmmm—swell." Gabrielle blocked the next yawn with the back of her hand and rubbed her eyes with the other, then shook her head. "Why'm I even bothering? Wake me when something important happens, okay?" She resettled her shoulders, folded her arms across her chest, and closed her eyes. Almost at once, her breathing slowed and deepened. Xena shook her head in wonder, then turned her attention to the boy.

"What next?" she asked mildly.

He shrugged. "Ukloss is bringing bread for you, from his bakery—I think his son Adrik is coming also, if he can find someone to tend the ovens while he's here. And—even if you don't want to listen," he said and hesitated. He eyed her sidelong, then went on, attempting to sound persuasive, "You'll have extremely good bread to break your morning fast with."

"That's—that was a good thought," Xena said finally. "Thank you."

"Well," the boy allowed with a faint grin, "you'd have had the same bread back in that cell—Ukloss has the contract for the market jail."

It was the last thing either of them said for some time. The lamp was beginning to run low on oil, the flame alternating between a meager flickering and a sharp flaring, resulting in an outburst of harsh shadows against the wall. Gabrielle had shifted, and now lay in a huddle, the top of her head braced against the wall, the rest of her curled in a tight wad, all deeply asleep. Kratos had wandered from the main room into the smaller several times; at one point he sat cross-legged on the floor to build an elaborate child's castle from the rubble of stones all around them.

He really is just a baby, Xena thought judiciously: dark tousled hair, a very young boy's soft cheek. Thick, black lashes lay across that cheek, and while he concentrated on the piles of stones and pebbles, his mouth had softened to a gentle, pink double bow—that odd shape that smiled even when the wearer didn't intend to smile. Etruscan, they called it. Charming, Xena would have called it instead. *His mother must warm clear through when she sees this side of him,* the warrior thought, and a faint smile touched her eyes and turned the corners of her mouth. She sighed quietly and turned away to study the far walls, and the shadows thrown by the lamp.

Some time later, the boy started as Argo lipped his hair; he glanced warily in the warrior's direction. She smiled faintly and nodded. The boy slid a nervous hand along the horse's golden jaw, down her throat, then, gathering strength, along her flank.

"He's very beautiful," he whispered.

"*She,*" Xena replied dryly.

"Oh—sorry, lady." The boy addressed the horse directly. He glanced, abashed, at the warrior once more. "Her skin is so warm. And so soft."

"You've never touched a horse before?" Xena asked, amazed.

"No one where I live can afford a horse—any horse," he replied simply. "And where I go around the city, I wouldn't dare lay hands on anyone's beast—horse or cow, sheep, whatever creature, they'd think I meant to steal it. Or hurt it," he added doubtfully. "Someone, last year or the year before, I forget, someone hurt someone else's horse; it was—it was bad. My cousin was weeping when he told me about it, and Helarion never weeps."

"It must have been bad, then. Better if he hadn't told you," Xena said. She wanted to touch him, to reassure him—but he squared his shoulders and turned away.

"No. Because if he hadn't, I wouldn't have known the new rule on the streets, and that's important for a boy like me. You know, my parents aren't . . ." He frowned, trying to find the words. "They don't have money, or a brother in the guard, or a cousin at court. Those who have those things—well, that isn't important—because we're poor people, we don't have such influence and we never will. So rich people like that can do what they want about the rules, but we can't." He shook himself, cast her another abashed look. "Sorry, warrior. Well—for a long time after that, no one dared touch anyone else's horse, not even my cousin."

"Sensible of them," Xena murmured. "A lot of people feel about their horses the way some feel about their children, or their closest friends." She shifted, and held up a hand when he would have spoken. "Someone's out there. Your friend the baker, maybe?"

71

Xena was right: It was Ukloss and his son Adrik, as well as another man.

Ukloss carried a narrow, long basket filled with warm, fragrant loaves and two large, glazed round buns. Xena was somewhat astonished—the man was larger than the brute running the market jail, but clearly without any of Mondavius's lack of personal charm, or dislike of bathing. The baker's son couldn't have been old enough to grow a beard and he was easily half his father's size—pale and freckled where his father was dark-skinned and brown-eyed. Wary, too—she doubted Ukloss had ever been in a situation where he felt the kind of uncertainty his son visibly felt at the moment.

Then again, men of the baker's size and obvious easy-going mien seldom were aware of outside threat, or anything remotely like it. A man that enormous wouldn't need to resort to violence, or even threaten it. People saw the size and assumed the attitude, even though the attitude didn't always go with the size.

"Warrior, the boy told me you were here, so I didn't dare bring less than my best." The baker's voice boomed, despite a notable effort to curb it; his son hissed warning and he smiled, shrugged, and balanced the basket on the tottery table. "Never mind, Adrik," he said soothingly. Gabrielle caught her breath in a sudden gasp and sat upright, knuckles digging into her eyes; Adrik gasped at the unexpected movement and sound, and fell back a pace, wild-eyed. The baker glanced in Gabrielle's direction, eyed his son with amusement, then looked evenly and pleasantly at the warrior. He smiled, even more broadly; there was a wide gap between his front teeth. "My son isn't used to intrigue; makes him nervous." He shrugged, and held out a fragrant, fruited roll; Xena smiled back and took it, then sank teeth into sweetened and raisin-laden bread. She raised her eyebrows in astonishment, and took another exuberant bite.

"It isn't that, Father," the boy murmured, and he sounded worried. "It's the— If someone out there heard voices where there aren't supposed to be people . . ."

"Well, then, they won't," the older man replied softly.

Xena tucked the bite in her cheek and spoke around it. "This is *very* good."

"Thank you, warrior."

She waved an arm, taking in the rubble of the hut, then settled her backside comfortably on one of the stones. "You might as well say what you came to tell me. But I just want you to know in advance what I've already told the boy: I don't know Athens, I don't know the people here, and I don't see any way I could be of more help to you than the King or his men."

"The King," the third man spat harshly; then he started as Gabrielle made a wordless, unhappy little sound. "Sorry, miss. It makes me that angry, though! No one bothers with the likes of *us;* we're too poor to matter, we don't supply the palace with anything it can't get elsewhere—"

"They can't get bread as good as Father's elsewhere," Adrik put in flatly.

"Hah. You notice they broke the contract with *him* matter of a season ago. Not long after *those* three came."

Xena cleared her throat, and held up a hand for silence. Adrik cast her a sour glance but his father laid a huge hand on his shoulder, and with a mumbled oath he subsided. "All right," the warrior said finally. "You're angry, you're frustrated. I already understand that. But—why? What three?"

"And where's Golden Boy?" Gabrielle put in sharply. She was rubbing her shoulders back and forth against the

73

wall to ease an itch; her eyes were fixed on Kratos, who shrugged.

"He said he'd come. He'll come."

"He'd better—"

"Gabrielle," Xena said warningly. "Hadn't you better eat that other roll, before I finish mine, and start looking for seconds?"

"Hmmm? Oh—thanks," she added with a warm smile, as Adrik handed her the soft, fragrant round of bread. He blinked, then shyly smiled in return before he remembered where he was, and why. His brows drew together and he moved back to join his father.

"I think she's right," he told his father as he gestured roughly in Xena's direction. "We know *them,* and we know how dangerous they are. We know how they react when they aren't obeyed. What makes you think these two women, all by themselves, could—"

He didn't finish the sentence; with an unpleasant oath, a quick bound and a snatch, Xena very lightly grasped his chin with her fingertips, looked into his eyes, then flipped him. He made some noise, the air gurgling in his pipes, but just before his head would have smacked into stone, the warrior caught him, spun him deftly back to his feet, and shoved him onto his backside on one of the low, flat stones that littered the ruin. He sagged, gasping. "For one thing," she said softly, "*I* don't take out my anger on people who don't know any better—at least, I don't let them land on their unprotected heads, do I? Sit still and be quiet, if you can't add anything sensible to the conversation." Her eyes moved from Adrik to his astonished father. She finally fixed a level glare on the third man. "What three?" she asked, deceptively languid.

He swallowed, nodded once, and said, "It's—they—two of them are ours. *Were* ours," he amended darkly as Adrik shifted in his corner and mumbled something. Xena cast him a sidelong look and he subsided at once, but she was relieved to see Gabrielle finish her roll, get to her feet, and sit next to the baker's son. The warrior was barely aware of their soft conversation behind her, but she could guess its substance. *Great, Gabrielle. Keep him quiet, keep him occupied, and keep him out of trouble,* Xena thought, as she turned her full attention back to the older men.

"The worst of the lot came to Athens only recently, the past winter, I think. From somewhere to the west, there was a man who sold weapons, not just to his own kind but to anyone who had coin, even to both sides of a war!"

"I know that kind of man, they're out there," Xena broke in. "Everywhere. Go on."

"Opher came from—a neighborhood or two away, near enough we knew who he was, but not so near we crossed paths often. His cousin Pixus and Pixus's brother Mideron grew up across the square from my family's house. Those two volunteered when the call went out for soldiers to fight in Troy, but they came back long before the war was over. No one knew why, but there's rumor they were stealing from their captain's tent." Xena cleared her throat ominously; the man looked at her resentfully. "Just making certain you know the whole tale," he said.

"You can't leave Athens until after full dark anyway," Kratos put in. A long, cold look came over Xena's face; Kratos gazed back at her with that open child's face so untrustworthy in a young street thief. She finally sighed and turned back to the men.

"All right, boy, you have a point. But *they* don't want to be stuck in here all day, do they?" Her gesture took in the baker, his son, their angry companion. "Go on."

"Here," the baker said soothingly. "Let me, Brezakius." He gave the warrior a broad shrug and a smile. "He doesn't think so clearly these days, ma'am; not since they took his son and his pa away, and left threats in their places. But I'm getting ahead of myself.

"Pixus and Mideron never was what you'd call nice boys, so it didn't surprise some of us when they turned into the kind of men they are: kind that even an armed company doesn't want around. They want coin and good food, a nice place to live—but they don't want to earn it. Opher moved down here with 'em after they came back from the army in—well, would've been disgrace for me or my son, they didn't much care since they had two pieces of silver as leave pay. Bribe, more like. Still, two pieces could take a man far if he wanted, especially if he had no family like those two—but they went through it in a matter of a few days.

"Now, you'd think an ordinary man would realize, after drinking down two silver pieces in a mere few days, that he would need to work to earn more, if only for the ale shops. Ordinary, dishonest man would think he needed to steal or lift purses for coin."

"This leads us somewhere?" Xena asked mildly, as he paused for breath. The baker nodded emphatically.

"Opher's nearly as big and ugly as his brother—fortunately, his brother's in the big cell outside the wine market and likely to stay there a while—"

"Wait a minute. You can't mean—Mondavius?" Gabrielle put in suddenly. Xena glanced back at her; her friend's eyes were narrowed.

"That's him," the baker said. He didn't sound very pleased. "Started a fight in the very midst of the market to cover that he'd stolen a merchant's purse, flattened five stalls and half a dozen guards. Last we heard, they won't let him go this side of next summer."

76

"Likely he won't leave *then*," Adrik growled. "One of his bullies was telling Pixus the man likes it there, calls it his own little kingdom."

"I've met him, and if I had to figure him, that's what I'd say, too," Gabrielle said flatly. "Ah—sorry for the interruption," she added brightly as Xena raised an eyebrow at her. The warrior turned away; the baker handed his angry companion a small, crusty loaf and went on as Brezakius bit into it.

"They came up with the plan amongst 'em, best any of us can decide: Opher, Pixus, and Mideron. Called themselves the House of Protectors and got a few of the neighborhood boys to steal *for* them. And at first, they chose careful-like, only the kinds of boys who would think it a fun new game. Boys whose parents wouldn't much care whatever they did. Then, when that wasn't enough coin for their greed, they picked lads who weren't sure about stealing but went along because there was no one to tell them not to. Though when *their* mothers and fathers found out . . . well, not important. Eventually, every boy and many of the young girls along our streets and around our fountain were working for 'em. Now, some still thought it exciting, and they were pleased with the coin or two the Protectors passed down to 'em. More were afraid to be thieves, but the Protectors found ways around that—like Kratos here, they threaten harm to his mother and father, unless he cooperated."

Xena shook her head. "Correct me if I'm wrong—but what they were doing is illegal, right? And none of you thought to go to the King at this point?"

"But, no one *knew* what was going on," the baker said apologetically. "I mean, what boy involved in something as complex as that would be able to convince his parents he was telling the truth about it? But—all right, say a father learns all at once that his young son has some copper coins.

Well, I ask you, what child in a poor part of Athens like ours would have more than a single copper come by honestly? And what child wouldn't immediately give that coin to his mother, to help feed his family? What would you think, if your son had a handful of coppers, and he wouldn't say where he got 'em? When the alternative is starving, it's not hard to convince yourself that your boy found the coin, or was given it by a kind stranger; the reality doesn't have much usefulness.

"But, say that much truth comes out—that the boy's been lifting money from people in the market—what parent would go talk to the other parents about it?"

"The King," Xena reminded them patiently. "You know—the ruler of Athens with the army of guards who are in charge of keeping Athens free of thugs like that? The man who's supposed to keep illegal things like this from taking over his city?"

"We *sent* someone," Brezakius mumbled around his bread. His eyes were black, all pupil. "Man we always went to with problems or concerns in our neighborhood. The man who made decisions for us that were too small to bother the King with. Sent Polydorus. He never came back."

"Wait." Xena held up a hand as she settled more comfortably on her stone, considered this for some moments, and finally shook her head. "It doesn't make sense! Are you trying to tell me that King Theseus had him—"

Brezakius flung his arms wide, and swore as his knuckles scraped across rough stone. "That's part of the problem! We don't *know* where he is, or what happened to him! We don't know if the King has any say in any of this! All we know is that anyone who's tried to get to King Theseus for an audience can't get past his first secretary—Idiometus, he's called; he's the man who decides what person gets to see the second secretary, who gets to pass on a message, and who gets put back out on the street without being heard at all. These days—you can ask anyone in the main markets, warrior!—most of those who go to the palace get to pass on their message, but hardly anyone gets beyond the first secretary. And blessed few messages seem to have gone where they're supposed to—at least, there's never an answer to such messages that we've heard about. And they say Idiometus looks like a man walking barefoot through asps.''

Silence. Xena broke it with a long, tired sigh. "Look. I'm *sorry*. But this still isn't something I can help you with—''

"You haven't heard all of it yet," Brezakius broke in; then hurriedly, warily, he added, "Your pardon, warrior.''

"That's all right. Tell me.''

"Well, we knew we didn't dare send anyone else to the palace, not until we knew what had happened to Polydorus. We aren't much help to our people here but we'd be of even less aid if we all disappeared. We got the truth of things out of Kratos here and two other boys, using hard threats that scared 'em half silly. Ukloss here and I paid a call on 'em—on the so-called Protectors—told 'em to go find somewhere else to live, they weren't welcome around *us*.'' He bit his lip; his eyes were suddenly haunted. "They didn't say much—other than to offer us wine in glasses none of us could afford to purchase!—well, they just smiled and nodded and acted polite. But even Ukloss got kinda nervous after a bit, and I was downright scared. They acted like they were just waiting to beat on us or even kill us when we least expected it. Or maybe,'' he chose his words with care, "maybe it was more like they knew they were so safe at what they were doing that it didn't matter what we threatened, they'd still win, and we'd lose. Hard.

"We left finally, and they were still being polite, kind of behavior'd make a mother proud, but when I got home that night, my son and my father were both gone, and my wife was hysterical, weeping so hard it took hours to get matters from her. Finally, she broke the bad news: they'd sent armed men, brutes with broadswords, to take my son and my father, and when she'd have shouted for help, one of 'em held a sword to my boy's throat—he's all of five years, warrior!" Brezantius's voice cracked, and he swallowed hard. The baker gripped his shoulder in wordless sympathy, and after a moment, the man nodded and went on. "They'd given her a message for me: 'Tend your own row and stay out of other people's gardens, do exactly what we tell you, if you don't want to get your loved ones back in forty pieces. Each.' Poor Silexia was half-hysterical."

"Understandable," Xena murmured as he raised red-rimmed eyes to look at her. "I don't blame her. Go on."

"Those two were the first—my Brenitus and my father. Then Kratos's pa. But they weren't the last. The Protectors have at least twenty of ours. I mean, men and older boys from this neighborhood. They're mostly the men who might have been able to fight for their people, if they'd had to. None of us ever have fought in any fashion, of course. But I know I would have fought with whatever I had to hand, if I thought it would mend things. Not—not now."

"They didn't take the women?" Xena asked. "I mean, I'd think a commander would do that; he'd assume that women would make easier prisoners to cow, and their men more likely to walk carefully because of their women."

"I'd have thought as much," the man agreed unhappily. "But the scroll merchant explained it to me: They find the men more use at hard labor wherever they are keeping them, and the women and children left here are easier to keep in line, since they have no idea where their men might be. And the women know full well whatever they do that the Protectors don't want 'em to do will rebound immediately on their missing loved ones.'' Bleak eyes met hers. ''But the worst is not knowing. Might be my son and my pa are already dead and left for the vultures to finish. If they never come home, how would I know?''

Ukloss mumbled awkward consolation. Brezakius shook his head and sighed, then finally went on. He'd lost much of his anger, and appeared suddenly lost, distressed, frustrated because a man of his size couldn't simply thump someone on the head and be done with it.

''I'm sorry,'' Xena put in finally. He glanced at her, then fixed his eyes on his hands.

''You have to understand,'' he went on stubbornly. ''How much that changed matters. I mean, some of our men would act first in anger, then think—if they were able. But everything any of us have ever heard says wives and mothers are the other way about. Our women realize there are lives out there in the balance; one can't just shout and shake his fist and make things right.''

''I understand that,'' Xena said as he hesitated. ''No one blames you for not fighting.''

''I blame myself,'' he whispered. The man shook himself. ''Well, we haven't much choice, anymore. Most of the children steal for *them* now, and a few of the women do, too.''

''Mostly they threaten beatings,'' Ukloss said apologetically. ''Beatings to those they hold outside the city, I mean. As surety, you know. Like Elyseba: They told her that Kherix, her husband, was stealing pigs out in the countryside, and that if she didn't leave her son alone so he could do his errands in peace—errands, they call it!'' he snorted. ''If she didn't, they'd knock Kherix unconscious and toss him into the sty.''

81

"Nice."

"And things are getting worse: the Protectors aren't content with the thieves they already have; they say that women aren't watched the way poorly clad boys or grown men would be; that it's easier for women to take things from the stalls and not be caught. Or even suspected." The baker sighed, shook his head. "And things keep getting worse. Some of us worry that they'll try to order our daughters and young wives to—I mean . . ." The baker fumbled with his words; he was very red in the face.

"I understand. Don't talk about it."

"They've got men in the guards who look the other way for *them*," Kratos put in suddenly. "Men they pay with the coins *we* steal."

The warrior caught hold of his near arm and turned him to face her. "How much do you know about this?"

"Not—very much. But I heard them talking about it, not long ago."

"Names? Any names?" the baker demanded.

The boy considered this, then shook his head. "I don't remember any names. Just that they have guards who will pretend they don't see purse snatchings if it's certain that we children are doing the work. And there are more men in the guards who can get people put in jail, like my mother was." His voice went high; he hiccuped and then fell silent. Xena caught her own breath sharply.

"Wait—let me see if I can't figure this out. Because you and I had a bargain," the warrior said thoughtfully. Her eyes softened as they met and held his. He nodded, bit his lip. "You wouldn't steal for them and they said they'd keep her there until you stole again, that right?"

His dark lashes suddenly were beaded with tears; he really was very young, Xena thought, and her heart unexpectedly turned. He nodded sharply and his voice was a thin, wavery thing. "They—I didn't even know where she *was*, that first night. Because I never would have let her stay in there! But . . . they . . . ." He swallowed; Xena wordlessly held out her arms and he walked into them, buried his face against her shoulder, and sobbed.

Silence followed in the small hovel, except for the boy's miserable weeping. Xena smoothed his hair, patted his shoulder, and murmured softly against her ear until he finally nodded and was quiet, though he didn't release his hard grip on her armor.

"You men," she said quietly. "I still don't understand. I've met your king; I know men who've served under him. This is *not* the kind of dirt he allows in his city! King Theseus is known everywhere as the man who protects the poor and the voiceless. The downtrodden. So why are these men getting away with something as filthy as this, right under his nose?"

"Don't know," Brezantius admitted with a shrug. "But there's rumor in the streets. The Protectors were afraid of our king early, but now they've got a new man to back 'em, and their new man has an ear of his own in the palace."

"Oh?"

"We don't know much, understand," Ukloss said diffidently. "Just that this man came from that weapons dealer's camp and fled, with as much coin as he could carry, after the dealer was killed by a slashing blow from some dreadful weapon—a round, killing thing, someone said—but we don't know of any such weapon . . . ." His voice trailed off; Xena smiled grimly and held up her chakra.

"It's *very* effective," she murmured, her eyes fixed on something beyond the filthy wall she stared at. "Mezentius." She smiled. It wasn't a nice smile. "This man have a name? Anything about him that could help me identify him? Anything at all,'' she urged as the two very pale, middle-aged men stared at each other.

"He's not much bigger than I am; he's got pale hair and a neat little beard, a small, tight mouth. And his name is Brisus,'' Adrik put in flatly. The baker gazed at his son, shocked; Adrik shrugged. "He talked to me recently, Father; you might have expected it, don't you think? The King's own baker—his ex-baker, sorry—doesn't respond to pressure, so let's find a way to pump his son for soft spots.'' He snorted. "Of course, he failed! But I'm not certain he realized that I was on to him from the first, or that I wouldn't have given him the time of day, even if they'd held *you* as surety.'' Silence. Adrik bit his lip. "Well, I'm *sorry,* Father! But there comes a moment when you have to tell yourself, if this goes on, no one is safe.''

"Including, apparently, your father,'' Ukloss said dryly. His son eyed him impatiently.

"I would have gotten you to safety immediately, Father, if I thought it necessary. But the man was bluffing, or testing me; he wasn't applying pressure.''

Sure you'd have gotten your father to safety. Young fool, Xena thought contemptuously. It was just that kind of swaggering bluster that drove situations like this one into bloodletting. "You're fortunate, boy,'' she said in a flat voice. "And so's your father. Brisus is no man to take lightly. I know.'' Adrik eyed her impatiently; she raised one eyebrow and offered him a chill smile that didn't rise above her lips, and he subsided immediately. "I've met him before—but that doesn't matter, not to you. If that's the kind of man your king's ignoring—if for whatever reason he's letting that kind run things around here—then I can deal with them.''

84

"Our—our families?" the baker asked, rather timidly. "I don't want to— I know you understand about who's out there as hostage—but—"

"But you think about this: If I agree to help you, then we do things my way. You might not *like* my way. Oh," she added sharply as all three men began to protest vigorously, "I'm not going to ignore the fact they're holding your people hostage, and I will not cause the death of an innocent. I'll swear that by whatever god you like."

Silence. Gabrielle broke it. "Ah—that isn't just words, trust me. She means that."

Xena cast her a brief smile; it faded as she turned back to face the baker. "And the first thing is, once I start the fight against these so-called Protectors and whatever scum they've hired, I follow it through right to the end, which means until they're in the King's prisons or they're dead. Do you understand that?" She waited. Silence. Three men gazed back at her, wide-eyed and unhappy. She sighed. "Because if they aren't in prison or dead, then they're mad and they want revenge." Another unpleasant little silence. The baker finally shook his head. "Good. You may not like what I do, or how I do it—or what I ask you to do. You'll have to deal with it. In return, I won't ask for more than any of you can give. And I'll get your people back."

"That's all we want," Brezakius said flatly.

"Fine. Now, maybe I can't do anything about King Theseus: I'm a warrior, not a statesperson." Another silence. Ukloss eyed Brezakius sidelong; the baker's son cast up his eyes.

Brezakius stirred finally, and would have spoken, but the baker gripped his shoulder and sent his eyes toward the small room beyond the partition. "I think we three should . . . talk," he said. "So's we understand each other, as well as this warrior."

"Talk all you have to," Xena replied flatly. She glanced over her shoulder. "Gabrielle? I think you and I need to have a short conversation about all this, too."

"Ahhh—hey! Whatever you want," Gabrielle replied, her worried eyes belying her cheerful tone.

The three men had gone into a huddle near the makeshift door; Kratos joined them, but his eyes were fixed on the warrior and her companion. Xena took Gabrielle's arm and led her over to the opposite wall. Settling on a flat stone, she patted the rock next to her. "Look," she said in a low voice that couldn't have carried halfway to the baker and his son, even if they'd been paying heed to her. "I've got something to say, and you're not gonna want to hear it. I—"

Gabrielle sighed heavily and broke in. "Don't tell me, let me guess. You're gonna try to convince Brisus you're still his kind of warrior, right?"

Xena's mouth quirked. "You kidding? He didn't trust me when I went into that arms merchant's camp."

"Oh. Yeah, right, I forgot." Gabrielle gave her companion a swift, sidelong glance from under her lashes. "Okay, it's not that. It's— Oh, no!" she said sharply. "You don't want me fighting with you, is that it?" Xena's mouth quirked again, and her eyes were darkly amused. Gabrielle's brows drew together. "What, you don't think I can—"

Xena held up a hand for silence; Gabrielle rolled her eyes and set her lips in a hard line. "Just hear me out, will you?" Xena implored. "Then I'll listen to whatever you still want to say about it. I don't want you with me out there, either rescuing those prisoners *or* fighting Brisus and whatever thugs and goons he's hired. That's not because I don't think you're good enough. You are."

"Oh. Thanks," Gabrielle grumbled. "I think." She went silent again as the warrior gave her a hard look.

"I'm not just saying that. But Athens hasn't been particularly good for you, has it? And there's a guard out there looking for you, on his own personal vendetta—something beyond the fact that he thinks you're a thief helping that boy, and that you should be locked up.''

"I can handle Agrinon." *I handled him just fine out there on the sand at the foot races,* she thought, *when he was bellowing at poor little Arachne. So he's holding a grudge because I made him look bad—I can still handle him.*

"I know you can. But what about Agrinon and ten of his friends? You've caught him off-guard before this; you won't get a second chance like that. That's part of it, but if that were the only thing, I'd want you at my shoulder, or guarding my back.

"Someone needs to get into the palace. Get to Queen Hippolyta.'' She tugged at Gabrielle's short brown skirt. "Find out what's wrong in there, and let her know what's wrong out here. That's your job.''

"Oh.'' Gabrielle considered this and sighed once more. "I thought we were *done* with 'You fight and I talk.' Weren't we?''

Xena grinned. "Who says you're gonna just talk? King's palace, remember? There's gonna be guards everywhere, maybe even household members who're being paid by Brisus. Remember the secretary who's walking on asps?'' She waited; an abashed grin was Gabrielle's response.

"Okay, okay, I'll do it.''

"Keeping in mind,'' the warrior cautioned her, "that it's better all around if you *don't* have to do anything but tiptoe in, talk, and get back out again.''

"Gotcha,'' Gabrielle said cheerfully. She looked around, wrinkled her nose. "So what—we meet back here?''

"Ah—warrior.'' The men shifted and Ukloss came back. "We—we thought, it's still dark out there, though it won't be much longer. Your horse—there's a smithy not too far away, my wife's cousin keeps it, your horse would be safe and well cared for. You could—you could stay with her, or in my shop.''

''Is that safe?'' Xena asked.

''Safer than here, most likely. Someone might come by; children do. They might talk—''

''I get the idea,'' she drawled, and got to her feet. She held out a hand. Ukloss eyed it nervously, then accepted it. ''Who's in your shop—besides you and your son?'' *Whom I trust as far as Gabrielle could toss him,* she thought.

''Just the two of us. My wife doesn't come anymore. There's a room where I store my grain, though there aren't too many bundles of that just now. It's not noticeable from the street . . .''

''All right. Let's get Argo off the streets before sunrise; I'll decide what to do once I see this stable.'' She looked down at Gabrielle, laid a hand on her shoulder, then beckoned to Kratos. ''You'll stay with her?''

He nodded. ''I can do that.''

''Good. You'll know where I am when Gabrielle needs to find me again, right?''

''I'll know,'' he said solemnly.

''Good.'' She tousled his hair and smiled at him. ''Don't get caught, all right?'' She wrapped an arm around Gabrielle's shoulders and hugged her briefly. ''Remember, quick and quiet.''

''Quick and quiet,'' Gabrielle promised. ''Um—remember, Athens hasn't been too lucky for *you,* either.''

Xena laughed shortly. ''It's gonna be even less lucky for Brisis and his friends.''

5

Gabrielle took more time than she needed resettling the door behind the three men, Xena, and Argo. Kratos sat cross-legged on the floor, looking up at her, his face expressionless and his eyes very wide. She smiled at him and settled on a stone, two of the baker's hard rolls in her hand. She held one out to him. "Well, I'd still like to strangle Golden Boy, but I guess it was all for a good cause, wasn't it?"

"I don't understand," the boy replied. "And you don't have to share that with me. Ukloss meant them both for you—"

"I already ate two," Gabrielle said firmly, and shook the roll at him. "So, we'll share. What don't you understand?"

"You should be angry—I mean, she's really angry with me, isn't she?"

"Oh, you mean Xena? Well, angry, sure but not the way you think," Gabrielle replied earnestly. "I mean, she gets cross when things get really complicated, like this has—but that's not your fault, and she knows it. She wouldn't blame *you*. And she gets upset when she sees things like

89

what your people are up against—you see, she really can't help herself. She's a hero—but don't tell her I told you that; she doesn't like me to say that about her.''

''Oh.'' He considered this gravely, broke his roll in half, and stuffed part in his pocket before he began to eat the rest. ''I—I didn't thank you for finding my mother in that cell, last night. If I'd had to go looking for her, we might not—''

''Oh, you'd have done just fine,'' Gabrielle assured him quickly as he swallowed, hard. ''Remember the scroll merchant was right there; he'd have helped you.''

''Maybe,'' the boy replied warily. Gabrielle eyed him, every bit as cautious.

''Ah—he's okay, isn't he? I mean, I only know him from the Bards' Academy . . .''

''He's okay,'' Kratos mumbled around a mouthful of bread. ''He's afraid of *them,* but so's the baker and—well, everyone but my cousin and the baker's son. Adrik is a fool—and my cousin's protected by his honored papa, of course,'' he added. He swallowed, broke off another bite, and tucked it in his cheek. ''All the scroll maker will say about them is that he doesn't like being hit. But I don't know anyone that does.''

''I'm with both of you: being hit is not fun at all. But, your cousin's protected? Ah. Gotcha.'' Gabrielle remembered suddenly. *Son of Hermes and under the protection of his father, my near foot,* she thought indignantly. *And my father is—is Zeus!* It made a picture; she bit back a grin, afraid the boy would think she was laughing at him, or his precious cousin.

They finished the bread in a companionable silence, which Kratos broke suddenly when he jumped to his feet and eased quietly across the rubble-strewn ground to the door. Gabrielle watched, every bit as alert, her hand moving toward a fist-sized stone. There was a faint scrabbling noise; the boy sighed quietly and scratched on the inner surface, listened again, then set his shoulder against the door. A long-fingered hand wrapped around the edge nearest the opening, and Helarion eased himself inside and pressed the door back into place.

He stood very still, gazing down at Gabrielle in the fading lamplight; she squared her jaw and looked right back, eyes level and opaque. It didn't work with Xena yet, but others could no doubt testify she was getting much better at the "look." The boy was apparently one of those; his eyes flickered, and he actually took a step back, against the wall.

He was older than she'd thought: maybe seventeen or so, instead of fourteen. There was a line of pale, uneven beard along his chin and jawline. Not quite as statue-beautiful, either: attractive in a way, but his jaw was too wide for her tastes, his nose a little too delicate and straight. His generous mouth tumbled into a spoiled-looking smirk as he gave her a very deep, courtly bow. "My little cousin says you want to pummel me for finding you accommodations and food last night. Well! Here I am: thump away!" He flung his arms wide and smiled. The effect was fairly dazzling, but not as heart-stopping as he clearly thought. Golden skin, a well-muscled body, a neat waist—he was certainly not the skinny little urchin he had appeared to be when she first saw him dashing through the marketplace.

"Thanks," she replied sweetly. "I'd rather wait and catch you off-guard. More fun for *me* that way—and a better payback." He blinked; the smile faded. She stood, folded her arms across her chest, and glared at him—straight across, he wasn't any taller than she. "I really would like to know *why* you did that, though. That was a low trick."

He shook his head, held up both hands. "Save the lecture, I've heard it before. It's boring. Next you'll tell me I had no business with the purse in the first place." He shrugged. "The man who had it dangling from his belt by one thin leather strap—now, that's the man who had no business with it. And besides, my little cousin got you out, didn't he? And you had Ukloss's good bread for dinner— I don't see what the problem is."

She stared at him, both shocked and astonished. "You really don't get it, do you?"

"I suppose I might, if I felt like it." Another exposure of even, white teeth, typically gorgeous eyes. "I don't."

"Cousin!" Kratos hissed urgently as he tugged at the frayed tunic; cloth tore with a rotten ripping sound and he snatched his fingers back as the older boy smoothed the ragged cloth back against his ribs. "She and the warrior are going to help us! Don't—"

"Kratos, no one is going to help you against the Protectors," Helarion informed him in a flat voice. "No one. The people around here can't afford to pay anyone for aid, and those men are well entrenched." He glanced at Gabrielle. "I've heard of the warrior—and I heard what you did to Agrinon. Obviously, you have skill with a weapon, and she's legendary. But this one will break her. *And* you."

"I don't think so," Gabrielle countered sharply. "Why don't you give it a chance?" Her eyes snapped, and her shoulders went stiff. "And who said anything about money? You don't *hire* Xena! Or me!"

He shrugged broadly; his lips moved once more in something like amusement. "Well, it isn't much to do with me, either way. I won't lift purses for *them;* there's nothing I can do to help anyone around here, either. If I die trying, what use is that to anyone?"

"Interesting attitude—but not mine," Gabrielle said flatly. "And you're wrong, I'll wager you anything. Well," she added hastily, as his mouth turned sly, "anything within reason."

"And who decides what's reasonable?" he demanded cheerfully.

"Cousin!" Kratos whispered angrily. "I knew you wouldn't help," he said, and his mouth suddenly drooped as Helarion lowered himself next to him to sit cross-legged. The boy's face was only just higher than his seated cousin's; at this angle, they looked very much alike, Gabrielle realized. Unnerving.

"You've always known what I'm like, Kratos. Don't act so disappointed."

The boy made patterns in the dirt with the toe of his sandal. "Well, but—oh, Helarion, if you talk like that, she might just get mad and go away."

"I won't," Gabrielle promised him. "I might thump your cousin a couple extra times, but I won't hold *you* responsible for him."

"Thanks," Helarion said dryly.

"Any time." Silence. It stretched. The boy finally cleared his throat.

"Well, I knew you wouldn't help," Kratos said resentfully. "But I need to get her—Gabrielle—into the palace, to see the Queen. So if you could at least tell me where to go once I get past the kitchen path . . ." His voice trailed away; Helarion was staring at him, his jaw trembling.

Another silence. Kratos stared right back. *So Golden Boy isn't beyond surprise after all,* Gabrielle thought. "You can't do that," Helarion said smoothly, but with definite finality.

"I can so! She has to get in so she can talk to the Queen! She doesn't know the way!" The boy squared his shoulders and his chin. "I can get her in there safely, if you tell me how. But I'm taking her, whether you tell me or not."

"You're mad, little cousin!" Helarion snorted. "You've been listening to that foreign scroll merchant again, telling you all the wrong kinds of tales." Silence. Helarion's voice had been light, but his eyes now brooded on the far wall for a long moment. Finally, he looked up at Gabrielle, and his generous mouth quirked into a small smile. "All right. Let's say, my *dear* lady, that—just perhaps—you thought I owed you an apology for last night's lodging."

"We could certainly say that, couldn't we?" Gabrielle began dryly.

He held up a hand for silence. "Indulge me. Say you thought that. Say *I* wanted to indulge *you*—for some foolish reason."

"It's called honor, but you probably didn't know that," Gabrielle murmured.

"I've heard of it." Helarion laughed; it wasn't a particularly amused laugh. "It's also a good reason so many young men are led down to Hades by my father each evening. Honor is one of those fool's notions that get you killed. Dead."

"Your father—I never heard that tale!" Gabrielle stared at him, fascinated then shook her head, sharply. "You're trying to distract me and it's not gonna work! Besides, you're wrong, honor and courage don't always, but— All right," Gabrielle said quickly as he rolled his eyes, "I'm *indulging* you. Go on."

"Say that I agreed to get you into the palace—and unlike my young cousin here, who has only gone as far as the kitchen pathway, I've *been* inside the palace, and I *know* I can get you where you want to go, without either of us being caught. Or even seen. Whichever part of the palace you have in mind. And I can get you back out again, particularly if you have to do that in secret." Kratos made a small, protesting noise and Helarion shook his head, then laid a hand on the boy's shoulder. "I'm not trying to insult you. You're good, cousin, but this kind of thing isn't really what you're best at. And my aunt Elyseba would make my life a misery if she ever learned I let you do this. Besides," he added lightly, "you're a marked boy at the moment, remember? Your mother's missing from the market jail and you've quit thieving for *them*."

Kratos shook his head stubbornly. "No one knows that it was me who got her out, and besides—"

"They'll learn soon enough. Trust me, cousin. You know how gossip is."

"Ah—look, can we continue this later?" Gabrielle broke in. "If he's marked, I'm *really* marked. There's a couple city guards who'd like to toss me back in that jail for a long time, and I am not gonna be pleased if that happens. I want to get this done, find out what I need to, and get back out of sight, okay? And I want to get this finished so Xena and I can get out of Athens before something else goes wrong. Okay?"

Helarion rolled his eyes and flipped a dismissive hand.

"Kratos," she added softly. The boy gave her a miserable look, then glanced away. "Don't do that, please. Honestly, I'm not trying to do what you think. You know, 'Oh, he's just a kid.' I was really, truly amazed when you got us out of that jail so quietly: that took courage, planning— most of the grown men I've ever met couldn't have done it. But if your cousin says it's that kind of dangerous for you—well, I have to think of your mother, because she'd hate me forever if I got you killed. And I have to think of me, and of Xena. We're both no good to anyone back in that cell, are we?" She waited. Eyes lowered, he finally shook his head. "And believe this, too: if there's a time when I need to trust you like I'm trusting Helarion at this moment, you're the guy I want at my side. Okay?'' A longer silence; the boy finally nodded. She turned to face Helarion, and her eyes were stormy. "So. When do we go?''

"Soon as you like," Helarion replied promptly; one long-fingered hand came out to ruffle his cousin's head and the boy managed a wry smile for him. "It's better if we hit the palace around sundown, though—the servants are eating, the cooks are preparing dinner, and everyone else— especially the Queen—rests before the late meal.''

"Fine," Gabrielle said.

"I can get you a scarf of my mother's," Kratos volunteered. He still didn't sound wildly pleased. "A long one. It'll cover your hair and face.''

"That would help a lot,'' Gabrielle said and nodded. "Thanks. One other thing,'' she added as she turned back to Helarion. "I need to go by the scroll merchant's shop and make certain they let him go.''

"The scroll merchant?'' the golden young thief replied with a shrug. "If he's out, I haven't heard of it.''

"He has an assistant. I need to tell him where Peder is.''

The thief grinned and ran a long-fingerd hand through crisp, golden curls. "Oh, well. If that's the most difficult thing you want of me today—''

"No guarantees on that. In fact, you'll be lucky to get off that easy.''

The sun was barely up, a dark orange ball against the eastern sea, when Helarion led her into the early bustle of the farmer's market. "Stay close, and ignore anyone who tries to stop you.''

"Ah—right. Why would anyone?'' Gabrielle caught hold of his elbow and dragged him to a halt. "I do better if I have a clue why things are going on, okay?'' He turned, impatience lowering his brows.

"To sample wares: fruit, bread, breakfast meats—some of the merchants can be pretty demanding. And I've heard about you and food, and your appetite—''

"Oh, yes?'' Gabrielle demanded softly; her eyes were narrowed under the soft gray scarf, and her hands shifted subtly on the staff she'd been using as a walking aid. Helarion gripped her near hand.

"Put that *down*! If you want to keep it, you use it like a walking stick, remember?''

"Don't you try to tell *me* what—''

He overrode her with an angry hiss. "You want the guard down our throats? Just avoid the food merchants, will you? You want to browse the stalls, do it on your own time! Right now it's gonna slow us, give the guard in this area a better look at you. You want that?''

"That was a dirty crack, about me and food,'' Gabrielle snapped back, though she was careful to keep her voice low. Her eyes were black, all pupil, narrowed. He rolled his own, dramatically. "But all right, I'll ignore them. So long as you get me to Peder's shop as quickly as possible.''

"I'm *trying* to, aren't I?'' He growled under his breath as he turned away and plunged into the darkness between a long row of fragrant booths. Gabrielle mumbled several impolite comments under her breath, and followed.

They made it through the farmer's market and into the potters and glazers before an angry shout slowed Helarion— briefly. He glanced over his shoulder and Gabrielle saw the wild amusement kindle in his eyes, the wide grin meant for someone behind them. "Don't look; you have the most dreadful luck, I swear by my father himself.''

"Luck?''

"Luck. It's your pet guard, wouldn't you know? And he's very angry," the boy said cheerfully. "I *said*, don't look!" he added sharply and, grabbing her near wrist, he sprinted down the crowded aisle, dragging her half off her feet and nearly costing her her grasp on the walking staff. He took two sharp changes of direction, past a man selling fragrant rolls from a tray and then around a richly clad, tall woman with a commanding eye and very red, plaited hair. Gabrielle followed perforce. The woman exclaimed and spun around to stare after them. Gabrielle briefly met the woman's eyes and shrugged helplessly, but Helarion was swearing good-naturedly as he dragged her between two stalls piled high with glazed and unglazed pots, cups, wine jugs, and platters. Another shout, more distant this time, and from behind the billowing canvas of an adjacent stall came the gallop of feet passing them at high speed. Helarion turned to face Gabrielle and laughed; his eyes were wicked and he wasn't even breathing hard.

More than could be said for *her*. She leaned forward, hands on her knees, fighting to control a wildly thudding heart and overheated face, to swallow air that whistled in and out of a tightened throat much too quickly. "Wha-what do you mean, pet guard?" she demanded finally.

"I was told you and the warrior were both in good fighting condition," he replied blandly. "You sound like my grandefer—my *mother's* father, that would be, of course."

"Of course? Oh," Gabrielle drew a deep breath, straightened up, and let it out slowly. "Of *course*," she replied dryly. "Since you're on a regular running program with Zeus, right?"

A corner of his mouth twitched impatiently. "I don't think we need to discuss this, if you're going to have an attitude like *that*."

"I don't care whether your pop's Zeus, or Hermes, or the stupid blind cyclops I just saw halfway to Thebes! I don't want to discuss it because I don't *care*!" Gabrielle shouted. At his sudden gesture, she glanced around, then lowered her voice prudently. "Look—can we get out of here, find the shop, and get out of sight again? Before something else goes wrong?"

"You!" A gravelly, unpleasant—and unpleasantly familiar—voice filled the area between the stalls; Gabrielle whirled, staff at the ready, to find Agrinon four short paces away—just out of her reach. His mouth was ugly; his eyes moved beyond her briefly and he nodded with grim satisfaction. "Knew you'd be with *him,* if we found you anywhere inside the city. So what—he's your lover, your brother—well, who cares what he is? Or maybe that warrior of yours likes 'em young—"

"Oh." Gabrielle managed a casual sounding laugh, though her hands kept a murderous grip on the staff. "Did you think that up all by yourself," she asked sweetly, "or did you have help?" His eyes narrowed even further and she laughed again, more normally this time. "Agrinon, you know what? I think you're gonna pay for that one, right here and now."

"I don't think so," he sneered. "Because you're both gonna come with us—"

"Not a chance," Gabrielle replied flatly. "So—what, you're scared of a mere girl half your size?" she added jeeringly. The guard snorted, his color suddenly high, and he drew his dagger. She leaped forward, and slapped the staff down smartly across his wrist, sending his blade flying. But the vibration along both hands and the rebound off his wrist cost her the staff at the same moment; it flew from numbed fingers to clatter to the ground well to her side.

"Little too crowded in here for my tastes," Helarion announced suddenly, and with a crowing, taunting laugh, he turned and ran. The second guard would have followed, but at a sharp gesture from Agrinon, he subsided warily.

"He isn't important. We want *her*," he snapped.

"You—get your skinny backside over here, you rotten little—" Gabrielle shouted, but Helarion was already out of earshot. A glance over her shoulder confirmed that; she turned back to face the two guards. Agrinon squared his shoulders, smirked nastily, and strode toward her. Her eyes flicked away from him; the red-haired woman she'd nearly run down moments before stood limned in the light of the little alleyway, hands on her hips and a formidable expression on her face.

"What's this?" she demanded loudly. The second guard whirled around sharply; Agrinon glanced in her direction, then ignored her, his attention all for the amazon-clad, pale-haired woman before him. Gabrielle offered him a faint, apologetic smile, then jumped, her legs scissoring sharply and unexpectedly. Her right foot caught him in the kneecap and he went partway down, cursing steadily; she spun halfway around, caught up the staff, and slammed one end into the ground as she kicked off. Both heels hit his temple with a nasty crack. He slid bonelessly to the ground, and was blessedly silent.

She spun around, staff at the ready; the second guard had backed away from his superior and their supposed prisoner. The tall woman tapped him on the shoulder and cleared her throat ominously. He gasped and spun toward her, but she already had her hand braced against her jaw, her elbow out. It caught him in the throat and sent him staggering; Gabrielle's staff slammed across the back of his head a moment later.

"Hey," she said finally as she looked up to give the woman a rather breathless grin. "Nice job!"

"I was curious," the woman admitted. "Oh—that?" She gave the fallen guard a distasteful look down the length of a slender, freckled nose, then began rubbing her elbow. "I had brothers. Learned that trick from one of 'em."

"I'll remember that, it's good," Gabrielle said. "But— you actually walked into this corner behind two of the King's guards because you were curious? I mean—that's nervy!"

"They can't touch *me*," the woman replied evenly; the corners of her mouth twitched with some kind of meaning. "And I was trying to sort out why an Amazon was wandering around the market with *that* particular thief, and covered by a poor woman's shawl. My curiosity overcame common sense, I suppose. Ordinarily, one avoids the King's guards these days."

"Oh—yeah. I gotta agree with you there," Gabrielle said with a sharp nod. "Now," she added as she looked around, and swore under her breath. Her companion raised one eyebrow in surprise. "That boy—I *knew* I couldn't trust him!"

"There isn't a merchant in this end of Athens who wouldn't agree with you," the woman replied. "I'm Cy-davia, by the way."

"Gabrielle. Ah—I don't suppose you'd know the way to a shop owned by a scroll merchant—a tall, pale-haired foreign one—named—"

"Named Peder, son of Wagt, village of Skjold? Don't look so surprised; there aren't that many foreigners in Athens, let alone men *that* foreign, and there's only one who's a scroll merchant," Cydavia replied crisply. Her eyes were amused, though. "I know where his shop is. Matter of fact, I was heading in that direction myself. So if you'd like a guide who isn't quite so—ah—fickle . . ." She stopped, the offer implicit. Low-pitched laughter interrupted her suddenly, and both women spun around, Gabrielle's hands

101

clutching her staff, at the ready. Helarion gazed down at the two guards, and as Agrinon groaned and stirred, the young thief slammed a boot into the side of his head. Cydavia eyed him narrowly and with open suspicion; Gabrielle winced.

"I cannot believe you'd remain here gossiping!" the market thief snapped. "What, are you waiting for them to waken so you can battle them again?"

"I can't believe *you* took off on me and then dared to show your face again," Gabrielle said flatly. "Are you always so dependable?"

"Most of my companions don't have the same talent for bringing guards down on us as *you* have," he replied pointedly. His eyes moved from her to Cydavia; they crinkled and his mouth twitched, but as the second guard groaned, he caught hold of Gabrielle's arm and hauled her behind one of the pottery stalls, down a long, narrow alley, and across a dusty, deserted square, eventually emerging next to a low stand covered in piles and hanks of spun wool. "We're close to the foreigner's stall," he said, the first thing either had said in a long time.

"Not that close," Cydavia's voice came from behind him, and he turned on one heel to glower at her. The glower didn't last long, though. His mouth twisted, his eyes lightened.

"I know you," he said finally. The woman folded her arms across fine blue linen and brought her chin up so she could fix him with a level, unsettling stare. "You're the woman who can't laugh and walk at the same time—it's all over the city."

"Can't—can't what?" Gabrielle asked, but certainty hit her before the boy could reply and she stared. "You!" she exclaimed as she spun around to gaze wide-eyed at the woman. "You're the merchant's wife who swore out the complaint against Peder, and got him tossed in that cell! How could you do that?''

"*I* didn't," Cydavia replied. Her eyes were momentarily angry. "My fool of a husband did. It wasn't his business to begin with and he won't do something like that again, I assure you." She moved her head slightly. "Not if he plans on using my father's money in his bid for the Agora this winter, he won't! Especially since I control that money." She looked from Gabrielle to Helarion and back again. "Never mind my fool of a husband. What's an Amazon doing in Athens skulking around with *this* creature?" A wave of her hand took in the market thief. Helarion grimaced.

"Good taste," he replied and Gabrielle elbowed him in the gut and cast him a sweet-mouthed, stormy-eyed smile as he choked and wheezed for air.

"I'm not really an Amazon— Well, okay," she amended carefully, "I was given Right of Cast under Queen Melosa. But actually, that was all kind of an accident. I'm— I travel with Xena."

The other woman had already gone wide-eyed, but at this, she caught her breath sharply. "Xena! Good gods, do you really? I've heard of her!"

Gabrielle shook her head and spread her arms wide in apology. "I— Now, listen, she isn't like that anymore, honestly—"

"No, I've *heard* of her!" Cydavia insisted. "She saved a village, a distant cousin of mine lived there; a warlord named Draco was ready to kill everyone and she—"

"Oh. All right," Gabrielle said with a sudden smile. "I guess you *have* heard of her. Great! But—"

The woman laid a hand on her arm. "And you've been with the Amazons? You know them? I mean—know them well enough that you could possibly give someone who wants to join them an introduction?"

"*Why* are we still standing here gabbling?" Helarion complained painfully from behind them. Both women turned and gave him a chill look; he smiled faintly and shrugged. "The shop is *that* way," he said bitingly. "We are here. The guards are god knows where—but everywhere throughout the market, and looking for you." He leveled a finger at Gabrielle. "And we—"

"And we are going, now," Cydavia cut him off imperiously. "She and I, that is. You can just be about your own business!"

It wasn't Xena's look but it was nearly as effective, Gabrielle thought admiringly. Down a lightly freckled, narrow nose, chin slightly elevated, nostrils compressed, and eyes utterly icy, dark blue slits. Helarion swallowed hard before he managed a would-be conciliatory smile.

"You may do as you choose, of course," he replied dryly. "But it happens I have business with Peder's assistant, Samilos. So we can go separately or otherwise, it's entirely your choice, ladies, but we'll wind up there together in any event, so why not—"

"All right!" Gabrielle gestured with her head. "That way, isn't it? Whatever! Can we do *something*?"

"I'd suggest we do," the other woman replied evenly and joined her. The golden-haired young thief swore in a picturesque fashion, then fell in behind them.

He didn't stay there long; but each time Gabrielle found herself hoping they'd lost him, he reappeared as if called, either at her elbow or just ahead of them. She jumped every single time; the red-haired Cydavia merely sighed with heavy patience and kept moving.

• • •

The scroll merchant's shop was smaller than she would have expected: a chamber no more than six paces by four, stacked floor to ceiling with finished scrolls all along the outer walls. There were no windows or openings of any kind, just a few thin slits at roof level for air. Narrow shelves spaced closely between the thick walls formed aisles and more scrolls towered above Gabrielle's head in what she hoped was a well-ordered stack. Other aisles held open scrolls, piled hides, parchments, stacked papyrus sheets, pale cream vellum, turned and polished spools, fancy ends for scrolls—all the ingredients which a scribe or a bard would need. Beyond this a set of shelves held already inked scrolls, and past that were incised clay shapes or glyphs to dip in ink or wax for easy illustration.

The infamous scroll that had temporarily cost the merchant his freedom was, Gabrielle saw with relief, nowhere in sight.

Helarion pressed past them and strode quickly into a small back room where a continuous grinding noise seemed to accompany floating wood dust. "Samilos—hey, are you in there?"

"Who else would be making this particular noise, in a shop like this?" a reedy voice demanded rudely in turn.

Gabrielle cast her eyes toward the low ceiling, then turned to smile at her companion. "So . . . Cydavia, isn't it? How come you want an introduction to the Amazons?"

The woman's mouth quirked, though her eyes remained dark. She shoved the pale blue scarf impatiently from red hair. "Because I'd like to leave my horse-rearing kin *and* my horse-rearing mate and go where horses are really appreciated, maybe? Because I'd like to ride whenever I choose, and I could do that if I were an Amazon?"

"Ah—wait," Gabrielle said with a sidelong glance. "Your family *and* your husband are horse people. You were raised with horses. You don't get to ride. Am I missing something?''

"My father wants to increase the family fortunes," the woman replied dryly. "My husband is the result."

"Ahhhh—got it." Gabrielle gave her a sympathetic look. "Your family and your man have these goals, all of which involve you playing the demure lady?"

"Right," Cydavia replied gloomily. "What I want— well, given the choice, I'd be out there on a white horse, riding with the Amazons."

"Don't lose that dream," Gabrielle urged quietly. "You just might get it, if that's what you really want." She recalled herself to the moment and sighed faintly. "Unlike me—I got one choice at the moment, and I don't like it much. I need to get into the palace, talk to the Queen. And I need *him*," she gestured in Helarion's direction, "to get me there."

"Oh, no, you don't," Cydavia replied vigorously.

"No?"

"No. He might be able to get you in and out. I can get you to see Queen Hipolyta, and back out again whenever you want. She and I know one another."

"Oh?"

"Well—she knows me the way a queen knows a wealthy merchant's wife," the woman admitted with a dry smile. "Still, she claims to like me because we can just talk about things—like horses. And that means that I can get into the palace openly. And though I don't generally bother, it's usual for a woman like me to have a servant along. Say," she eyed her companion up and down, "say a woman of nearly my height, pale hair covered discreetly by a dark scarf that belongs to the woman who actually does keep my chamber, and under the scarf, Amazon's skirts?"

Gabrielle laughed. "Hey. Hey! Like it!"

"You *would*." Helarion spoke from just behind her, and she jumped. "It's a fool's notion; don't listen to this woman," he urged as Gabrielle spun around to glare at him, arms folded across her chest. "She's— I mean, look what she did to the scroll merchant!"

"She didn't," Gabrielle said flatly. "Her husband did. And *I* laughed at that stupid scroll myself."

"You can't—All right," he said. "You go in with her, you maybe get to the Queen, you maybe aren't detected, you *maybe* get back out again. And then what?"

"And then I get out of your life forever—which sounds really good to *me* at this point," Gabrielle retorted.

"And if you need to get word out of the palace to your— ah, your *other* friend while you're deeply in the midst of— call it the enemy camp—then what?" Helarion pursued.

"Well—okay, then I—ah—" Gabrielle glanced at Cydavia, who shook her head so the red plait slapped both shoulders. "Well, we—okay, then we what?"

"Then," Helarion replied evenly, "we signal to Helarion from the Queen's windows," he laid a finger across the bridge of his slender nose and rubbed it, three times, "and Helarion gets word to the warrior and her allies, and—well, you claim to be intelligent, lady bard, you work it out."

"I'd like to work it out on your—" Cydavia began angrily, and her hands bunched into fists. With a would-be cheerful laugh, Gabrielle edged between the two.

"Well—great. I just knew we could sort things out, if we cooperated. Helarion, I guess we won't see much of you once we get going, but you'll be out there, right?" He eyed her, his eyes sardonic. "Because if you aren't, you don't want to think what Xena's gonna do to you, right?"

He sighed, shook his head. "Right. Okay, fine, right! I'm with you. I— Who's that?" he demanded as the slender shaft of sunlight coming through the shop door was suddenly cut off.

6

It was the scroll merchant himself, a little worse for the wear, who came slowly into the shop, eased into the shade between two long aisles of scroll paraphernalia, and slid bonelessly down the nearest shelves to sit, cross-legged, in mid-floor. He swore in what must have been his northern language, a nasty sounding mess of fricatives.

Gabrielle hurried over to join him, sat knee to knee with him, and laid a hand against his cheek. A faint line of near-white beard prickled her fingers, and he smiled faintly.

"I was sure you'd keep your promise and come to check for me, Gabrielle. Thank you. But it's fine," he added, and a corner of his mouth attempted a smile. "They had no choice but to let me go, and leave my shop be—for the moment, that is." He glanced up as Cydavia came over to join them, winced as his eyes met hers, then managed a smile in her direction.

"I told Berdris to drop all mention of a charge," she said firmly. "The whole matter is between me and you, and none of *his* business. I wasn't angry with you, merchant. My husband won't do that again."

"I am delighted to hear it," Peder replied wearily. He glanced up as his dark stick of an apprentice came out of the back room to stare at him curiously. The merchant stiffened, and Gabrielle slewed around to see the erstwhile son of Hermes peering over Samilos's narrow shoulder. "Don't you dare to steal anything, you sun-haired menace," Peder ordered flatly. "Not so much as a fallen fragment of clay, or a rag of papyrus—"

"What would *I* want with such nonsense?" Helarion demanded. "I don't read or write, and I can't see the point of either, as you well know. It keeps no one fed, after all."

"It keeps *me* fed," Peder replied crisply.

"Well, but I've sworn to you before not to take the least pebble from before your shop. Sir," he added, and made the word sound almost like a curse.

"I know you've said so," Peder replied darkly. "And we both know I trust you as far as *my* chief god's favorite son could hurl a hammer. That's a long distance, before you ask." He turned back to Gabrielle. "You shouldn't have come out during the daylight, you know. In fact, I'd've thought you'd be long gone from Athens, you and Xena both."

"Well-l-l . . ." Gabrielle stretched the word out, and finally shrugged; her cheekbones were pink.

The merchant smiled; the skin around his blue eyes crinkled. "You're helping them—staying to help Kratos and his people, aren't you? You know—I just knew you would, once you heard—"

"We're gonna try," Gabrielle said and cast a meaningful glance in the direction of the apprentice. Peder nodded.

"He's all right. But! He should be working on those new filials for the order of scrolls the Academy placed, shouldn't you, Samilos?" he added meaningfully. Samilos mumbled something and was gone. Helarion had vanished quietly sometime before, Gabrielle wasn't exactly certain when. "I trust Samilos entirely," the merchant said.

"Well—all right," Gabrielle replied. "I think you ought to know, Xena isn't totally happy about all this. I mean—she's helping, of course. Something—a mess like this, of course she'd help people like Kratos and his mother! But she's not thrilled with the situation, so it wouldn't hurt if you avoided her for the time being."

"I'll avoid her," the merchant said hastily.

"I'm just trying to figure out, though," Gabrielle went on, "why you aren't doing something—anything!—to help Kratos and his mother and the rest of them. I mean, what if Xena and I hadn't been here, what if we hadn't been tossed into that cell, or *her* husband hadn't made a complaint against you?"

"Oh—that? It's called Fate," Peder replied grandly, with a sudden return of the amused corner of his mouth that passed, in his condition, for a grin. "We were fated to meet, all three of us; the Norns planned it—"

"You would *never* get the Fates interested in a mess like this," Gabrielle said flatly. "Whatever you call *your* Fates, ours wouldn't touch the current situation. They'd be laughing too hard about the irony of it."

"Nonsense," he said, and waved a hand. "Three Norns, three Fates. And mine are just as amused by irony as yours, but that doesn't mean they stay out of human affairs."

"Well, *Xena* isn't amused at all, just now," Gabrielle told him firmly. "Just—keep that in mind, will you? And, really, Peder, I want to know how come you aren't helping Kratos and his mother. I mean, really, all those poor, desperate people—"

"You see this shop?" the merchant broke in, and he waved both hands. "A poor thing but mine own—that's a quote, by the way—and the way things are just now in

110

Athens, I could lose it at any time, and wind up *working* my passage back to my uncle Erkkh's longhouse. I'd rather not; the Phoenecians are kindly shipspersons, but there are others who believe in things like leg irons and whips. I'd be even less pleased to be dead of stupidity; the Valkyries would not only leave me here to rot, this far south, but they'd laugh at me—"

"Later," Cydavia broke in firmly, hands on her hips. "She asked why. That isn't an answer."

"It is so an answer," he replied, his voice vaguely resentful. "There is nothing I can do for those impoverished people but talk to the wrong people and get tossed back in that prison cell. Or die doing something stupid that would probably get half of *them* killed as well. I don't know King Theseus and I certainly don't know which of his huge household can be trusted. I don't fight—I'm a *scroll* merchant, by all Valhalla! And you've met some of the King's guards, you know what they're like! I did what I could, I *found* them a fighter. Two fighters," he added cautiously as Gabrielle gave him a sidelong look and gently cleared her throat. "I'm sorry if it doesn't answer anything for you," he said finally. "It's how things are. You do what you can, with what you've got. That's realistic."

"I— All right." Gabrielle sighed and drove her fingers through her hair. "You're right. And I'm sorry. It's just that—"

"When you hold a pen, everything looks like a scroll," Peder replied.

"Well—yeah. That's right. Hey—like that; mind if I borrow it?" she asked.

He smiled suddenly, that sly turning of the corners of his mouth that reminded Gabrielle of the statues she'd seen of satyrs, and brought his open hands gently together. "We're even, then, I think," he said.

"Stop that," Gabrielle said sternly, but she spoiled the effect moments later by laughing. "All right, you got me. Pay me back with some information, and we'll truly be even. Who do you know in the guard, besides that awful Agrinon, who maybe isn't being paid only by the King?"

"Dirty guards, paid to look the other direction, you mean? More of them than any of us would like," Peder replied thoughtfully. He shrugged finally. "There's Agrinon, his usual partner Xedimal—but they're so obvious I wonder the King himself hasn't shoved them into a cell. Normally, Theseus walks the city, or rides about, keeping an ear on things, paying attention—*real* attention, mind you—to complaints, and actually seeing something's done about such matters."

"I know. Everyone says." Gabrielle sighed.

"They're right," Cydavia put in. "It's only the past half a moon-season that things have gone from unpleasant to unbearable."

"Fourteen days or so? Well—that's something to know," Gabrielle said.

"Guards . . ." Peder had been mumbling to himself. He finally shrugged. "One or two in the palace, or so I've heard, but I don't have names for you."

"Well—at least I know to be careful, then. Right?"

"Careful," he murmured, and eased stiffly to his feet. "*You* take care in that palace," he warned. "It's a Minotaur's paradise, all long corridors and—"

"I can guide her," Cydavia said quietly.

"Oh—oh. Yes. Well, then." The merchant inclined his head in her direction, kissed Gabrielle's thumb, and stumbled back toward the small chamber where his apprentice was grinding away at the day's labor.

• • •

112

A mere breath later, Helarion tapped Gabrielle's shoulder; she gasped and Cydavia swore softly. The boy turned to stare at Gabrielle in wide-eyed astonishment. "You can't let this woman take you in to see the Queen," he said flatly.

"Oh?" Eyebrows raised, the woman in question challenged the thief.

Gabrielle looked from Helarion to Cydavia and back, sighed quietly, and finally nodded. "As much as I hate to admit it—he's right. Things go wrong, they always do. I call it the '*that* wasn't supposed to happen' problem: the moment when the things that aren't supposed to go wrong *do* go wrong. Xena would flatten me like one of Peder's little winged creatures if I let something bad happen to you."

"It won't—" Cydavia began firmly, but Gabrielle was shaking her head and she held up a hand for silence.

"I know. I always think that, too: of course, it won't. Yeah, right. Helarion here has a stake in that neighborhood, and you don't. And you have important things you want to do with your life, if you get the chance. You won't if one of the wrong guards spots us and kills you, will you."

"I—" The woman hesitated, and fetched her breath with a little sigh.

"Bruised hurts. Wounded hurts," Gabrielle went on earnestly. "But dead is for always. And all of those things can happen so fast." There was an uncomfortable little silence. "I'm sorry," she said helplessly. "All I can say besides that is if there's any chance I can do it, I'll pass on a message to let Queen Melosa know you'd like to at least talk to her, maybe become one of her family. I'm sorry there may not be any way I can introduce you to Xena; I mean, you admire her and all that—but you know how it is, things are pretty hectic . . ."

"I'd like to think I could have helped you," Cydavia said softly. Her shoulders and her mouth drooped. Gabrielle patted her shoulder, then gave her a quick hug.

"Well, but, you did. That second guard, remember?" Gabrielle smiled. Her red-haired companion returned it after a moment, then gripped her near hand; her face turned serious.

"Send word to the scroll merchant, here, if you find you need me or my aid after all," she said, then turned and left the shop.

Silence followed, except for the sound of wood being sanded, amid an undercurrent of male voices. Gabrielle turned to gaze squarely at Helarion; reciprocating he eyed her in a seemingly candid fashion. "Remember," she said finally, "that I chose your help instead of hers. If I chose wrong, I swear you'll regret it."

"You terrify me," Helarion replied dryly, and with a sharp nod of his head, he indicated the back chamber. He went; she followed. But just before the narrow entry to the little workroom, he shifted direction and eased between two high-piled shelves and into the open. Gabrielle stayed right on his heels. But once in open air again, he stopped so suddenly she slammed into his back. "See?" he added cheerfully. "I wager that merchantess wouldn't have known about *this* way out, would she?"

Gabrielle leveled a finger at his nose. "Do you say, 'Greekess,' too?" He grinned; she scowled. "Helarion. Don't *start* with me, all right?"

"Who, me?" he demanded, then shoved the finger aside and spun around to swiftly lead the way down a narrow, shadowed alley. Gabrielle glared at his back, but as he turned to gesture urgently, she hurried to catch up with him. *I asked to meet him, on purpose,* she told herself flatly. *Bet his honored papa was laughing all the way down to Hades.*

Helarion stopped a few paces farther, and pointed along the dirt track between low, flat-roofed buildings. "See the loose bricks down there?" It took a moment for her eyes to adjust; she finally nodded. "There's another baker's—not as good as my uncle Ukloss, but Eketeron will feed me anytime I like." He pursed his lips. "And he likes a good tale, well told, so you won't find it hard at all to earn your own bread, will you?"

"Bread?" It seemed, suddenly, forever since that wonderful fruit-and-nut roll, and the crusty chunk of bread she'd eaten after. Her stomach growled, and Helarion grinned widely. Gabrielle gave him a sour look and a shove. "Go on. I can do that—even better, if you're still alive to introduce me."

"You frighten me," he said, and followed it with a chuckle as he headed toward the baker's. Gabrielle cast up her eyes and swore evily under her breath.

Night: the sun had barely dropped behind the mountains when Helarion led her back up the alley. Gabrielle cast a worried glance over her shoulder, in what she thought might be the direction of Ukloss's bakery, and whispered, "Xena, you be careful out there."

She and Helarion dodged down alleys and across busy streets, through one market, then across a crowded square, where a monk in a tattered loincloth exhorted violence against those who enforced poverty. Two guards stood nearby—she wasn't certain whether they meant to arrest the monk once he said something sufficiently anti-Theseus, or if they were there to protect the man from the muttering listeners. Another alley, and then another, which snaked around so much she completely lost what little sense of direction she'd had to begin with. Helarion drew her to a halt at the end of it, and indicated direction with his chin.

"Palace," he whispered.

"Oh, *really*?" she murmured sarcastically in reply. If there was ever an edifice that couldn't be mistaken for anything else, this particular set of walls and buildings was it: the fabled palace of the kings of Athens, the glorious whited walls of legend. Gabrielle, to her astonishment, felt tears prickling at the corners of her eyes; she turned aside to blot them on her fingers. The boy wouldn't understand; he'd laugh at her, if he saw.

But when she did turn back, she could see his young face was solemn, and his jaw was firmly set. *Not completely without a sense of history, or something like it. Even if he hasn't any other kind of sense,* she decided, and despite her better judgment, she warmed to him. A little.

"We'll stay here," he whispered huskily. "Until full dark. All right with you?"

She shrugged. "You're the one leading me; I don't know the area, and besides, I'm guarding your back, remember?"

"Guarding . . . ?"

"Your honored father will be on his way to Hades, won't he?" Gabrielle replied sweetly. It was Helarion's turn to cast up his eyes.

Ukloss's bakery was busy all day long, and crackling with news of the audacious jailbreak. Two guards arrived from the market jail, come to pick up the loaves and rolls for their prisoners, and—in low, excited voices—to add their own version of events to the soup of rumor that flowed through the city: "They say, Baker, the Trickster god himself came from his errands for Zeus and Hera, to open the cell. After all, who better to steal unsuspected through the night *and* to break open a lock with no violence and no sign—and scarcely anyone missing? There were forty-seven in that cell and still forty-four when we discovered

116

the door, and all those sleeping as though the god himself had put a spell upon them.''

''Well—'' The baker sounded worried to her ears but he seemed to gather strength for whatever reason as he went on. ''They say Hermes is not in favor of beings of any kind being caught within a cage, don't they? I mean—only look at his path across the sky, unfettered by anyone's rule!'' A little silence; the guard began to laugh, and after a moment, the baker joined him.

Xena, settled into a corner under the baker's long counter, smiled grimly. Not everyone would believe that kind of nattering, including one of the guards, though the second sounded fairly awed. She decided the baker was only making polite noises. And, of course, he'd agree with anything that kept the King's guardsmen from actively seeking out a very human rescuer, utilizing a very real key.

No mention of who had escaped—the baker didn't ask and the guards weren't forthcoming with more information.

Maybe she and Gabrielle stood a chance of helping these people after all.

She shifted uncomfortably; hiding out in a baker's in the midst of a city the size of Athens! *I cannot believe I was persuaded into this.* As the guards left, the baker murmured something to his son, who stepped away, then came back, a soft, sweet breadstick dangling from his fingers where Xena could reach it. She sniffed gingerly, then accepted the offering and bit it in half. Almost as good as those goodies she'd had every night while living in a king's palace and posing as his daughter, Diana.

The afternoon passed slowly; she listened to conversations, spoke with Ukloss or his son on the few occasions when the shop was empty. Now and again, she dozed, shoulders shoved against one rough wooden wall, feet braced against the other. Late in the day, there was a rush of customers who came to buy bread for their evening meal, then another long, quiet period. She heard Ukloss's voice, high above her, a low murmur—she couldn't catch the words, but a moment later, Kratos slid in under the counter next to her. Xena sat up a little straighter, shifted the sword scabbard away from her left shoulder, and gave the boy a smile.

"Gabrielle spoke to the scroll merchant, and Helarion took her to safety for the day." He was keeping something back, Xena thought—those sidelong glances from under thick lashes and the way he pursed the corners of his mouth.

"She's all right?"

He nodded emphatically. "She's fine. The sun set only a little while ago, and they left for the palace. They'll probably be inside pretty soon, so I have to go back. I thought you'd want to know," he added, with another of those sidelong looks.

"That was nice of you," she said and ruffled his hair. "If you get a chance to talk to her, tell her I said not to do anything foolish, and to stay out of fights."

"Ah—nothing foolish, no fights," he said, then scrambled to his feet and ran off. Xena gazed at the place he'd been and sighed. Dinars to small coppers, Gabrielle had already found trouble out there somewhere. Behind her, she could hear the baker and his son once more, then the scraping of wood against wood, and the slam of a door.

"Warrior—you can come out now," Ukloss said softly. He stepped back as she uncoiled herself, stood, and stretched. "Brezakius and one or two of the other men will be here in a moment; you can talk to them, whatever you need to do."

"All right. You warned them not to speak of defying your so-called Protectors, didn't you?"

The baker shook his head. "I told 'em. But there isn't a one of us who'd dare say boo to his neighbor just now, for fear it would get back to *them,* and they'd take it the wrong way."

"All right," Xena replied calmly. She could only hope it was true: men like the baker and his friends seldom realized how difficult it was to keep a secret from men like Brisus—men like Brisus saw conspiracies against them under every rock, while men like the baker didn't think in terms of conspiracy, and therefore didn't watch their words closely enough. No point in mentioning that now; it would serve no purpose but to make Ukloss and his son nervous. She turned to give Adrik a hard-eyed look. "You found that wagon?"

The look he gave her back wasn't friendly but he nodded. "And the stablemaster says he'll have it hooked to his best donkey; the beast is quiet and doesn't balk like some. That's what you wanted, isn't it?"

"Near enough," she said. "Ukloss, you're certain about your own cart?"

"It wasn't in such good condition when *they* stole it from me," he said. "Because there hadn't been time for me or my son to grease the wheels in some time. Last time I saw it go by, the noise set my teeth on edge."

"Good," Xena replied softly. "When's their man go out?"

"I told you—" Adrik began, but his father laid a hand on his shoulder, silencing him.

"Not always every night, but most nights. I start the morning's batters at full dark, to give them time to rise. *Their* man comes about then, on the nights he goes from town. He takes whatever loaves I still have, piles them in a basket, and shoves it in the back of my cart. So you'll be able to hear and see him." His eyes went vague and distant for a moment, then he crossed to the nearest shutter to peer skyward. "Matter of another hour at best," he said. "He comes back with the cart piled high: food and goods—we try not to imagine too hard how the stuff came into their hands."

"An hour," Xena murmured. "All right. That gives me just enough time to go fetch Argo—and for you," she added to Adrik, "to get that donkey harnessed to the cart. Because when Brisus's man goes out, we're going to follow him." Silence. She waited. "And we're going to get your people back. Tonight."

For a long, tense moment, she thought the baker's son was going to protest—and from the look in his eyes, he was. But the anger went from him all at once, and his shoulders slumped. "Warrior—you can't! I mean, we can't! They— There's no safe place to—"

"I think," Xena said between clenched teeth, "that we agreed I was the one deciding the rules?" Adrik's eyes kindled, but his father tugged at his arm and spoke against his ear urgently. "Good," she said as neither man spoke again. "We can't do anything against your Protectors until we find your people and get them to safety. We don't need to have a fortress for them, just someplace they can hide for a day or so, until we remove the threat of your so-called Protectors." She eyed both men sternly. "We tell no one else what Adrik and I are doing tonight, you got that?"

Silence. The baker nodded timidly; Adrik gave her a harsh stare and demanded, "Why?"

"Because the fewer of us who share the secret, the fewer there are who might give it away—not deliberately," she added sharply as both men started and eyed her in sudden anger. "There are plenty of ways a secret can be broken, and the easiest is to share it. The three of us are the only ones who know—I'm not talking to Brisus, and neither of you are going to have the chance to say anything on purpose or accidentally, are you?''

''Never mind, Adrik,'' the baker said soothingly. ''I understand what she means: people don't mean to break a secret but it happens. Remember the picnic for your mother's birthday last year, boy?''

''I don't— Oh.'' The younger man considered this, then finally sighed, and let his eyelids sag shut. He nodded. ''All right, warrior, you win. I'll do as you say.''

''Exactly as I say,'' Xena corrected him gently. Another silence followed; the baker prodded his son in the ribs. Adrik nodded again. ''Good. So—get me back to that stable, so we can be ready to follow when Brisus's stooge heads out. Baker. You think of a place we can hide those people, once your son and I get them safely back here. Not long,'' she added as he frowned and stared at his hands. ''A day, two at most. The quicker we act, the more surprised Brisus will be.''

An hour or so later, Xena crouched along the outer wall of the bakery, Adrik at her elbow, and listened to Brisus's man—a sturdy fellow shorter than Gabrielle, with dark, close-cropped hair, opaque brown eyes, and an irritatingly reedy voice. ''All right, Baker. You want to be sure your big friend's son is still alive? Is the boy's favorite toy a painted wooden serpent?''

''I know it is, Mikkeli,'' Ukloss said evenly. ''I helped Brezakius paint the pieces so it would be done for the boy's fifth birthday.''

''You want the boy to see a sixth birthday, behave yourself,'' Mikkeli replied flatly. He dragged the heavy basket of bread from the shop with the baker's help, shoved it into the back of the cart, and tied it into place, then got onto the narrow, high seat. "Remember, you and your dirty kind are all dead, if we decide you are," he said, and shook the reins. The ancient donkey ambled off amid a horrid screeching of wheels and groaning of joints.

The baker was a dark shadow against darker walls. "Warrior?" His voice quavered, and she heard him swallow past a very dry throat.

"Baker," Xena replied softly. "It's all right. This Mikkeli will never hear a thing until much too late. We'll bring your people back, alive and unharmed." She gripped his shoulder briefly, then swung onto Argo. Adrik patted his donkey, then clambered onto his own cart and clucked at the beast. Its ears twitched, once, but it obediently moved out, behind the warrior.

Xena stayed close behind Mikkeli—near enough to keep the noisy, creaking cart in view, though it was seldom visible except as a dark moving blot against a darkish, empty street. Once outside Athens's sprawl, she drew back to speak to Adrik. "All right. You can still hear him, right?"

"Right," the boy replied flatly.

"You can see me, right?"

"Ah—I can see you," he said doubtfully. The moon was hidden behind clouds. Xena clapped him on the near arm.

"Don't worry. We're on the main road, and he won't leave it soon if I remember correctly. There's nowhere he can drive that cart and keep it in one piece if he gets away from the road. But if he does, I'll hold back so I can direct you the right way. Stay where you can hear him as well as you can now; don't come closer, where he might hear you."

"Got it," he said tersely, and dragged at the reins briefly. Xena gave the donkey an uncertain look, but it was truly a well-behaved beast. She stood in her stirrups, and relaxed again as the distant shriek of wood against wood assaulted her ears.

They went in such fashion for at least an hour; the moon was a fingernail paring, casting little light across the empty road, and most of the time it was behind clouds. The noisy cart that had been the baker's was loud enough to occasionally set the warrior's teeth on edge, but never quiet enough to lose. Only once was she forced to drag Argo to a halt so the baker's son could catch up and find the narrow track which dove between dry, aged oaks. The sea lay that way, she thought; a moment later a faint breath of wind, with the hint of salt and chill air, confirmed the nearness of the ocean. Adrik was mumbling under his breath just behind her, but at her sharp gesture, he was quiet once more. Ahead of them, the baker's aged and ill-treated cart groaned and creaked on.

Then there was sudden silence. Xena drew her mount to a halt. Adrik, warned by the lack of sound, dragged on the reins, fetching up next to her. She cast him a teeth-only grin, a white flash in the gloom, and murmured, ''We're near. Stay with me and keep quiet. Follow my lead.''

''Yes,'' he whispered tersely in reply, and with a sharp nod of his head, he eased from the seat to take the donkey by the harness and walk it down the road. *Not as stupid as I'd have thought,* Xena decided. Then again, it could have been *his* father they were coming to rescue; maybe he'd begun to realize that. ''His friends, his family, his neighbors,'' she whispered to herself, then shook her head. Whatever. Just maybe, he wasn't going to be a liability.

She could only hope.

The cart ahead of them was suddenly quiet, but the donkey was braying and someone was shouting at it, someone else bellowing at the shouter to shut up. Other voices were abruptly silenced. Xena flipped her right leg across the saddle and slid from Argo's back; she caught hold of Adrik's shirt and murmured against his ear, "Chaos up there; we take advantage of it, right?"

Silence followed, then a sudden dim smile. "Right," he whispered. "What do I do?"

"Tie the cart off, come with me." She waited briefly while he wrapped the reins around a slender aspen, then stole along the narrow cart track. One building—no, two, she thought. Hard to tell. Several figures milled around, involved in some unseen activity. A reedy, irritating voice cut across her thoughts.

"Hey—hey! Give me a moment, will you? There's a basket of bread, plenty for all of you and—heh—a mouthful or so each for your labor force," he finished with a nasty laugh.

"Hey—labor force?" a jeering, even reedier voice answered him. "Like they're doing anything for us to speak of?"

"Better be," Mikkeli replied flatly, "or they aren't doing anything for anyone, remember? You gotta guard on 'em tonight?"

"Guard? What for? They know what happens, they try to pull anything."

"Fine. Brisus said to remind you of that, no point wasting anyone's time baby-sitting *them*."

"Yah!" Someone else was laughing so hard he could barely be understood. "Well, they know all right. Shoulda heard what Xenozik told 'em—" He was violently shushed by three men, and someone dragged him off his feet. "Hey!" he grumbled in a hurt-sounding voice as he yanked free and stumbled back into the building.

Mikkeli laughed cheerfully. "Hey? Who cares? Just do what Brisus says and everything's okay, right?"

"Hey—hey, Mikkeli, don't we do everything Brisus asks of us?" another man hastened to say. "I mean, he changes the rules alla time, but we try to keep up with him, don't we? And we haven't lost any of those guys over there yet, have we?"

"Ahhh—forget that crud, Philosopher!" More laughter. "What you got to send back with me, so Brisus ain't snarling at me on account I ain't got him good stuff? Keeping in mind, the last four times I come out here, I ain't got anything *he* thinks of as good?"

"Brisus gonna be surprised this time," the one Mikkeli called Philosopher replied cheerfully. "Got a couple of the bigger guys into that rich guy's summer compound, down the road that way. Got the woman's jewel baskets and one cache of coin."

"Just one cache?" Mikkeli jeered. "You know these rich pigs, they always got lotsa caches; they didn't try hard enough. Or *you* didn't."

"Hey—who you talkin' to, Mikkeli?" another demanded. He sounded half-drunk.

"I'm talking to *you,* every one of yas, straight from what Brisus told *me,*" Mikkeli responded. "You want him to come out here, tell you personal-like?" Uncomfortable silence. "Okay, then. Let's get this bread in and maybe you can share some of what Knolio there has been drinking—if there's any left, that is."

"Plenty left," the Philosopher mumbled. "That was the other thing they found, was the wine cellar. Really *big* wine cellar."

Xena caught hold of Adrik's arm and drew him back into deeper shadow as the men surged around the baker's noisy cart and two of them hefted the large basket of bread from the back. When he was about to whisper something, she shook her head, laid a hand against his lips, and left it there until the men had gone inside and the door closed behind them. No light shone around the door, through openings of any kind—or between the boards. And the sounds of conversation and coarse laughter were so muted she couldn't make out words at all.

"Okay, fine," she whispered close to his ear. "Keep it down. You heard, no guard on the other building. You go in there alone." He started, and began to protest in a nervous whisper. She swore under her breath and shook his arm, hard. "Listen to me! They know you, they don't know me! You tell them what you have to, no more, enough to get them *quietly* out of that hut and into the cart, so we can get them out of here. I'll be at the door, listening; you need me, or there's trouble with them," she gestured toward the well-built, closed-up hut where Mikkeli and the others were eating and drinking, "and I'll be right there. Make it quick and quiet, and there won't be a problem. Got it?"

For a long moment, she thought he was still going to protest, but finally he slumped in her grip and nodded. "Fine. Get going, I'm right behind you. Stay in shadow, much as you can," she added, and, her hand still on his arm, she guided him out into the open area, where a little thin moonlight was casting shadow. He gave her a sour look, but went obediently. Xena slipped her sword loose in its scabbard, flexed her hands, and followed.

7

To his credit, once Adrik found out he had no choice but to take charge of the ramshackle hut where his people were being held, he did a good job of things: Xena watched him vanish into the shaky little structure, and heard one very brief, very loud creak as his foot came down on a particularly bad place in the floor. There was an eerie silence during which she could almost feel his cautious, furtive movement across the floor. She guessed he was letting his eyes adjust, testing each step before he put full weight on it. She heard nothing for a very long moment. Then a low, bewildered voice reached her from well inside and she froze, but this was followed by an extremely low, hurried conversation she couldn't hear. Xena finally nodded in satisfaction, then slid her boots carefully along the dangerous little pile of rotting boards that might once have served as a porch, eased down, and moved light-footed across dry, gravelly dirt to the next building, so she could press her ear against the outer wall and listen.

Movement the other way—Adrik and a much larger man aiding someone small from the wretched hut. A breeze that was right off the ocean slid across her shoulders and moaned through the broken walls and sagging doorway of the hut. Her skin prickled. It was cool at the moment— rather pleasant. By morning, it would be downright chilly. *And not two blankets among all of 'em, I'd wager,* she thought angrily.

Her eyes narrowed and she leaned against the wall of the headquarters building. The shutters here had been recently replaced; she could smell fresh-cut wood, as well as the faint, pungent odor of a wood fire inside. *All the comforts of home, in there.* She glanced over her shoulder; Adrik had just stepped inside once more, and the larger man cast her a brief glance, then nodded sharply as he followed Adrik into shadow. A board creaked sharply, and was silenced almost at once. The big man came out a scant moment later with a small child draped across his shoulder, skinny arms dangling loosely and head lolling—still asleep, apparently. Adrik was right on his heels, someone even smaller cradled in his arms. Behind them, two ragged, exhausted-looking men tottered down the rough steps, half-carrying a third.

Harsh, loud laughter brought her attention back to the main building. The three men froze, pale faces turned her way. She waved them urgently toward the wagon, then pressed her ear against the tightly fastened shutter. "Not bad stuff, Philosopher!" That was Mikkeli's reedy voice, hard to mistake for anyone else's—and probably the only one she'd be able to hear at the moment. Much more wine in him, though, and she wouldn't be able to understand his words. "Gimme another, and don't be so stingy! Brisus don't gotta know how much they hauled outa that estate for you, does he?" More laughter.

She straightened, looked along the wall one way and then the other. What she wouldn't have given, just now, for a better place to listen, where she could hear more than Mikkeli's slurred, reedy speech. Adrik stole close, gestured toward the hut, and leaned close to her, to breathe against her ear: "All but seven out of there—but the cart's packed."

"You can't get the rest in somehow?" She eased away from the wall, pulling him with her, stopped in deep shade next to the sagging wall of the prison hut, and whispered, "Try, will you? Better if that thug heads back to Athens tonight not suspecting anything. If we have to take his cart, and—well, guess."

He sighed, very faintly, but finally nodded. "I understand. But the donkey won't pull much more weight— Well, we'll try." Xena gave him a small shove between the shoulder blades, and indicated the interior of the other building with a sharp jerk of her head. He nodded again, eased away from her, and took a child from the large man who'd just come out. She stepped back to her original listening post.

"Hey—hey! You guys think you're bored here, try the city!" Mikkeli was shouting over a babble of angry yelling. "I mean, we don't do *nothing* Brisus don't okay, even if the Protectors say it's all right to do whatever we want, ya know? I mean, no women! Not . . . even . . . one! And hardly any wine, and we can't even lift a purse ourselves or smack someone around just for fun! Why? Whadya mean, why, Knolio? You got wine where your brains used ta be! 'Cause Brisus don't want nobody having fun, that's why! He's got a mean little mouth on him; he don't drink or party with the girls or nothing! I swear, all *he* thinks about is profit!" Someone else spoke earnestly, then Mikkeli continued. "Okay, awright! I know what he tells *us* is he don't want the King's honest guard should catch on too soon. But that's stupid, who cares about them? We got the King under control; his men get outa line, we flatten 'em like flies, right?''

The Philosopher's voice was raised, briefly, so she could hear a few words. ''. . . easier if the city runs as it normally does . . .''

''Philosopher, who *cares* about that? I mean, lookit this pretty bronze thing I got, fits over all the knuckles of your favorite fist—bought 'em back when—can't remember!'' he added in surprise. ''But I spent the coin on the bronze thingies instead of drink, and why? So's I could take out punk types like those snooty, better'n'you guards! Or those snotty, better'n'you Athenians with their posh chariots and sniffy 'we got stuff and you don't' attitude—and now, all of a sudden, Brisus says, don't mess with 'em! Oh, right! What's that about? Yous guys outside the city got— Hades, you got wine, got goodies from estates like that one yonder, the one you just pillaged; you got people who aren't snooty like the city types. Hey, you even got women!''

''Like Hades we got women!'' someone bellowed in re-ply. Knolio, she thought. He sounded as if he couldn't even stand at this point. ''Where we get any women that Brisus don't hear about it, or the King don't? We ain't that much better off'n you, Mikkeli! Food's lousy most of the time, and last time we had wine was . . . was . . .''

Mikkeli's high-pitched laugh interrupted him. ''Women! Ya know? *Those* things?'' Laughter interrupted him. Xena's eyes narrowed, and a corner of her mouth twitched. ''Hey, you got a couple-three okay women out in that hut over there!''

''Mikkeli, Brisus said—''

''Brisus can jump off a tower!'' Mikkeli shouted the Philosopher down. ''A really tall one! *I* ain't so dumb, I know how to have fun *and* get the lady to keep her mouth shut about it, too!'' More laughter. ''Wanna see?''

She heard voices, a muted scrape and thump—a chair or bench going over, it sounded like—then the clomp of heavy booted feet, and Mikkeli's voice at the door. "All right—but remember, it was *my* idea first! Yous all know what that means, right?"

Light flared as the door opened, and loud laughter and coarse remarks from half a dozen men, well on their way to being seriously drunk, assaulted her ears. "That's right, mine *first*," he shouted. "My idea, so my woman! You wanna play after me, you draw lots!" Adrik stood frozen in the doorway of the disheveled little hut, his arm around a tattered, thin wreck of a grandmother; she leaned against him, breathing heavily, her eyes closed. Xena gestured furiously for him to retreat; he licked his lips, bent down to speak to his companion, and dragged her swiftly and silently back out of sight. The warrior had one brief view of a pale, deeply seamed oval face, frightened eyes, and sagging lips.

Great. She could only hope the other man, wherever he was, was smart enough to stay out of the light, and out of Mikkeli's sight.

As for Mikkeli—he was weaving a little but his eyes glittered unpleasantly in fire- and lamplight, and with a flash of teeth, he dragged the door to with a healthy slam. He drew a deep breath of night air, coughed a little, then eased himself down the two shallow steps, and, whistling in a would-be casual fashion, started down the short, narrow path that would take him to the second hut. At the edge of the porch his foot hit a broken board and he nearly fell; clinging to the creaking rail, he swore under his breath, then straightened up and swaggered across the threshold. "Yoo-hoo," he chirped. "Papa's here. Let's play house."

He staggered a few steps into the room, and stopped short as a tall figure loomed up before him, a hand against his chest. Xena laughed low in her throat, gave him a flash of teeth, and then kneed him hard between the legs. The air whistled out of his lungs and with a pained groan he slowly began to topple. "I got a better idea. Let's play nap!" she murmured, and brought the edge of her right hand savagely down on the back of his neck. Dust rose in a cloud from the filthy floor and a board cracked as Mikkeli landed hard. She nudged him with her foot—out cold. "You go first," she added evenly, then turned to face the interior of the hut. It reeked; without the wind whistling through broken wall boards and up through the floor, the smell of unwashed bodies, fever, and sickness must have been unbearable. It still couldn't be called pleasant. "Adrik," she hissed. "Get the rest of them out of here, fast as you can. Use the second cart, it's okay."

"But . . . but you said—I mean, they'll know!"

"This nasty little drunken sot at my feet says they'll know anyway. They've been drinking hard, but they'll miss him pretty quick." The limp Mikkeli moaned very faintly, but as she nudged him with her boot, he slid from the middle of the floor, and once she had him out of the way, she kicked him. Hard. "Time to go."

"I won't do it alone—" Adrik began warily.

"I'm gonna help, all right," she replied grimly. She stopped, laid a hand on his arm, and tightened it when he would have spoken again.

Outside, there was light once more and the Philosopher's voice as the man opened the other door and yelled into the night, "Hey, Mikkeli! Ya didn't say nothin' about keeping the women to yourself out *there*! What, your nose not working or you just like a big audience?" Someone behind him jeered derisively—she couldn't make out the words. The Philosopher snarled something in reply, then shouted, "All right, Mikkeli, you don't come back in here time I finish this cup of high-class wine, I'm comin' out! We all are! Got it?''

Adrik, his arm still around the limp woman, stared up at the warrior anxiously. Xena smiled unpleasantly. The light in the ugly little wreck of a room went as the door on the other building slammed echoingly. "I'm gonna help. But not the kind of help you have in mind. Get them out to the cart, and get a couple of these people to locate all the horses they've got, and get 'em tied to the carts. These low-lifes want back in Athens, they walk." Her fingers dug into his shoulder and he gasped. "Do it now," she hissed, then spun on one heel and strode into the open.

There was moon again: a break in the clouds, she saw as she glanced up. Just enough to let her reach the steps, and then the door, in complete quiet. The latch wasn't hooked; probably the Philosopher didn't expect anyone but Mikkeli to push it open. She smiled faintly, eased the door inward the least bit, and stood listening. Adrik went back and forth twice with people from the little hut; two of the larger and apparently less weakened men carried others out. Finally, the baker's son indicated the hut and spread his arms in a slashing gesture: *No one left inside*, she supposed he must mean. The two large men spoke with him for some moments, then all three slipped around the ocean side of the delapidated hut and vanished. Gone to retrieve the horses, or so she hoped.

Inside, there wasn't much going on at the moment: the muted clink of cups, someone hiccuping now and again. Knolio, she remembered, and long memory put a face to the name: he'd been one of Draco's or one of hers, until some village or other had given him nightmares, and set him to drinking hard. *Mine*. She remembered all too clearly, suddenly: the private killing spree that had pushed him over the edge, why she'd sent little Mannius to sneak him out of camp. From the sounds of things, he'd been trying to lose himself in a wine jug ever since.

She shook her head. Knolio wasn't her problem; he'd made his own problems, and his own living version of Hades because of them. *The people he was keeping imprisoned here—that's your problem, Xena,* she reminded herself grimly. Knolio had chosen the wrong side once again. Too bad.

Someone else spoke in such a soft, slurred voice, all she could catch was "Mikkeli." Coarse laughter buried the rest of it. Her eyes narrowed; the fingers of her left hand moved to ease the chakra loose.

Movement seaward: Adrik stood in the thin moonlight, his left hand jabbing in an exaggerated fashion toward the rear of the hut. He nodded several times, then plunged out of sight once more. Xena cast her eyes up. *Shoulda come up with basic signs; I guess he means they got the horses and they're bringing them, and he's gone back to help.*

It had better be just that, she decided a bare moment later: the Philosopher's voice had caught her attention. "Hey! What's he *doin'* out there?" Jeers, catcalls, and hiccuping laughter answered him. "Shaddup! Ya—you all know what I mean! Told him, finish the cup, then we head out and help him—and lookit, aren't I a generous kinda guy? I finished that cup, then had another, nice and leisurely, and he still ain't in here! Think we oughta—that we better—"

Xena straightened, squared her shoulders, then took the small step that placed her squarely in front of the door; a kick sent it slamming against the inner wall, and she was inside before it could rebound into the frame. "Don't worry," she said with a dangerous smile. "There's plenty for everyone." Six men stood—or tried to stand—and stared blankly at her. A seventh—Knolio, though she could barely recognize the man she'd known in the wreck she saw—was making distressed little sounds and trying to right the wine jug. He hiccuped and the jug jerked out of his hands to roll across the table and smash on the floor. Moaning, he fell heavily to his knees and went after the pieces.

Another of them, a tall, slit-eyed fellow who reminded her unpleasantly of the Egyptian back on Ithaca, shoved his way to the fore. An even taller, gray-haired fellow in a long, wine-stained tunic that might once have been white, murmured at him, "Clopateros, wait, let me."

Clopateros shoved thug-class tatters and remnants of broken, ill-cared-for, and downright filthy fighting garb away from the hilt of his sword with one hand and pointed at the warrior, rather unsteadily, with his other. "I know who you are!" he snarled. "Brisus tol'— Brisus told us all about *you*!" The Philosopher stared at him in turn. "That's Xena! He said, she shows up, don't you listen to her, anything she says 'bout bein' one of us, 'cause she ain't. Ain't one of us, I mean. She's here for *them* guys!" he added as he flailed out with his left arm to indicate the other hut. His elbow caught one of his companions in the belly; the man choked and fell back into the wall, then slid limply down it.

"Them guys? Oh, no," Xena purred. "I'm here for the babies and the women, too." Stunned silence. "And I'm gonna leave you a little advice, in payment for all of those impoverished Athenians. You fellows had better leave Brisus and his bottom-line, profit-only way of thinking, before it costs you plenty. Like breath."

"You can't kill us all!" One of those who'd been knocked flat was climbing cautiously back to his feet. The Philosopher held up a hand for silence.

"Ah—Nelos, if this is really Xena, though I wouldn't bet coin on that, she quite likely can do just what she says. But if you're really Xena," he addressed her directly, "then you know Brisus makes a bad enemy."

"You're assuming he's going to survive this latest scheme, aren't you?" she asked evenly.

"And—you don't *kill* people anymore, everyone knows that," the Philosopher countered. His smile and his eyes were smug.

"Don't wager on *that*. I don't kill people *unless I have to*." She smiled unpleasantly and flexed her hands. Three of the men retreated, stumbling over their fallen companion. "But it might not be my decision; Athens isn't my city."

"You think their king's gonna take Brisus out?" Nelos jeered. "Guess you don't know what's happening in Athens after all, do you?"

"I know enough," she countered. "And I've got friends who know more. But that doesn't concern you. The people I just pulled out of the pigsty next door do. And that two-footed vermin I left in there. Way I figure it, you *owe* those folks."

"Yah." Nelos spat, drew his dagger, and started for her. "Who's gonna make all of us pay—you?"

She took one long step forward, slapped his dagger aside with her own, caught him up by his greasy leathers, and smacked his face three times, hard, then released him. Two of the fallen drunks who'd just tottered back to their feet went down again, under Nelos. The Philosopher shouted a warning, went into a crouch, and drew his sword as two of his companions eased around him on both sides, hoping to catch the warrior in a pincer maneuver.

As Xena watched them come, she seemed relaxed, even bored. But to the careful observer she was alert, thrumming like a bowstring, alive to every movement of the men surrounding her, from the sound of their sandals as they shuffled nervously across the floor, to the murky smell of their sweat, to the taste of their fear. Suddenly one of them feinted, and the other lunged, his hands clumsily scrambling for her throat.

Xena dodged to the side and, grabbing the man's wrist, yanked his arm behind his back, twisting until she heard a loud pop. The man began to scream. His comrade, the other half of the pincer movement, dashed forward, more in an effort to escape than anything else, but Xena gripped his shoulder as he went past and drove her knee into his stomach. His eyes bulged and he made a sound like a fish that wasn't quite dead.

Near the stone fireplace, three men, including Nelos, staggered upright, but the Philosopher was already moving to attack, his short, heavy sword held low and with something like professionalism. Xena waited until he entered the first posture of attack, and then somersaulted forward, trapped the blade between her thighs, and easily vaulted back to her feet, plucking the sword from the man's hand. Releasing the weapon, she offered it, pommel-first, to the stunned Philosopher.

"You dropped something."

As he pounced on the blade, she spun, swinging her leg around in a heavy, vicious arc; the round kick knocked him to the floor.

Xena turned back to Nelos and the two others: one was fumbling an arrow into his bow, while his companion tried to wield his dagger and stand up at the same time. Nelos was probably the best off; he had successfully drawn his sword and was furtively moving down the wall toward her. Xena uttered her trilling, unnerving war cry—deafening in such small quarters—and then ran straight at the two men.

Thinking they were being attacked head-on, both flew into a panic. One released his arrow too early; it passed harmlessly by Xena and thudded into the wall next to Nelos, piercing his shirt and pinning him there. Oblivious to all this, the one with the dagger managed only to cut himself a little before he finally had the weapon pointed in the warrior's direction.

But to their surprise, Xena ran *between* them, then up the wall *behind* them. At the height of her momentum, she reached down and placed a hand on each of her attackers' head, and then pushed off with her legs. Bringing her feet over her head and pushing off of their handy skulls, Xena began to sling her long, muscular body across the room. This maneuver was one of the most difficult; her abilities were stretched as far as they ever had been, the hard, slender muscles in her arms weeping with the strain. Nevertheless, she couldn't resist grinning at the shocked looks on the faces of the two men as she smashed their heads together, sending them into unconsciousness.

Now to finish it. Looking down the length of her body, she could see Nelos, struggling to get free of the arrow's grasp. He should have tried harder. Her feet struck him first, and then the full weight and force behind Xena's deadly acrobatics exploded across his chest. Just weight now, he sagged against the arrow; the shirt ripped finally, and he tumbled to the floor. Landing lightly, Xena bent over and checked his pulse. He still had one.

On the far side of the table, Knolio hiccuped and began to whimper; Xena could see him, crawling from cup to cup, setting them carefully upright, fumbling across the floor for fragments of the jug that still contained wine. She ignored him; he was too drunk to notice the fight raging all around him, let alone contribute to it.

The Philosopher was on his feet once more, pushing away from the door, trying to fumble a dagger from beneath his tunic, when the door burst open, sending him flying. Xena sidestepped him easily, gave him a shove with her foot. Mikkeli stood in the doorway, dagger in his left hand, bronze device fitted over his knuckles. An evil smile split his dark face and glittered in his eyes.

"Got me by surprise," he said. "That only works once."

"So—who needs surprise?" Xena murmured. "Come on, *big* guy, I'm *really* scared!" she added throatily. The little man's eyes were suddenly wide and all pupil; he shifted the dagger deftly from left to right, back again. The warrior laughed, spread her arms wide, then strode forward to rake the dagger from midair as he sought to flip it again. She shrugged in mild amusement as he swore furiously, and clamped down on his right wrist. Mikkeli yelped angrily, then more shrilly as Xena snatched the bronze knuckle device away from him. She gave him a teeth-only smile, clutched at his close-cropped hair, and slammed the knobby bit of bronze into his forehead, hard. His eyes rolled up and he sagged. She let go, and watched expressionlessly as he went flat on the neatly planked floor.

There was movement behind her; Knolio was still whimpering over spilled wine, trying to rescue what he could, but off to one side, the Philosopher, eyes narrowed, was licking his lips, visibly trying to figure out how to sidestep her and win his way free of the small, well-constructed hut.

The warrior flexed her hands and smiled at him. The Philosopher froze, then straightened and spread his arms wide. "I'm unarmed," he said calmly. "And I don't want to fight you."

"Maybe that's not your choice," she replied.

"I understand that. I would like to offer a proposition, however. That poor man," a cautious gesture indicated Knolio, "was one of yours, if I've understood his story correctly."

"He was. I did what I could for him; the rest was up to him."

"I've done what I could for him, too—"

She laughed sourly, and he bit his lip. "What?" she asked. "Getting him in with Brisus? Seeing he gets enough wine and women?"

"Look at him," the Philosopher said. "This is the first wine he's had in months. I'd have kept him away from that estate if I'd known he'd find it—well, that's past, too late. It doesn't do good things for me, either."

"I noticed." Silence. Someone groaned against the far wall, and outside, she could hear soft voices and a horse whickering.

"A proposition," he said finally. "Let me take Knolio with me, now. We'll take the coin and jewels, return them to that estate, and I'll try to get Knolio somewhere he won't get into trouble anymore." Another silence. "You owe him that, warrior."

"I don't. Not the way you mean. And I don't know that I trust you with all that wealth—"

"You have your hands full: those people, Brisus, the men he's suborned in the palace, and the guard." The Philosopher folded his arms. "We don't return it, the owner of that estate will be no worse off than he is right now. I'd give you my word, sober, but I doubt you'd take it."

She held up a hand. "Shut up a minute, and let me think." Off to one side, Mikkeli began mumbling under his breath; she sidestepped and kicked him hard, and he went limp and quiet again. The Philosopher closed his eyes and bit his lip, then backed away and squatted down next to Knolio and began talking to him, very softly. Xena finally sighed heavily. "All right. And I have a suggestion. You know a guy named Mannius?" The Philosopher shook his head, but Knolio looked up, a frown drawing his brows together.

"Hey—hey, it's Xena!" He looked at the floor in surprise, as though wondering how he'd gotten there, then caught hold of one of the fallen chairs and began to laboriously work his way upright. "Hey, Xena, how ya doing these days?" He hiccuped, then blushed as the warrior cast up her eyes. He swayed in place, until the Philosopher caught hold of his shirt and held him steady. Knolio didn't seem to notice. "Ya look good. Ain't seen you in . . . in . . ."

"Been a long time, Knolio," Xena said softly. "But you don't look good at all. You picked the wrong kind of friends again, didn't you?"

"I was just— I— Brisus just came along and he—"

"Yeah, I know. Never mind. Knolio, I'm going to let you off easy this time, but you're going to have to promise me something in return. Okay?" She folded her arms and waited. He gave this serious consideration, and finally nodded gravely.

"Anything—anything for you, Xena. Swear!"

"All right. Your friend the Philosopher here says he'll go with you, you two will return the money and jewels you took from that house—"

"Not the wine!" Knolio protested thickly.

"No, not the wine. You're going to walk away from the wine, Knolio, leave it all here. It isn't good for you."

"Aw!"

"You're going to *do* it, Knolio," Xena said flatly. The drunk eyed her glassily, swayed back into his companion, and bit his lip. "Because you start drinking that stuff, you forget how to take care of yourself, you start hanging out with guys like Mikkeli. I don't want to find you with guys like this again." She waited.

"Okay," he finally managed to say, unhappily.

"Good. You're going to return the stuff you helped steal, and then you're going to leave Athens. Tonight. Right away, and for good. You'll head for Thebes, up the coast road." Her eyes shifted to the Philosopher, who nodded. "Mannius is up there, taking care of a cyclops—"

The Philosopher started and nearly dropped his companion. "Cyclops? You don't take care of—"

"This one's blind and he prefers mutton to man, these days." She touched the drunk's shoulder, rousing him from a half sleep where he stood. "Knolio, you'd like to see Mannius again, wouldn't you?"

"Mannius—he's my friend. Where's Mannius?" Knolio peered around doubtfully.

"Not here. You'll go find him, help him out. Philosopher, you'll like this cyclops. And if you and he run out of things to talk about, there's always the Sphinx."

"Sphinx! But they—she eats—"

"She likes to talk more than she likes to eat. It's better than staying *here,* don't you think?"

The Philosopher gazed at her for a very long moment, then beyond her. He shook himself finally. "We could go anywhere once we leave here, you wouldn't know."

"Or care, at least in *your* case," she agreed. A corner of her mouth twisted as she looked at the swaying man between them. "I'm doing this for him, and he needs a keeper just now. Take my suggestion, for his sake, why don't you? And yours."

"The pastoral life," he said gloomily, and brushed at his stained robes. "I left my father's goat pens for the city—"

"And look where it got you," Xena said. She glanced over her shoulder as a board creaked behind her. Adrik stood there, shifting from foot to foot. She turned back to the Philosopher. "Where's the bread?" she demanded. The

Philosopher pointed—a large larder box attached to the wall near the fireplace held a basket, still piled high. She pulled a double handful of loaves from it, and shoved them into the tall man's arms. "Here. That's to make sure he stays fed. If I were you, I'd get him out of here right now, before *they* start waking up." She hauled the basket out of its box, brought it outside, and shoved it into Adrik's arms. "Pass those around, and get the wagons started out, now. I'm right behind you."

"Hey, Xena." Knolio straightened up and managed a shaky smile. "I'm glad I got to see ya again."

"Knolio." She gripped his shoulder, and held her breath as he coughed, expelling a cloud of sour wine smell. "Let's not meet again like this, okay?" The hand tightened and he winced. "Because if there *is* a next time like this, I'll break your head, I swear it."

He gave her the same wide-eyed look young Kratos had. "Xena, I swear—"

"Don't swear, Knolio. Just do it, okay?" Her eyes moved to the Philosopher. "Grab whatever else you need, and get going. Now."

"All I have to grab is *him*," the Philosopher replied evenly. But he fished a leather pack from a pile in one corner, shoved two small baskets into the bottom of it, then dropped the bread in on top of the baskets and hauled the straps across his head. He took hold of the swaying Knolio then and led him outside. "Come on, my friend," he said soothingly, "little fresh air, little bread, you and I take a nice long walk, all right?"

"Sure." The drunk seemed to have forgotten the eventful evening—he didn't even seem to recognize Xena. She shook her head and stepped onto the path, where it wound beneath a stand of wind-bent oak, to watch as they vanished northward.

• • •

The baker's cart was already gone; Adrik, his cart now full of exhausted, gaunt people, was waiting for her by the rear wheel. "We can catch up to my father's cart anytime," he said. "I know what you told Father, but I think it's a bad idea, taking these people anywhere near Brisus. He might be waiting at the bakery, or his men might. And you said quiet . . ." His voice trailed off.

"Using your brains, I like that," she said. Momentary silence followed. "Back to the stable, where we started, then, how's that?" A woman's nervous voice rose in protest; it was as suddenly buried by half a dozen other people, all speaking at once. "Wait!" Xena said loudly. "I'll explain, if you'll listen! We rescued you tonight so none of you would have to suffer out here one more minute. But we haven't cleaned up in the city yet, so you can't just go home; that could be dangerous for everyone. We'll get you home as soon as possible, believe that, and your people will know right away in the morning that you're safe! Now, we've got to get out of here, right away, so please, stay calm; we won't let anything else happen to you. There's plenty of bread, and we'll stop for water very soon. And we'll get you someplace warm as quickly as we can."

"Stables first," Adrik said in the sudden silence. "Then to Netteron—there'll be time before dawn, if we go now."

"Netteron," Xena said. "Man who's hiding Kratos's mother?" He nodded. "Has room for all these people?" Another nod. "Who *is* this Netteron?"

"Priest," Adrik replied. "Keeps the temple for Hermes."

"Hermes," Xena said darkly as she swung onto Argo. There was entirely too much of the gods' favorite trickster in all this for her tastes.

8

Full dark descended rather quickly on Athens; the sky had been cloudy off and on most of the afternoon, but as the sun dipped behind the western hills, fat clouds in a heavy mass rolled off the ocean, bringing cool air and a hint of fog. Gabrielle wrapped Elyseba's thick scarf around her arms and tried to find a more comfortable way to sit in the sheltered little corner between a stable and a leather finisher's buildings. *At least this close to the palace, the shops and stands are clean,* she reminded herself. All she could smell here was warm animals and fresh hay, now and again interlaced with the lanolin used in good wax. And now the smell of the ripe, heavy peaches Helarion had just brought to go with the cold and tough-crusted bread left over from the baker's blotted out everything else.

He held out two of the large fruits so she could choose first; Gabrielle rubbed hers on her sleeve then paused, peach halfway to her lips. "You *paid* for these, right? With that coin I gave you?" she whispered. He rolled his eyes, fished in his pocket, and wordlessly held out a small copper. "Wow, that's all that's left? Two cost *that* much?"

"Doesn't anything satisfy you?" he grumbled. He dropped the copper in her hand; she shoved it back into his pocket.

"This will," she said, and settled back to enjoy her peach. Helarion finished his in half a dozen quick bites, then turned so he could watch the street and the sky. Gabrielle had already checked the sky; it was darker but not dark enough yet, and according to Helarion, dinner in the palace was served later than most people ate anyway.

She inhaled, and sighed happily. Either the boy or the stall owner had picked out one of the best pieces of fruit she'd eaten in a long time. *I hope he really did buy them. The copper could have just been—* She shook her head. She could drive herself crazy, trying to second-guess Helarion. She wiped juice from the corner of her mouth, finished the bread, and stretched, hard. "Everything all right, out there?"

"It's been better," he mumbled, then glanced at her sidelong. Gabrielle's eyebrows went up, and he blushed. "I mean—not you or *her*. It was just—there's guards everywhere this evening, it took forever to get where I wanted to be, half the people who usually tell me things wouldn't talk because they were afraid the guards might see me with them. Poor old Mama Omoria." He sighed. "Her peaches," he added by way of explanation. "I'll have to pretend to steal something from her, if your friend's plan doesn't work. Otherwise Agrinon will think she's my friend and have her tossed in that cell as a way to get to me."

"That won't happen—" Gabrielle began automatically. He gave her a sardonic look, then turned back to study the street. "All right, I said it myself, stuff happens you don't want to happen. But not when Xena says she's gonna fix it."

"She's really that good, is she?"

''Better. I told your cousin, she doesn't make promises she doesn't intend to keep. And she's a hero— Don't look at me like that,'' she added in irritation. ''You'd think you'd never heard of them!''

''Our *king* is supposed to be a hero, too, and look at Athens,'' Helarion countered sourly.

''But Theseus *is* a hero,'' Gabrielle said. ''I mean, you ever hear any of the stories about him? How he saved Athens's best young men and women from the Minotaur?''

''I've heard the *story*,'' he replied.

''Well, it just happens to be true. And—and he was on the hunt for the Caledonian boar. I know that's true because Atalanta has the boar's hide and *she* said he was there. And besides,'' she added, ''yes, *look* at Athens! You've got some bad problems right now, but how long has that been going on? And how bad was it before that?'' Silence. He glanced at her sidelong, then turned back to gaze at the sky. ''And, I mean, you know how many cities there are where the people get to decide a lot of what goes on, and the King says, sure, that's what the most of you want, fine with me?'' Another silence. She waited; he shrugged, his back to her. He was getting hard to see, in the gathering gloom, she suddenly realized. ''None, that's how many. How much longer we gotta stay here?''

''Not long. Just— Ssst!'' He came to his feet in one lithe movement. Gabrielle got up a little stiffly and shifted the staff to her right hand, but it was only Kratos, a little out of breath from running. He slipped past his cousin and leaned briefly against Gabrielle.

''Xena's going with Adrik and a cart, to find our people and bring them back.''

Helarion frowned. ''Already? Isn't that—''

''If she's doing it that way, she has it planned out,''

Gabrielle broke in. "And I meant what I said, she doesn't make plans that fall apart."

"I was thinking of Adrik," the thief grumbled. "He can't do anything but complain."

"Yeah," Gabrielle said pointedly. "Sounds like someone I've spent the whole day with." Helarion turned to give her a narrow-eyed look, but the corner of his mouth twitched and he started laughing. Kratos tugged at his shirt.

"They're putting the tray together for the Queen right now," he said. "And the cooks are getting food ready for the servants and the guard hall."

"And how do you know *that*?" Helarion demanded. "I thought you weren't going onto the palace grounds alone!"

"I never promised. And you needed to know that, right? And I thought, if I got caught, the cooks would just yell at me, but *you*—"

"And if you got caught, little cousin, how'd we have known the meal was almost ready if you couldn't come back to tell us?"

Kratos's brows drew together. Gabrielle stepped between the two. "Okay, that's all settled, guess we'd better get moving, hadn't we?"

Helarion sighed heavily and let his head fall back so he could address the sky. "I wish someone would tell me what I did to deserve *this*?" No answer, of course. He sighed again, moved quietly forward to eye the street, then slid into the open, his left hand gesturing urgently for the others to join him. Gabrielle gave Kratos a quick hug, and followed.

Xena wouldn't like it, knowing he's with us tonight, and his mother would probably have fits. Rightly so. The boy was of an age to be attending one of the free open-air schools King Theseus had brought about—learning to cast verse in iambic pentameter instead of how to separate a merchant and his purse. *I sent that merchant woman—Cydavia?—yeah, her—sent her away so she wouldn't get into trouble. Hurt feelings are better than wounded or dead or in prison, after all.* She drew a steadying breath and turned to Kratos—he wasn't there. She looked all around: deserted street, quiet everywhere except for the occasional clatter of plates or low-voiced conversation inside one of the shuttered houses.

Helarion was four or five paces ahead of her, his back close to a low wall separating the street from several old, well-kept houses. His head moved continuously, watching for any sign of trouble. Kratos was right next to him—the boy'd somehow gone around her and on up the street, and she hadn't seen or heard him. "Leave it be," she whispered tiredly. Boy who could move that quietly and invisibly might prove useful after all. And she had a sneaking hunch that even if she ordered him to go home, he'd ignore the command and stay close by anyway. At least *this* way, she and Helarion had half a chance of keeping him safe.

A little to her surprise, though the main gates to the palace were barred, the small doorway next to it was open and seemingly unwatched. Helarion led them past this, sticking well to the opposite side of the broad avenue, around the next corner, and then down near the far end of the next wall, where a smoothly paved road led onto the palace grounds. She could make out tall, narrow trees on both sides of the road, fronted by hedges, while beyond, barely glimpsed through the branches, there was an expanse of lawn. The inner walls were white, too; they gleamed when the moon briefly broke through the thick clouds. As the sudden luminescence washed across the grounds, Helarion dragged her hurriedly into the bushes.

They were too fragrant—and prickly. Gabrielle bit back a curse and hastily pinched her nose to keep from sneezing. Helarion was a dark shape against the warm light spilling from a wide-open double door near the end of the road. He leaned down to whisper, "Kitchens." She nodded. He turned her a little, and indicated direction with his chin. "Just beyond it, in the dark there? Pantries."

"Kinda *light* down there," Gabrielle whispered, and indicated the kitchens with a small jerk of her head.

"Follow me," he replied softly, and, with a swift glance in both directions, he rustled through the bushes and vanished between the trees.

A tug at her skirt; she leaned down so Kratos could whisper against her ear. "There's a little space here; one of the trees didn't grow as fast as the rest. Come on." He took her fingers, looked around as cautiously as his cousin had, and drew her with him. There *was* a narrow opening, just as he'd said. It wasn't as big as she'd have liked, and she emerged on the other side with bits of broken branches stuck in her hair and down the front of her shirt. But Helarion was already beckoning urgently from across the lawn, and Kratos still had her hand.

Helarion waited only long enough to make certain they were following him, then skirted a long stone bench and a pool, a small stand of flowering bushes, and a statue—she couldn't make out who it might be, or even which sex, it was suddenly so dark.

Either we went around a corner from the kitchens, or they shut the doors. It was unnervingly dark, particularly since she was in an unfamiliar place—a place with so many guards they needed their own hall. *Guards,* she thought gloomily. Well, Agrinon wouldn't be one of them, at least.

Kratos seemed to have good night vision, though; he drew her steadily on, avoiding the occasional barrier and finally fetching up against a pale stone wall. She could smell apples and grain somewhere close by. The darkness was nearly absolute; except for the white wall, she couldn't make out anything but an occasional darker shape. She had no sense of how far anything was from her, either.

Kratos let go of her hand and moved quietly away. Someone else gripped her shoulder and pulled her close— Helarion, she realized after one heart-stopping moment. He still smelled like fresh peaches, and all that bare skin was surprisingly warm. She leaned against him, let her eyes close. He hesitated, then briefly wrapped an arm across her. "All right," he whispered finally. "That's the pantries."

"I can smell them," she began breathily. He gave her a little shake.

"Not so loud! There's a door on this side for the merchants to bring stuff, but there's another on the palace side. This time of night, someone could—"

"Fine, I get the idea." She cut him short. "Where from here?"

"Queen's apartments," he whispered, before drawing her several steps along the wall and giving her a half turn away from the fading smell of apples. One long-fingered hand tilted her head back.

"Up?" she asked warily.

"Of course, up. Queens get the view, remember?"

"I should know that, by now." The moon sailed into the open once more; Helarion pulled her back into shadow, but not before Gabrielle got a good look at the palace wall on this side. The outer wall was thick—probably a walkway on top for the guards, she thought unhappily. The palace itself was even more open than Odysseus's—unshuttered windows everywhere, broad doorways which let out directly onto a broad terrace at ground level, and, rising three stories above the terrace, row upon row of balconies. Lights were visible on a number of these, and in one or two cases, shone through ornate balcony railings. Helarion tugged at her hair to get her attention as the moon sank into cloud and the outer wall vanished from sight. "Queen's apartments," he whispered, and pointed.

Gabrielle sighed. "That's all the way *up*. You aren't planning to climb those balconies, I hope!"

"No. *Or* go inside, before you ask. Over here, way we came." He led her, one hand lightly encircling her wrist, about halfway back to the pantry. Here was the faint but nose-wrinkling odor of a long-dead fire; her free hand encountered rough, unglazed pottery. A huge expanse of it. "Winter oven," he explained. "They do some of the cooking out here; the chimney heats the inner wall of the servants' quarters.

"So?" she asked. A flash of teeth was her only answer and at that moment, realization hit. "I'm supposed to—Oh, no! I'm not going up a chimney!"

"They *said* you were strong. You can't climb that far? It's easy; you just put your back against the inner wall and use your feet to—"

"And when I get out, I'm completely blackened and I go visit the Queen like *that*?"

"Keep your voice down," he hissed. Then he was silent for a long moment so he could listen. "This is a palace, remember? They clean it every spring, *really* clean it. I know. When I was younger, I was one of the lads they paid to scrub the uppermost levels."

"All the same, I don't think—"

"You want to go first or second?" he broke in with another flash of teeth. "There's probably spiders . . ."

"So I either break through the webs or the ones *you* knock loose fall on me anyway, right? I go first," she added before he could say anything else—and before she could think about a chimney four stories high and one solid mass

152

of web. "That way, if I fall, *you* can catch me," she added sweetly. He merely bowed and waved her on.

No sign of Kratos. She hadn't seen the boy since he'd left her by the pantry, she suddenly realized, but as they climbed, she began to suspect he'd preceded them up the chimney. The walls were surprisingly smooth, the only odors those of baked clay, and the least hint of wood smoke. No spiders, but once, a fragment of web wrapped itself around her fingers. She fought a shudder, rubbed it off on her skirts, and kept going.

The boy was waiting for them, crouched near the chimney on the inner side of the low wall that surrounded the roof. Gabrielle dropped down cross-legged next to him to catch her breath. Helarion, to her disgust, didn't even seem slightly winded as he eased out of the chimney and knelt next to his cousin. "Everything quiet up here?"

The boy nodded. "Someone came up to collect the bedding from under that awning where the King sleeps sometimes."

Gabrielle peered across the roof. A sagging awning stood near the opposite wall, a goodly distance away. "King's apartments are under that," Helarion breathed against her ear. "There's a stairs down. Then his throne room on this side of his apartments, and then the Queen's rooms. I'm not sure how many she has, but at least six, including her bedroom. I can get you into her private dining chamber or her bedroom."

"I might need both," Gabrielle said uncertainly.

"Both is fine, too," he said, then rose fluidly and held out a hand for her. A thin shaft of moonlight raked the roof, and slowly faded. Helarion was as clean as he'd been earlier, and her own hands and arms looked fine. Kratos touched her hand.

153

"I'm waiting here, in case you need help or if there's a message."

"Great," she whispered back. Up here, there seemed less chance he'd get into trouble. *No one's gonna get into trouble,* she told herself firmly, and followed Helarion along the shadowy roof.

He halted at a narrow stairway, turned, and eyed her critically, then drew Elyseba's scarf over her hair. "Stay close," he ordered, and took the steps two at a time. She glanced back toward the chimney—no sign of the waiting boy—then followed.

The hallways were darker, older, and more richly worked than those in Penelope's palace. Of course, Athens and this palace had been here for at least a hundred years before the palace in Ithaca was built—and the kings of Athens had a greater pool of craftspersons and artisans to draw upon. *Too bad I won't get the chance to really look at this place,* Gabrielle thought. Helarion tugged at the end of her scarf impatiently, and she picked up the pace.

She could hear voices now and again, but they were all distant, or muffled behind closed doors. At each corner or bend, Helarion paused to listen. Often, he slowed to turn and walk backward so he could check the corridor behind them. Only once did he gesture urgently and draw her into a niche behind a tapestry. Finally, when nothing happened, he shrugged, led the way back out, and went on again.

At last, he halted with his hand on an ornately worked bronze latch. "Reception," he murmured and laid his ear against the wood. Gabrielle gazed anxiously up and down the corridor, but it remained deserted, and finally Helarion pressed the latch, eased the door open, and pulled her into the room.

It was small, and dark except for an oil lamp in the shape of a rearing horse that flickered on a table near the balcony. There was a low couch here, near her feet, and close by the lamp sat a high-backed chair. *Throne*. That and the horse went a long way toward relieving a concern she hadn't realized was gnawing at her until now: Helarion *did* know his way around the palace. "Hippolyta—horse," she murmured. The boy hissed a faint warning in her direction and she fell silent. He held up a hand indicating she should wait, then eased around the throne and onto the balcony. Count of four and he was back at her side.

"Light in the next chamber and the one beyond. Private dining and bedroom," he whispered. "There's a door over there." He pointed toward the wall on her right.

Swell, Gabrielle thought. *I just walk in there—and what if she isn't in the dining chamber, and other people are?* But the time was past for stealth, she decided. There wouldn't be guards in the Queen's own private rooms, and servants wouldn't be a threat to her—not once she spoke to the Queen, gave her credentials, and asked her help. She hoped. She leaned close to Helarion. "Fine. I'm going in. You stay out of sight, but don't leave, in case I need help getting out of the palace for some reason."

"You—"

"Things happen, remember?" she murmured. "And I'm not Xena." He considered this, and finally nodded. She started around the sofa, toward the door, then turned back as something else occurred to her. "Don't steal *any*thing!" But he was already out of sight and the little reception room was very still. Gabrielle cursed faintly, then felt her way over to the inner door.

The dining chamber seemed almost too brightly lit, after the darkened reception room. She blinked furiously, one hand on the latch, but when she could finally see, there was no one in sight. The room contained a long table which held nothing but a matched pair of horse lamps and a tall pottery stand holding a bowl filled with fruit. Four couches surrounded the table; two polished bronze lanterns hung from the ceiling and these cast the bright light over the chamber. She shot a nervous glance toward the darkened balcony, crossed the polished floor quickly and quietly, and stood a long moment, hand on the latch of the next door, listening.

It seemed quiet enough; she eased the latch free and edged the door open the least bit. The lighting in the next room was subdued. She could hear a woman's low, pleasant voice, though not the words. *The Queen? But who is she talking to?* To her astonishment, and as if in answer, she heard the thin wailing cry of a very young infant, suddenly cut off, and the woman's voice again crooning softly. Eyes wide, Gabrielle eased the door wide and walked into the Queen's bedchamber.

Queen Hippolyta lay on a low, well- but plainly-cushioned couch, coverings pulled partway up her body. It could be no one else, Gabrielle knew: the dark hair woven into those distinctive plaits that only an Amazon would wear, and the badge of family she still wore, despite her marriage, embroidered on the right shoulder of her thin gown. No fear showed on her long, pale face, although it must have been surprising at the very least to have a stranger walk into her bedroom. The bundle in her arms—nothing was visible save fine white wrapping cloths—shifted restlessly. "Do I know you?" the Queen asked finally; her voice was low and she had the least hint of a foreign accent.

Gabrielle went to one knee and briefly averted her face. "Ah, I'm sorry, no, but you know my friend, Xena," she said rapidly. "I'm Gabrielle, I travel with her, and I have Right of Cast under Queen Melosa."

"I know Xena. And I know *of* Melosa," Hippolyta said warily. "But why are you *here*?"

"Because there's trouble in Athens," Gabrielle said. "And people are worried because the King isn't doing anything about it, and it's getting really bad in places and—"

"The King," Hippolyta broke in, and sighed. "I haven't seen my husband in five days—more than that, I've lost track. Since before—" She smiled at the bundle in the crook of her left arm. Gabrielle came farther into the room as the Queen smoothed soft cloth back to reveal a small, pale, dark-haired baby. It couldn't have been more than a few days old.

"Ohhh," Gabrielle whispered. "It's adorable! I mean—he?"

"My son," the Queen agreed, and ran a finger across the thatch of hair. The baby's tiny hands were clutched into fists and he seemed deeply asleep. "Hippolytus. *Our* son."

"But—but the King. I don't understand," Gabrielle said. "You just had his son, and he hasn't been in to see you?"

"They said he was ill, a fever, and he was afraid I'd catch it or the baby would. I— Of course I was disappointed, but it was only sensible. But since then, I haven't heard anything. My servants don't answer my questions. And when I try to get up, they find reasons why I can't . . ." Her voice trailed off. The baby made a faint fussing sound, but when the two women looked at him, he was sound asleep once more. "You don't suppose— You said, something wrong," she said suddenly. "In the city. What is it, and where is Xena?"

Gabrielle glanced cautiously around, then drew a low chair next to the Queen's couch and made a reasonably succinct story of it. The other woman listened intently, interrupting only once or twice, and then with intelligent, terse questions. "Anyway," Gabrielle finished up, "the street rumor is that someone in the palace is helping those men, but nothing's been said about the King himself, and personally, I wouldn't believe King Theseus was letting that kind of thing go on if he knew about it."

"He wouldn't, ever," the Queen agreed. "But this is worrying. Things haven't been right, really, since his new accounts keeper arrived somewhere around mid-summer."

"New accounts keeper?" Gabrielle asked.

Her companion shrugged, resettled the child. "He came from King Nestor with such glowing testimonials, and Theseus has always liked Nestor, so even though he didn't really *need* another accounts keeper, he let the man stay.

"Well, almost at once, Mesmer—that's his name, Mesmer—began finding errors in the previous accounts, and then actual thefts of funds. Theseus was particularly angry, I remember, because the money had come from funds that were to have gone to one of the poor neighborhoods. There had been a fire in the spring, so many houses and shops were destroyed, and the money was supposed to help those people. And it was—just gone. Theseus had his old accounts man tossed into the cells down in the basement; for all I know, he's still there. And Mesmer took his place."

"Mesmer," Gabrielle repeated thoughtfully. "Are you *sure* he came from King Nestor? I mean, why would he have sent someone like that if your husband hadn't asked about a new accounts keeper?"

"I asked that myself," Hippolyta admitted. "Theseus got angry with me, something he rarely does. But I have a temper, so of course, I got angry right back and we wound up not speaking for several days. And then, not long after that, we had pirates off the coast, and he went out with the ships as he always does, to make certain—well, you know.

158

Has to see it done himself, he really doesn't delegate much, and never delegates anything to do with fighting.

"So it was another—I can't remember, quite a few days—before he returned. And he seemed—I don't know, distracted. Subdued. Not— I still can't decide if he remained angry because of our quarrel; maybe he found it was easier to talk to me, just the few words that needed saying now and again, rather than not speaking at all. Or maybe he was already ill, trying not to let it slow him down, but not wanting me to know. He's a man, you know," she added with a faint smile. "They get these moods, and they're so odd about illness."

"Yeah. I know," Gabrielle replied feelingly. "Some of 'em, anyway. So, thing is, you haven't seen the King in a while. But the servants? I mean, you've asked where he is, how he is, and they don't tell you? They aren't keeping you a prisoner in here, are they?"

"It's not that, just that they tell me I shouldn't get up yet. I've never had a child before, so I don't know for myself whether it's safe to ignore what they say."

"Well, I don't know a lot about it," Gabrielle admitted, "but I grew up in a village and there's some basics every girl learns. If you didn't have any problems when you were carrying the baby, or during the birth—"

"None."

"And it's been how long?"

"Four days—no, five."

"Then there shouldn't be any reason why you can't get up and walk around, if you don't try to do something like walk the length of the palace the first time you're on your feet. Have you been up at *all*?"

"The necessary few times that one has to get up," the Queen replied, and the corners of her mouth quirked.

"Nothing hurt? You didn't get dizzy?"

"No."

"Someone's trying to keep you in this chamber, then," Gabrielle decided. "That's not good. Maybe that new accounts man is—your servants haven't changed? I mean, they're the same people, just acting strange? With what's happening in the city, I mean, what if someone scared them to do what he said, or paid them, or something?"

"I don't think you could *pay* my servants to betray me. But fear, especially for someone you loved, a child or a parent—it could be. If I hadn't been in this situation, probably I'd have paid more attention to them. I know these people very well." Momentary silence. "I knew I didn't trust that Mesmer," Hippolyta added grimly. "Men who won't meet your eyes and won't answer an ordinary question . . . I can't think why Theseus would keep someone like that around, it's not his way." She considered this briefly, then eased the child away from her side and held him up. "Take him, please." Gabrielle took the boy, smoothed the wrappings around him, and watched as the other woman began edging up onto one elbow, then swung her legs over the edge of the couch. Gabrielle almost protested as the woman got to her feet, swaying, but she bit back the remark. *You got in here for her help, and you told her things. You shoulda known this would be her reaction.* And the Queen might not know much about her body's reaction to bearing a child, but she was, after all, an Amazon. She'd know how much strength she had, and how best to use it.

It was *her* husband whose city was in turmoil—her city as well, really. Her husband who might be in peril himself. *Or dead,* Gabrielle realized. Very likely, that particular realization had brought the new mother to her feet.

The Queen took back her son, lightly kissed his cheek, then laid him in the high-sided, canopied basket at the head of her couch. He shifted a little, pursed his lips, then settled once more. Hippolyta smiled. "His father makes that same face, just as he falls asleep." But her eyes were grave as she met Gabrielle's. "Carry his basket, will you, please? I don't dare leave the child here alone, and I don't know which of my women I'd dare trust with him."

Gabrielle eyed the child thoughtfully, then transferred that look to the mother, who simply stood and waited. With a mental shrug, then, she hefted the basket by its handles—fortunately, it wasn't weighted down with much besides the infant—and looked back at Hippolyta.

"Fine," she said. "Let's go find my husband."

"All right," Gabrielle replied. "But—ah, remember that I sneaked in here, you know, and if the wrong guards find me out in the halls . . ."

"They'll obey *me* when I tell them to leave you alone," the Queen said flatly. "They'd better."

"I truly hope so," Gabrielle said. She settled the infant's basket on the crook of her left arm, took up her staff in the right, and set off, back the way she'd come. The Queen eased around her once they were in the private dining chamber, so she could open the door into the reception room.

"I used to keep chobos in here," she said. "But I gave that over a long time ago; Theseus reminded me it wasn't polite in Athens to keep weaponry close to hand when you greeted your people. Showed a lack of trust, he said." The corners of her mouth quivered. "It's too dark in here," she added as she thrust the door open and stepped inside. "I've told them I want light enough in these rooms that no one falls into the furnishings."

"Sensible," Gabrielle replied. "Too bad about the chobos, though." A pair of Amazon short fighting sticks would've been handy—maybe the Queen wouldn't have enough strength to make use of them, but the guards wouldn't necessarily know that. They *would* know chobos in the hands of an Amazon could be a painful weapon, and often a deadly one. Hippolyta picked her way through the chamber, eased the door into the corridor open, and stepped out. Gabrielle waited until the woman nodded, and caught up to her as she started down the hall toward the King's chambers. But she stopped short as they crossed a passage going toward the front of the palace; Gabrielle, her scalp prickling, eased the basket as far behind her as she could and awkwardly brought the staff across her body in a one-armed grip.

The breath and the tension went out of her, leaving only weak-kneed relief and irritation. "Helarion! What are you doing all the way down *here*?" she demanded as the boy spread his arms wide and ducked his head in the Queen's direction. The Queen's eyes narrowed.

"Helarion. I've heard of *you*," she said. "Gabrielle. What are you doing in the company of this market gadfly? And why didn't you mention him before?"

"Well—I didn't mention him before because I knew if you'd heard of him you'd react just like—like you're reacting," she finished in a small voice as the Queen transferred a "look" the equal of Xena's in her direction.

Helarion cleared his throat and waved both hands for attention and silence. "Ah, Gabrielle, and—um—lady, I'm here right now because there are guards coming this way, from the main gate."

"They're my guards and my husband's, young man," the Queen replied stiffly.

"Maybe not," Helarion replied quickly. He gave Gabrielle a sardonic grin. "It's your friend again; I don't know how you and he are bonded, but—"

"Agrinon!" Gabrielle hissed. Her eyes narrowed. "Your Majesty—"

"Hippolyta," the Queen corrected her. "You're a sister, remember?"

"Hippolyta, then. If it's Agrinon—that guard I told you about?—then he's definitely *not* yours. Or the King's."

"Which way are they going from the gate?" the Queen asked Helarion. "Which passageway?"

"Which—oh. I see. They came through a side entry, someone let them in, I didn't see who. And they're coming up the back passages, but not the servants' ones."

"Don't want to be seen," she murmured.

"I'd say not," Helarion agreed. "They're being very quiet. I think they were making their way to the King's small reception room on this top floor, but I had to back away before they saw me. And so I could warn you."

"Good job," Gabrielle said. She turned to the Queen. "How far to the small reception room?"

"That way," the Queen said, and set off, moving a little more quickly than before; her face was pale, and there was a small line between her brows. Gabrielle shook her head, turned to Helarion, and thrust the basket at him.

"Here. Take him."

He automatically took the handles, and peered doubtfully at the contents. "Take . . . ? I don't tend babies!"

"I don't either," Gabrielle said. A tug at his shirt got him moving, trailing behind her as she hurried to catch up to the Queen. "But I *do* fight, and you don't, right?"

"I can; I just choose not to," he spluttered indignantly.

"Well, I choose *to* fight, and I'm pretty good at it, too. What you do well is fade out of sight and move fast, when you have to. And you have a good eye for where the danger is. That's the main reason you're carrying the baby—it's hers."

163

"It's— Beloved bright Father, you can't ask me to hold the heir!"

"Oh, yes, I can!" Gabrielle replied. "Come on, we can't let her get out of sight!" This as the Queen abruptly turned up another of the many side passages and vanished. Helarion grumbled unhappily, but settled the basket on his arm and lengthened his stride. Fortunately, the Queen hadn't gone very far—fortunate, because the passages in *this* end of the palace snaked every bit as much as Peder had warned. Nothing was straight, and narrow or wide corridors went everywhere, branching without much pattern. "Look," Gabrielle added persuasively as they came up behind Hippolyta. "You've got a heart under that hard exterior—"

"Says who?" he demanded.

"Says me. I saw you with your cousin. You really care for him, don't you? And I'll just bet you spent a lot of time with him when *he* was a baby." She glanced at him sidelong; to her surprise, his face softened and he smiled, a genuine, sweet smile that wholly transformed him.

"He was so little, and so cute—all right. I'll take care of him. Don't blame me if you look up and I'm not there."

"Absolutely not," she replied firmly. The Queen turned her head, gave him a long, appraising look, then nodded and lengthened her stride once more.

9

Gabrielle caught up with the woman once again as she hesitated by a narrow, shadow-filled doorway. Hippolyta plunged into the opening, eased the latch aside with the faintest of clicks, and listened for a long moment. Silence. She tugged at Gabrielle's shirt, and breathed against her ear, "It's the back way into the throne room. The old king had his secret advisors use it, to eavesdrop on anyone coming to petition him."

"Sneaky," Gabrielle whispered back; the Queen sent a grin in her direction and nodded.

"We've thought of blocking it. Just as well there hasn't been time, under the present circumstances." She gave the door a shove and walked into the room.

At first all Gabrielle could see was a small, empty space, dimly lit and overlaid with shadows. As her eyes adjusted, she realized they were behind two high-backed thrones. Lanterns swung from several brackets on the other side of the chairs, casting heavy shadow in this secluded area.

To her right was another of the ubiquitous balconies, this one flanked with painted wooden shutters. The walls and low ceiling were dark blue and gold, painted in an abstract pattern that must have cost someone dear, both to plan it and to commission it. But the room didn't seem very large and, when she followed Hippolyta through the narrow gap between the thrones, she discovered it wasn't nearly as finely furnished as she'd have thought. The double doors were clearly made for defense rather than beauty: they were heavy wood fitted with braces for a bar. The bar itself had been swung upright on a hinge. "Oh," Gabrielle said, her voice flat. The Queen turned and raised an eyebrow. "I mean, it's nice, I guess. The paint and all. Just—well—kinda plain," she finished lamely.

"It's the small room," Hippolyta assured her; the Queen's eyes were alight with dry humor. "The fabled great reception room with the huge circular fire pit where the heroes roast their sticks of meat, all the rest of it— that's on the main floor in the corner. We use *it* only when Theseus or I need to impress someone."

"Oh—right. Gotcha."

"This chamber dates from the siege by Minos." A gesture took in the bar across the double doors. "Some say we shouldn't be using it at all, too much emotional pain for not only us but the Minoans. I don't entirely buy that."

"I don't either," Gabrielle replied. "And I know all about the argument. The Minoans made their own path, decided what was right for them—they failed. Why should you apologize, or try to pretend it never happened?"

"Why indeed?" The Queen's mouth quirked once again. "I like this room—well enough. One day, I hope to redo the paint, the ceilings, everything. Anyway, for everyday sessions, this room is much more practical than the formal chamber—" The Queen stopped as the latch on the main double doors clicked loudly and they began to swing inward. Gabrielle caught at the Queen's arm and dragged her swiftly back out of sight. Helarion stood, basket in hand, at the secret door, ready to ease it open and flee. Gabrielle signed him to stay put, then slipped up next to Hippolyta, who had edged around the far side of the nearest throne, still well in shadow but where she could see what was going on.

One door slammed against the wall; the other drifted slowly in and swung partway back. A small, dark, slender man in plain shirt and breeches came in, followed by a slightly taller man in a long robe heavily embroidered with gold at the cuffs and hem. "My husband," Hippolyta breathed anxiously against Gabrielle's ear.

"Ahh—nice robe," Gabrielle murmured; the Queen shot her a startled look, then shook her head.

"That's Mesmer in the expensive garb; Theseus wouldn't waste good coin on such clothing."

"Oh. Sorry." The Queen laid a hand on her arm, and pressed a finger to her own lips for silence. The King looked dazed or ill—his face was too pale for a fighting man's. The man with him, by contrast, had that well-fed, sleek look that suddenly reminded Gabrielle in a way of Draco. *Smug. Full of himself. Mistake him for the King— right.* The King crossed the room, stumbled at the edge of a small rug, and settled on a low couch near the throne farthest from the women. Mesmer smiled unpleasantly, and took the throne for himself.

Hippolyta's eyes narrowed, and the hand on Gabrielle's arm tightened briefly. Painfully. Gabrielle clenched her teeth, touched the woman's fingers to get her attention, and indicated the hand with a glance. The Queen started, and released her.

"You are tired." Mesmer's voice was low, soothing. "Very tired. Your duties are wearing you down. You are so *very* tired."

"Tired," the King agreed dully.

"You wish nothing more than sleep."

"Sleep."

"And while you sleep, your good friend Mesmer will deal with the petty details that wear you down. You will sleep, and Mesmer will do the work."

"Sleep. Good . . . friend . . . Mesmer . . ."

Gabrielle's eyelids sagged and she fought a yawn. The Queen eyed her sidelong and gave her a pinch; she yelped. Mesmer came to his feet in a bound and ran to the center of the chamber. The King didn't move.

"Who's there?" Mesmer barked. Gabrielle struggled to her feet but the Queen was already on hers and striding into the room. "I— Your Majesty!" he added in a surprised voice as he went to one knee and lowered his head. "Such a surprise to see you here. But are you certain it is safe for you to be on your feet, so soon?" He stood again, looked her squarely in the eye, and began to murmur in such a low voice Gabrielle couldn't make out all his words. ". . . rest . . . birth of a first son, so tiring . . ." Gabrielle was swaying on her feet when Helarion came up behind her and gave her a little shove. The Queen cleared her throat ominously, and the accounts keeper fell pruently, warily, silent.

"I know what you're doing, Mesmer!" Hippolyta snapped. "Amazon healers know that particular technique, and it won't work on *me*! Release my husband, now, or I'll—" She took a step back and raised her voice. "How *dare* you draw a dagger in this chamber!"

Gabrielle snatched up her staff and hurried to place herself in front of the Queen. Mesmer opened his mouth to say something, but at that moment the doors crashed open again and guards surged into the small chamber, Agrinon at their head.

"Mesmer, that woman's back in the market! And if *she* is, then Xena—" He stopped short, and half a dozen men slammed into him; the rest spilled around him, filling the doorway and the whole far end of the small reception. "You!" he hissed, and his eyes narrowed.

"Hey, old friend!" Gabrielle gave him a positively evil grin. "Wanna try and even the score? Way I figure it, I'm up, two to one, and *you* didn't even get to land a blow the time *you* won!"

But he backed away, sidestepping into the far corner of the room until he bumped up against a huge bronze jug on a small, low table. At his gesture, two of the guards closed the doors and stepped back to block them. "Get her!" he shouted. "Get them both!"

"Fourteen to one?" Gabrielle eased into a crouch and began feinting with the staff. "Bad odds for you, Agrinon. Don't move, okay? I'll come for *you*." Behind her, Hippolyta dove for the nearest throne, and Gabrielle risked a quick glance in that direction. "Good idea, sister! You get out of reach and I'll take care of—" Her voice faded and her eyes went wide as Hippolyta came back to her side. In her hands were two short, slender royal scepters, one knobbed at the end in silver, the other etched with a rearing horse. The Queen smiled grimly. "Hey!" Gabrielle managed to say brightly. "Nice set of chobos!"

"They'll do," Hippolyta replied softly, and with a bound, she closed the distance between herself and the nearest three guards, who had been trying to stalk around behind the two women. A blur of motion, several loud cracks, and three men lay groaning on the throne room floor. Gabrielle blinked, then jumped forward, catching one man under the chin and the fellow next to him in the gut. Two steps back, Hippolyta leaned against her shoulder, then half-turned to set herself against Gabrielle's back.

She didn't *look* as exhausted as she must already have been, after birthing her first baby and spending several days flat on her back. Gabrielle braced her feet to take what weight the Queen was putting on her, then almost fell when the woman snarled a particularly unpleasant oath and moved out suddenly to attack another guard.

In the corner, Agrinon was shouting; seven men had gone down to the women's joint attack, but three of those were already back up and only one looking the worse for wear. Another of them retreated toward the doors and would have gone through them, but at another yell from Agrinon, one of those holding the entry brought up his dagger in a meaningful gesture. The would-be retreater backed away, eyes searching the chamber for another way out. His lips moved, shaping the word "Balcony," and, cautiously skirting Gabrielle and with a doubtful look for the King, who hadn't moved or so much as blinked, he eased around him, too, and dove behind the thrones. A loud crash and the floor shook as someone fell, hard; Helarion eased into the open briefly to give Gabrielle a cheerful grin. A large shard of pottery dangled from his upraised hand. Gabrielle returned the grin, then jerked back to the moment as someone grabbed the end of her staff.

She shook it, then yanked, hard. The guard—the one from the market earlier in the day—gave her an unpleasant grin and yanked back. Gabrielle spun into him, drove her elbow into his belly, freed her staff, and brought it down across the back of his head. She spun back as he fell, staff moving, eyes searching for the Queen.

Hippolyta had moved away from Gabrielle, setting herself between the guards and Theseus. Her left leg was braced against the King's throne, the chobos a blur of movement. None of the guards seemed to want to come near her. *Great, Gabrielle thought. She doesn't need the workout just now. I hope Helarion got that baby somewhere safe before he stuck his nose in just now—* Two more guards threw themselves at her, and the thought went unfinished.

Another bellowed command came from Agrinon, who was very red in the face and so incoherent with fury that she wondered how any of his men could understand what he was shouting. *She* certainly couldn't. One of the two men guarding the doors moved to the center of them; the other drew his sword, shifted his grip on the dagger, and began trying to work his way around the outside of the room, behind the King and possibly behind the thrones. Gabrielle dropped another man; when she dared risk another glance in that direction, she saw that the Queen had backed the man with the blades against the wall.

She sent her eyes back the other way. Agrinon was edging toward the doors, and from the look on his face, she thought he intended to escape that way. She sent the staff sharply left and right to clear a path, and then started for him. He eyed her warily, then drew his sword and backed away into his corner once more. He glanced along the other wall, perhaps in hopes of reaching the secret door. Maybe he thought he could sneak behind *her,* but that wasn't going to happen. Four men stood between her and the door guard at the moment, and most of those who were down were down for good this time. If Agrinon tried stealth, it wouldn't work; she didn't have that many enemies to watch out for anymore. *And if he tries to escape, well, he's Helarion's problem,* she decided.

The Queen brought both chobos down in a slashing cross-armed blur, the head of the unfortunate swordsman between them. A loud double crack, and he swayed back into the wall and slid bonelessly down it. Hippolyta turned back to place herself between the main part of the room and Theseus once again. She was very pale now, and sweat beaded her brow. ''Better finish this fast!'' she shouted.

''Like it!'' Gabrielle shouted back; she feinted with the staff for one of the men facing her, and when he jerked back out of range, she switched her attack and slammed the staff into him like a battering ram, then took hold of the weapon two-handed and brought it around in a hard backhand swing. It caught another guard, throwing him into a third and fourth.

Agrinon was making straight for the main doors this time, but he stopped half a dozen paces short of them: the guard he'd left wasn't there anymore, and someone had dropped the bar across the doors. With an oath, he ran over and threw down his dagger so he could tug the bar free, but it wouldn't move, not even when he let go of his sword to shove at the bar two-handed. His fingers moved along the brackets and he swore furiously. ''Where's Gnerios? And who wedged this door!''

''I did it—with my little hammer!'' A singsong, irritating voice just behind her left ear made Gabrielle jump. Helarion came into the open, easily and gracefully dodging the two nearest guards who were snatching at him. Agrinon roared in a wordless, ruddy-faced fury; Helarion made faces at him, then laughed and danced back out of sight.

''Get him!''

But the two men who started to obey Agrinon's order had to get around Gabrielle first; she bared her teeth at them, and snapped the staff first across one's forehead, and then back across his kneecaps. The other simply shook his head, dropped his weapons, spread his arms wide to show he wasn't holding anything else, and sat in the middle of the floor. Gabrielle glanced around a room suddenly quiet and filled with fallen men. Hippolyta managed a faint, triumphant smile before she weakly sagged onto the King's throne and let the scepters clatter to the floor. Gabrielle nodded in satisfaction, then started toward the wedged doors, staff at the ready and a gleam in her eye. Agrinon backed away from her, toward the corner he'd held earlier, but as he reached it, a finger tapped his shoulder. He caught his breath in a gasp and spun around. Helarion stood behind him, a beatific smile on his face and the large bronze jug poised upside down over his head.

"Catch," he said softly, and dropped the pot. It came down squarely over Agrinon's head and shoulders, covering him to the elbows before the bottom cracked down on the top of his head with a muted clang. The man's knees buckled and he slowly toppled over.

Silence. Gabrielle drew a deep breath and leaned into her staff, eyed the fallen men warily, then worked her way through and around them to the Queen's side. "Hey? Are you all right?" she asked softly.

"A little . . . tired," the other woman admitted breathlessly. "But fine. Theseus, though . . ."

Gabrielle patted her shoulder. "He looks all right—I mean, I'm sure he'll be okay. First thing, though, we gotta do something about these men. Fighting them once was enough." She turned and gazed around the room. Helarion had vanished but he emerged from behind the thrones, basket in hand. He set it at the Queen's feet, smiled down at the baby, then glanced at Hippolyta.

"Never even woke up."

"His father's like that," the Queen agreed. She regretted her words as she turned to Theseus, who stared at the wall, dazed. She sighed heavily. "All right. What *do* we do about these men?"

Gabrielle shook her head, set her hands on her hips, and thought, hard. Nothing suggested itself. "Isn't there anyone in this whole building you can be absolutely certain of?'' she asked finally.

''No time to go searching for anyone,'' Helarion said and shoved one of the guards with his toe. The man had been groaning softly for some moments. ''I suggest rope.''

Gabrielle eyed him tiredly. ''Rope. Where'd you find rope in a palace?''

''Oddly enough, *I* know,'' Hippolyta put in. ''Up on the roof, there's a pavilion where Theseus and I often sleep, in summer at least. There are ropes to keep the poles upright and extra lengths of rope everywhere because the wind sometimes springs up and the poles need reinforcing. If you can find the proper stairs to the right part of the roof—''

''I can find it,'' Helarion said immediately. He was half-way to the main doors when he stopped short, spun partway around, and gave the women an apologetic grin. ''Sorry. Forgot how well I blocked that entry. I'll be back.''

''Great—I think,'' Gabrielle mumbled as he vanished. Moments later the door banged behind him. ''Um—if you'll help me keep an eye on these men until he *does* get back with the ropes, I swear I'll think hard in the meantime and see if I can remember ever hearing about what that guy Mesmer was doing.''

''I know what it is, just as I told him,'' Hippolyta replied calmly. She pushed to her feet, shoved the basket back out of the way a little farther, and scooped up the two scepters once more. ''Some Amazon healers use it for everything from easing a headache to making a wounded warrior relax so she can be stitched back together, without pain. I . . . I remember someone saying it also makes people do what you want them to.''

''Makes . . . people—'' Gabrielle swung around to eye the King warily. ''Really! You think that's what that Mesmer guy was doing?''

"I'd wager on it," the Queen replied grimly. "But I'll be able to ask the man when he wakes up—and I think he'll find it a good idea to answer what I ask him."

"Ah—yeah. Bet he will. So—what d'you do to make it go away? I mean—I've seen people drink too much ale and get kinda like that, but all they gotta do is sleep it off and eventually they're okay." Gabrielle frowned, shook her head. "Well, unless they start drinking again soon's they wake up. But this—if it's just done with words . . ."

"But words can be very powerful, Gabrielle."

Gabrielle flashed her a smile. "Yeah, I know. I'm kind of Xena's unofficial bard, after all." She spun partway around and delivered a hard, cracking blow to one of the guards who was on his hands and knees, trying to sneak away quietly. He went flat; the Queen winced. Moments later, the secret door opened and Helarion hurried into the room, his arms piled high with coils of rope; ends dangled all around his legs and trailed after him. "How'd you get down from the roof without breaking your neck?" Gabrielle asked.

"I'm good, of course," he replied and dropped the rope with a flourish on top of Agrinon.

Gabrielle gave him a hard look—her best copy of Xena's "look"—and said warningly, "Helarion—"

"I know. 'Don't start with me,' " he chorused, then bent down and gravely handed her a length of rope.

It took time, even with all three of them working as quickly as they could. Once there were only four or five men still unbound, Helarion left them to it and went to pry his wedges out so the main doors could be opened. Gabrielle wrapped rope around Agrinon's ankles and tied it, hard, before swinging him around and hauling the pot off his head. He glared up at her, his hands clawlike and ready to snatch, but he didn't seem to have the strength to move. Gabrielle smiled sweetly. "Ah-ah-ah," she said and held the staff where he could see it. Muttering under his breath, he slowly relaxed, rolled his eyes, and allowed her to wrap rope around his wrists and tie a snug knot. "Look at it this way," she said as she stepped back to admire her handiwork, "all this adversity you've had lately will do *great* things for your character!" He snarled wordlessly. Gabrielle smiled back.

Helarion had the bar loosened in its braces, but when he went to ease it free, Gabrielle touched his arm and shook her head. "Maybe they had backups; leave it where it is for now."

"Maybe we'll never *know* which of them is dirty," he retorted. "I mean, how are you gonna find out?"

"Mesmer is going to tell us," Queen Hippolyta broke in. A grim smile turned the corners of her generous mouth. She stood near the wall, fists on her hips, staring down at the richly robed, supposed accounts keeper. "Because if he doesn't, my *sister* and I are going to put him through an Amazon gauntlet. Aren't we, Gabrielle?"

She didn't look up; Gabrielle gaped at her blankly until Helarion nudged her with his elbow and indicated the fallen Mesmer with a sidelong jerk of his head. He wasn't unconscious, though his eyes were still closed; his body was tense and he was holding his breath. Gabrielle nodded and in a deep, would-be menacing voice said, "Yeah! Not just the gauntlet but the *long* version! That's the one with the . . . with the . . . I can't say it out loud, poor Helarion will have bad dreams for a month," she added in desperation.

He blinked at her. "I will?"

"Trust me," she added earnestly. The fallen Mesmer blinked rapidly, glanced in Gabrielle's direction, then squirmed and tried to move away from the Queen's feet.

She stepped on one flowing sleeve, holding him in place. "Do you want to know how that works, Mesmer? Because *I'll* tell you, right now, in full, rich detail. Every cut, every bruise, every—"

"No!" The man's voice came out as a strangled squeak. "Not—no, don't, please don't, I'll— Anything but that!"

"Then talk to me," Hippolyta snarled. "Tell me who hired you to come here, who in the palace is in your pay."

"You don't want much," he complained faintly.

"No—just everything. If you'd rather hear me describe the alternative to you, in full, rich, bloody, bruised, broken, slashed, mangled detail—"

"No! I'm— All right, I'll tell you." He was whimpering faintly, but as the Queen stirred and flexed her hands, he managed to pull himself together and make a reasonably quick confession. "The guards—twenty-seven who are ours . . . the man who came in, leading those men just now, he has names, all the names. The rest—there aren't many yet—the rest are afraid for their families. Others in the palace—one man in the King's employ, the secretary Hadrimos, no one else." He scowled up at the Queen. "They all *like* you and him too much; you think this was easy?" She bared her teeth and he shivered back away from her, went on with his rapid confession. "In the city—a few men under someone called Brisus plus another twenty or so, mostly kids, working for the Protectors—there's three of them. Out in the countryside, there's an old farm . . ."

"That's being taken care of," Gabrielle said. "That's— that's really it? All of them?"

The man cast her a bitter look. "We've only had something less than a moon season! With another, or maybe two more, we'd have been so entrenched you'd never have taken us this easily. Half a year or less, we'd have had all Athens!"

"Maybe," Gabrielle said. "But I don't think so. So, Hippolyta, what do we do with this roomful of scum?"

She considered this and shrugged. "Cells in the basement. I never cared to have them there, and they've been empty for years, but just now I'm glad."

"They may not be empty," Gabrielle said. "Remember the other accounts keeper? The real one? And—I might be wrong, but I think there's a poor city man named Polydorus locked in down there."

It was getting late, Gabrielle realized; the King's guards had come at the Queen's summons and taken Agrinon, Mesmer, and the others away. The King's guard captain remained behind awhile, listening as the Queen gave him a list of orders: scour the castle for anyone who didn't belong, find the proper accounts keeper and have him restored to his apartment, locate Polydorus if he was within the palace, and set up interviews with the entire staff to make certain no one was acting according to Mesmer's orders, either willingly or under duress. Then send word down to the kitchens to send a late—and large—dinner to the King's small reception room. "All that fighting gave me an appetite," she told Gabrielle as the captain bowed and left; his men followed with the prisoners. Agrinon spared Gabrielle one last black look; she smiled cheerily and waved as he was hauled away with the others.

"Appetite—yeah, know what you mean," Gabrielle replied. "Helarion, why don't you go fetch Kratos down here? After all, he did a lot to help us; I think the Queen would like to meet him. And I'll bet anything you like that he's hungry, too." Helarion cast his eyes up but went without comment. The Queen sighed and eased herself back down on the edge of the King's throne. Theseus hadn't moved so much as a hair, despite the noise and traffic through his chamber, and just now he sat unblinking, staring right through his Amazon wife.

"I should have asked Mesmer how to break the spell," she said worriedly. "But I probably wouldn't have trusted his word on *this*." She reached with one long-fingered hand to caress her husband's cheek. Gabrielle glanced over her shoulder as a clatter of footsteps came down the hall, but it was only Helarion bringing a wary and shy-looking Kratos.

Hippolyta roused herself and smiled at the boy. "Gabrielle tells me you've been helpful. Thank you, on behalf of King Theseus and myself, and all Athens."

"Um—Lady," he said hastily as Helarion hissed something against his ear. "I was just trying to get my mother safe."

"That's a good cause. Here," the Queen added as two large men carrying wide, high-piled trays came into the reception room. "I think we have dinner. You look like a boy who could use a good meal." Kratos eyed the trays with astonishment. But when Gabrielle glanced away from him to see how Helarion was taking things, she saw that his expression was the twin of his young cousin's.

It was one of the stranger meals she'd ever eaten, Gabrielle decided later: Helarion and Kratos, wildly ill-clad for this comparatively sumptuous chamber and bountiful meal, but unself-consciously eating like two healthy young men who had a chance at not only great quantities of food but a variety they might never sample again; herself and the Queen of Athens—a woman as strong in her own way as Xena, who asked Gabrielle to call her sister, and who shared a plate with her newfound friend while openly nursing her infant son; and behind all this, King Theseus, who sat unblinking on his bench, oblivious to anything around him.

His appetite finally slaked, Kratos went to one knee and glanced up at the Queen from under long lashes. "Um—Lady—" Helarion hissed urgently against his ear and the boy gave him a frown before turning back to the women. "Your Majesty," he corrected himself carefully, "I think I would like to go back to my neighborhood and see if my mother is okay, and see if Xena's got back with our people. Um—if you don't mind, Your—"

"Lady is just fine, Kratos," Hippolyta informed him gravely. Her free hand came out to ruffle his hair, and he grinned up at her, abashed and very pink across his cheekbones. "Go to your mother, Kratos, and tell her the Queen says she has a son to be proud of."

"She won't ever believe I met you, or that you said that," Kratos said doubtfully.

"She will. Because once this is all over, you'll bring her here at my invitation, so she and I can talk about how to make things better where you and she live. So her son doesn't have to steal coin purses in the market, ever again."

"I'd like that," Kratos whispered; he got to his feet, turned, and walked quickly from the reception room.

Behind him, Hippolyta sighed quietly. "I fear for our children. For my own son. Because, if—Gabrielle?" she added sharply as the other woman clutched her temples and closed her eyes.

Vision assaulted her. *I can see it! This room, but it's changed somehow, and a haggard-faced, tiny, gaunt woman is being married to a man—it's Theseus but he's older, his hair's graying and he's still pining for his first, dead Amazon wife. But the woman—I can tell what she's thinking; she only wants the boy—Hippolytus, it must be him, but look at him, he's tall and handsome and—and*

180

beautiful. Things shifted blurringly; time passing, she thought. When the vision steadied once more, she saw less, felt more of the mood. *The whole palace is sick with that woman's desire and the poor boy only wants to remain pure and serve the Huntress.* Vision after vision slipped through her mind, jealousy and fury, recriminations and then the sand where Atalanta had run—a deserted winter beach, a chariot, a snake the size of a mature oak rising from the ocean, and the boy, half-dead, lying in the wreck of his cart while King Theseus knelt and wept. *Oh, dear goddesses, tell me Xena is right after all, that my visions aren't real but the product of too much imagination!* Gabrielle was panting for air as she opened her eyes, and her brow was damp. The Queen was staring at her wide-eyed, and so was Helarion, who had her by the shoulders. She managed a smile, tried to force the smile into her eyes. There was a taste of bile in her mouth, burying the subtle and wonderful flavors of the dinner she'd just finished. "Ah—sorry, I get these attacks, you know?" She could feel the blood warming her entire face, but that was a good thing: the Queen was too polite to press matters. "So— what are we gonna do to get the King back to normal?"

"My Theseus." The Queen, properly distracted, set her infant son back in his basket and got to her feet. "My poor beloved," she whispered and laid a hand along his jaw. Gabrielle's eyes prickled with tears; she turned aside to wipe them roughly away.

Helarion got to his feet. "He doesn't seem too harmed, really. Just—not with us. Maybe, once the magician is gone, the spell will fade away. Or maybe go just like— that." He snapped his fingers. Theseus shivered, blinked, and stared wildly around the chamber. His eyes focused on his Queen's feet, moved up her body, rested on her face.

"Beloved?" he whispered in a rusty voice. "Hippolyta, it *is* you! But—but they said, they told me you were so angry, and then, that you and our daughter—that you fell, and that you went into labor, but that she—" He frowned, and transferred his wide-eyed, confused gaze to his hands.

"They lied," Hippolyta replied evenly. Her own face was very white. She dropped to one knee, cupped the King's face between her hands, and moved it so his gaze fell on the basket between the two thrones. "Theseus, I would never be so angry with you as to desert you, no matter what! And I didn't fall, nothing bad happened. Theseus, look. That's our son. Yours and mine."

"Son," the King whispered. "My— *Our* son. Our *son*." He considered this and shook his head; his dark eyes softened and he looked at Hippolyta anxiously. "Our child. My horse maiden, how are you faring? And why did you not ask me to come, when you felt the hour upon you?" Hippolyta, apparently at a loss for words, shook her head and bit her lip, then glanced at Gabrielle, who got to her feet.

"King Theseus," she murmured and ducked her head. "Things have gotten a little—well, a little strange in Athens lately. There was this guy, Mesmer . . ."

"Mesmer." Theseus's dark eyes went wide and blank and his voice became a low drone. "He said I needed to rest, to sleep, to relax, to . . ."

"Husband!" Hippolyta shouted. Helarion snapped his fingers once more. Theseus blinked and came back to the moment. Gabrielle stopped swaying in place and shook her head sharply.

"Oh—sorry," he said in a much more normal voice. "Why are we here?" he asked mildly. "In this room? I don't recall coming here at all—in fact, the last thing I remember is seeing to the horses after I drove my chariot along the sand at low tide . . ." He stared in rising concern as Gabrielle clutched her temples; vision was rising once more, the near-dead boy a mangled wreck of blood and exposed bone ends . . . She shook her head to clear it again, managed a smile.

"Headaches," she murmured apologetically. "Sometimes—ah—sometimes *apples* give me these headaches; someone suggested I really should peel 'em, guess I'll have to try that."

"Oh," Theseus replied. He eyed her doubtfully, and turned back to Hippolyta. "Strange things in Athens, she said. I don't remember hearing about anything wrong in the city."

"They've kept it from you, somehow," Hippolyta said. "Let Gabrielle tell it."

As Gabrielle spoke, the King rose and began pacing the small throne room. Occasionally he glanced at her; Gabrielle wasn't certain from the look on his face whether he simply didn't believe her story, or thought her mad. *Guess I'd think I was mad, too, if I'd been watching me just now— that vision and all,* she decided. When she finished, he was quiet for a long moment, one hand thoughtfully rubbing his chin as he paced. Finally he turned, set one booted foot on the seat of his throne, and looked at Hippolyta.

"It's what comes of delegating," he said.

"No," the Queen replied firmly. "Of delegating to the wrong people, that's all. But that's not important just now; fixing the problem out there is."

"Well—a company of guards," Theseus began uncertainly. Gabrielle cleared her throat.

"Um—sire, if I could suggest something? Xena's already out there, like I told you. Probably she's got those kidnapped people back, but we don't know that yet. So a straight attack might not be a good idea. And—and you don't want your people even thinking that you'd send an army into the streets, do you? Because some might be grateful, but most of them would wonder—''

''I take the point,'' he said as she hesitated. ''So, what do you suggest, just let Xena finish the job for me?''

Gabrielle shook her head. ''I was gonna say, if you picked a few men and went yourself, you know, enough men to overwhelm the Protectors and Brisus and whoever they've got. Enough men for that, but not enough to scare the ordinary people. And—and so they could see you personally, so they'd know you don't tolerate men like that.''

''They should know that already,'' Hippolyta put in. She was frowning. ''Husband, I don't like the idea of you being out there with only a few men.''

''Particularly when *you* aren't in fit condition to protect my back, is that it?'' he asked with a smile. The smile faded. ''I'll be at least as safe out there as I was in the palace, Hippolyta. Safer than I was on ship when we attacked the pirates.''

''Safe as you were on the boar hunt?'' she asked dryly. ''Remember to have someone guard your back.''

''Of course.'' He looked at Gabrielle. ''Are you coming with us?''

''Actually, I thought I would go find out if Xena's returned. I'd be better with her, if we have to fight any of those guys. And we really can't do anything if she hasn't rescued those people. So I can send someone back with a message, as soon as I know, and then we could meet at first light at the baker's. His name's Ukloss, and it's the street of the Blue Horseshoe. Can you find that?''

''I know it. My guardsmen can find it.'' The King let his foot down from the throne and came across to clasp Gabrielle's arms and pull her close briefly. ''Thank you for helping my wife and son, and my city.''

''Well—sure.'' Gabrielle nodded; her face felt warm. ''But thank me after we do something about Brisus and the Protectors.''

10

The back streets of Athens were cool and damp at the moment, and there had been fog down along the shore most of the way into the city. Xena stepped out of the stable where Argo was being curried. There was silence all around, except for the very distant sound of men laughing raucously—a tavern over a street or so, she decided.

Just the three of them occupied the dark, deserted, and narrow track.

Adrik eased around her and started back toward the baker's. Xena loosened her dagger in its sheath and followed. She cast a tired glance at the small woman by her side, invisible in the gloom except for the pale scarf across her hair. Elesyba, aware of the movement, looked up and immediately away. "Warrior," she said quietly, "I know you don't want me out of that temple and in the open again. But I know my son, and I worry. Poor Kherix—Kratos's father will do better without me fussing over him, he'll sleep. And there's no threat left that they will take us away, is there?" Silence. The woman glanced up at her, and Xena saw amusement in her face but also a surprising strength.

"I can't see your face to read your lips, and you don't know my hand language, so it seems you'll simply have to make do with me."

And I thought Gabrielle could be stubborn, Xena thought. At least with Gabrielle she could make her arguments in return; in this case it was absolutely impossible.

Of course, she couldn't blame the woman for wanting to be with her young son—but the threat was only partly removed. Well, maybe she would serve as a stabilizing factor for young Adrik, who at the moment seemed to think his rather minor part in vanquishing Mikkeli and the rest of them had made a warrior of him. *Look at him,* she thought, *swaggering down the street like he owns it.*

Well, but—that couldn't be such a bad thing: gods knew the boy'd been shoved around enough by men like Brisus and Mikkeli. He deserved a sense of victory, even if it didn't last for long. And the self-confidence it gave him might prove useful when they took on Brisus and his cohorts. *Yes. Might get him killed, too. Remind him of that, before he leaps two-footed and blindly into danger.*

She easily knew the route between the stable and the baker's by now, having traveled it three times. But it was useful at the moment having Adrik just ahead of her with his eyes and ears open, so she could consider what to do next.

It was so gods-blasted complicated! Not knowing why a normally concerned and caring king had turned his back on his people; not knowing which of the guards—besides the all-too-obvious Agrinon—were taking coin and goods from the Protectors and betraying their king and his people not knowing if Gabrielle had succeeded tonight . . .

Not knowing what Brisus was up to. *Brisus,* she thought flatly and her eyes narrowed as her hands flexed. He'd been responsible in part for the blow-up in Mezentius's camp that had resulted in Marcus's death. Brisus and his personal shrine of profit . . . he was the blacker side of that dark coin Gabrielle had complained about a mere two nights earlier on their way out of Athens: those who sought wealth and status and didn't care about the cost to anyone else; who counted wealth as the only measure of a man's or woman's importance and who'd willingly tread the less important people underfoot. "I can afford the best so I have a right to it," she murmured, and her eyes narrowed. Brisus was about to find out what the best was going to cost him. She was going to flatten him like one of that scroll merchant's little winged things.

All the same, it wouldn't be wise to underestimate the man. Brisus was obsessed by profit but he wasn't stupidly narrow of vision in his quest for it—he could plan. He claimed to have cut his teeth on warriors' board games and she'd seen him play, years earlier. He was very, very good at them, particularly the ones that required lots of pieces and lots of moves. Brisus was the kind who'd be thinking five moves ahead of his opponent. *But then, I was pretty good at the board games myself, once I learned about them,* she recalled. Once she'd left her village behind and joined up with fighting men.

Better at them than Brisus, she thought judiciously— after all, they were simply battle tactics in a bloodless format, and unlike most of the men she'd played, she never lost her temper when things started going against her.

All right, think, she ordered herself. So far as she could tell, Brisus must know she'd been in Athens: both that little adventure with Atalanta *and* their stay in the market jail would have made juicy gossip, and of course, Agrinon could have told him. He might hope that once she and Gabrielle had escaped last night, they'd keep going, right out of Athens. He wouldn't count on it. But he wouldn't know, or even suspect, anything was up until Mikkeli went missing.

Too bad she hadn't asked Mikkeli when he was expected back. Brisus might have put the man on a tight schedule; Brisus might be asleep or passed out by this hour, but he might be waiting for a delivery that was at least an hour late. He'd surely know by first light that something had gone wrong, though; the baker said the cart always left and returned during the night. Brisus would assume the worst and be deep in plans for some counter move long before the eastern sky turned pale.

There were possibilities within possibilities, from that point: she couldn't decide what course he'd take, once he was sure Mikkeli wasn't coming back. He'd immediately dismiss the notion the man had taken the pickings and run. *He'd be right. Those who'd think about doing such a thing would be too afraid of him. Mikkeli's the type who'd be happy with his pay, however much he griped out there about conditions under Brisus. And most likely there was rarely very much to steal.* Brisus wasn't expecting his little camp to provide him with gold and jewels; that cache had been an unexpected find, according to the Philosopher.

So. Brisus would assume Mikkeli had been attacked or ambushed—by the men of this neighborhood, maybe; maybe by the King, or the King's honest guards. *Or me.*

There were too many factors, too many loose ends, and too much depended on Brisus, the warped, mean-minded little beast. Surely his first move would be to send someone down here to find out when Mikkeli had left and if he'd been seen since—frightened locals wouldn't lie to him if their loved ones were threatened. *So I get back into the bakery as quickly as I can, and I stay there. And hope Gabrielle shows up soon.* She considered this as Adrik eased around a corner and momentarily out of her sight. *Maybe she's already there.*

Gabrielle. *There* was a wild piece on the board, if you liked: Gabrielle on her own in Athens, accompanied only by an absolutely amoral market thief who thought himself the son of a god. She wondered how things had gone at the palace; the girl had been safe up until sunset, at least— thanks to Kratos, she knew that much. Of course, the boy could have been lying—she was fairly certain he'd been holding back something. *More likely, Gabrielle got into some kind of trouble—minor stuff—and told him not to worry me with it.*

Gabrielle was like that. But she was also smart; she'd be extra careful, knowing how much depended on her tonight. And both those boys were resourceful, out of necessity: between them, Kratos and Helarion would find a way through the King's guards and servants. And if Gabrielle had actually gotten into the palace and reached the Queen, if she had managed to talk to the woman, then they could count on the Queen being persuaded something was desperately wrong in Athens. Whether the fabled Amazon really had power of her own, as they said—whether she could do something about the current situation on her own, if need be—well, no point in worrying that, until it became a problem.

The snap of cloth brought her back to the moment and warily halfway around, but it was only someone's breeches and long shirt hanging out to dry, and flapping in a momentary gust of wind. The next high stone wall came between her and the breeze, and by the time they'd cleared it, the wind had faded again.

There could be reasons Theseus hadn't fixed matters already, she supposed. If so, and if Gabrielle was able to speak to the King tonight, then by morning Brisus might have nothing more to worry about but an aching head, and keeping his share of bread from that hulking brute who ran the market prison. The warrior considered this; a corner of her mouth quirked in an unpleasant grin. *And she and I can leave Athens without a running battle in these narrow streets. Like that notion.*

The grin faded. There were still too many problems. The Athenian palace was a regular warren, or so they said: hallways going everywhere, chambers, secret hallways, other hidden chambers. Every bit as bad as the older and poorer neighborhoods, like this one, and nearly as bad as the labyrinth on Crete.

Of course, that was supposedly why the young Theseus had kept his head when he'd been tossed into the Minotaur's maze. The warrior's mouth quirked again and she cast her eyes up as the moon rode briefly from behind the clouds. That story Gabrielle had invented to entertain those villagers back in Ithaca, about the Minoan king's young daughter falling in love with Prince Theseus and handing him a ball of twine so he could escape the Minotaur's maze, was really sweet, but who'd ever believe such a pat story? Any more than they'd believe the honorable Theseus would steal away from Crete with young Princess Ariadne, only to desert her the first time the Athenian ship sought shore for water and meat.

She heard the faint sound of unsteady footsteps and a sandal slipping across loose stones, and sidestepped several paces, eyes intent on the far side of the narrow street. No one in sight, but the footsteps were fading and now she could hear someone drunkenly singing, and someone else yelling at him to shut up and go home. Nothing to do with her. But a moment later she caught hold of Elyseba's shoulder and drew her to a halt; Adrik was running straight for her.

He was breathing hard, trying to be quiet about it. "Warrior! There—there are men in the bakery with my father! I—I don't know who, I couldn't see, but they must be from the Protectors; they're shouting and cursing at him, it's—it's horrid! They're threatening to . . . to . . ." His fingers caught at one of the leather bands around her biceps.

"All right," she replied softly. She pried his trembling hand loose and transferred it to Elyseba's shoulder. "I'll take care of them, make certain your father is safe. You stay with *her,* and make sure she stays here, well away from the bakery. Make sure you do, too."

"But—"

"You're supposed to do what I say, remember? You don't want to become a hostage, do you?" Silence. His shoulders sagged and he finally shook his head. "You don't doubt they'd do just that, do you?" Another silence, another sigh. "Fine. I swear he'll be okay." The moon fortunately chose that moment to sail from behind a cloud. Xena caught Elyseba's arms between gentle hands and when the woman looked up at her, she edged around so the light fell on her face and said, "There is trouble at the bakery. I am going to fix it; you will stay here with Adrik. Yes?"

She half expected revolt, but the woman merely nodded and then said, "Yes, I'll stay."

Xena freed a dagger, sheath and all, and shoved it into Adrik's hands. "Wait here," she said. "I'll be back." As she eased quietly down the street, she could hear sharp whispered conversation behind her, but it was abruptly cut off. The moon vanished; the street was all uneven cobbles under her feet, close walls, disorienting shadows. A brief wail of wind slid through a narrow opening; the sound halved, halved again, and was still.

Complete silence followed for a breath or so as she quickly and stealthily moved along the road. All at once she could see the squat shape of the bakery and smell the biting odor of rising batters. A low, grating voice was interrupted by the baker's high, frightened yelp; this in turn was cut short by both the grating voice and another, shouting at once. She edged around a corner, peered cautiously out, and then eased slowly back into shadow.

Three men stood outside the main door of the bakery, half a dozen horses with them; they were trying to look casual, but their eyes weren't missing much. *All right,* she decided cooly. *They haven't seen me. I could take them, they're nothing—and then the human crud with the baker hear the noise and they use him as a shield. And maybe I can take the human crud out, before they hurt him—and maybe not.* Things happened. She needed another way into the bakery. She cursed softly. Why hadn't she asked Adrik about that, or checked with the baker earlier? There was one door—the one being guarded at the moment—and other than that, there was only . . .

Only the hatch. An unpleasant smile curved her lips, and she began easing around the building, and around the next corner, until she was almost opposite the single door. The hatch had served plenty of people both early in the day and late in the evening, when there were too many coming to buy bread for the next meal to all fit into the shop. She could see Adrik in her mind, surrounded by baskets of long loaves, handing them out and taking coin as fast as his fingers could move. He'd been shaded, even though the hatch faced west: shaded by a small, neatly patched canvas awning, as she recalled.

The awning was still there, now pulled down across the opening. She touched the frayed end hanging down below the sill, then moved away as someone inside snarled out a string of ugly oaths. A wary glance around, then two steps back: she leaned against the wall, her eyes fixed on the covered hatch, and frowned. A shutter on the inside—had there been one? She didn't recall a shutter. Inside the building the man who'd been cursing was now shouting—not at the same person, she thought, because someone else hurriedly crossed the room with a lantern. Light made the canvas pale and the patchwork stood out sharply as darker marks against the light-colored cloth. She ducked down as light stabbed through a narrow slit between the awning and the hatch; then she began to move sideways, cat-footed, her back to the wall. The light followed her for several steps, flared brightly across the canvas, and moved away, into the far corner. She smiled grimly: no shutter.

The smile faded abruptly as the baker yelped in pain, then shouted, "But I don't know what you want! My son's gone to deliver the late baskets of bread, and I haven't *seen* your man!" A snarl of low-pitched words followed; she couldn't make out what the other man was saying, but the baker's frightened response filled in the blanks neatly for her: "Pixus, I swear to you," he shouted, "I have no idea where that stupid Agrinon is, I haven't seen him in at least a day. He's probably back sleeping with that poor young weaver! And it's no good Brisus getting fussed about his horrid little man and my cart; I saw them off hours ago, and I haven't seen them since! That's truth, I swear it!"

"Keep it down!" someone shouted at him. "If you're trying to attract help by yelling, the King's guards don't come this way anymore, and there ain't anyone around here to help *you*! What—think your son's gonna show up with the King and a whole army at his back?" Half a dozen men laughed raucously. Xena flexed her hands, took a running start at the awning, and dove through it.

• • •

She came out of a tight tuck and sprang to her feet. Several silent, stunned men stared back at her, jaws sagging. It would have been almost comical except for the heavyset bearded thug in a filthy silk robe that might once have been red-and-blue striped; he held the baker in front of him, one hairy hand wrapped around Ukloss's collar. The other hand steadily held a broad-bladed dagger across the man's exposed throat. Ukloss's eyes were wide, black disks surrounded by white. The eyes shifted suddenly; she sensed rather than saw movement just behind her right shoulder. She lashed out with a sharp backfist; it met stubbly greasy beard, then slammed into bone; the man behind her stumbled back into the wall and collapsed soddenly to the floor. She took two steps in the other direction, just in case the fallen man wasn't as out as he should be after a hit like that, or in case he'd had company. She smiled at Ukloss. It wasn't a reassuring smile, but the baker seemed to take a little heart from it.

"I know about you, you're Xena!" Pixus shouted and pointed at her with the knife. His voice was even more grating and unpleasant in close quarters—the kind of voice his sort deliberately cultivated, to overwhelm men like Ukloss. "One more step and you get a bath in the baker's blood, you want that?"

The smile spread; she shrugged. "It's supposed to be good for the skin, isn't it?"

He blinked, thrown momentarily by the unexpected remark, and before he could regain control of the situation, she had snatched the chakra from its sheath and sent it flying. The baker gasped and squeezed his eyes shut, but the deadly flying circle missed him by a full hand's width, to slice across the heavyset Pixus's dagger hand; the blade clattered to the floor. The chakra ricocheted off the wall to ziny sideways at one of Pixus's men, who yelped and threw himself flat as it whizzed over him; he leaped back to his feet and began pawing through his ragged garb for a weapon. Too late: the weapon hit a pole and slammed into the back of his skull. His knees went loose, his eyes rolled out of sight, and he went flat again; this time he stayed down.

Pixus had ducked reflexively each time the chakra hit something, and now he crouched in mid-room, sucking his cut hand and staring wildly all around. Sparks flew as the chakra careened off the small bronze counter; Xena snatched it in mid-flight, slammed it home, and swung around briefly to check on the first man she'd hit. He was groaning, slumped against the wall, eyes still closed.

Pixus was staring in blank astonishment at the line of blood welling along his hand, then at the dagger on the floor some distance from his feet. He bent to snatch it up, dragging the terrified baker down with him.

"Ukloss!" Xena shouted. The baker roused at that and began to twist frantically in the other's grasp, but Pixus was at least as large as Ukloss and much stronger. Xena swore, threw herself into a tight forward roll, spun halfway around, and caught hold of Pixus's grubby robe and his sandals. "Ukloss, go!" she shouted again, and yanked, hard. Pixus flailed for balance and went flat on his face, the air driven from him in a loud grunt. The baker went flying into the wall, and almost out the hatch.

Five men were still on their feet: they glanced at one another grimly and drew their swords as one. Xena grinned tightly, and shouted out her piercing, warbling war cry. One of the men turned white, dropped his sword, and went flat. She bounded forward, grabbed the two nearest by the scruffs of their none-too-clean necks, and slammed them together. There was a painfully resonant clunk, and the two collapsed in a heap. Beyond them, Pixus was staggering to his feet once more as the door to the shop slammed open to reveal three heavily armored men caught in the opening. One of them was yelling furiously and trying to shove the other two aside so he could enter the bakery; another seemed half-witted because he kept trying to fight his way past the middle man and get inside. The third was cursing steadily; from the sounds of things, some part of his armor had caught on one of the other men's and they were hooked together. The middle man was shouting too loudly to hear anyone but himself.

Xena laughed and shoved Pixus with one foot. Still off-balance, he went over in a tangle of robes.

The men in the doorway were still yelling, and two of them swore in fury as the middle man—a short, square-faced fellow with the body of a wrestler—stiff-armed his way through. With a shriek of tearing metal, the other two went flying in opposite directions. The middle man leaped into the room, a stubby-handled trident in one hand, a tangle of net in the other. Pixus flailed himself partway upright and yelled, "Gornius! Get her, but don't kill her; I want her alive!"

"You're even stupider than you look, Pixus," Xena commented as she went into a crouch. Gornius advanced on her cautiously, jabbing his way with the trident. Unfortunately for him, the net was in as much a snarl as Pixus's robes, thanks to the confusion in the doorway; when he tried to flail it at her and catch her feet, it bounced limply off the baker's table, then settled around one of Pixus's sandals. Pixus snarled out a curse and yanked; Gornius roared wordlessly, red-faced, and yanked back. The warrior laughed again, bounding forward and ripping the net, sandal and all, from the short man's grasp. With an accomplished flick of her wrist, she flipped it down over his head and knocked his feet from under him. The trident went clattering across the floor; she scooped it up and slammed it deeply into the floor, pinning the net and the wildly struggling Gornius in place.

Ukloss yelled a wordless warning; Xena took a step back, arms out and hands flexed. The two who'd been shoved aside were through the door; one of them, a tall, skinny man she vaguely recognized was trying to flank her, dagger poised. The other was coming straight at her, sword poised for a downstroke. She bared her teeth and leapt into the air; letting her momentum do the work, Xena waited until the sword was just a flashing arc before striking out with a devastating kick. Though he went down hard, yelling and bleeding profusely, the man was back on his feet almost immediately. One hand clutching his nose, sword forgotten, he snagged a nasty-looking dagger from his belt and ran at her with it. Unaccountably, he suddenly staggered and went flat again. Xena glanced down in surprise, and saw a basket that had become tangled up in his legs. She heard a horrified gasp, and looked up: Adrik, his face white and his mouth sagging, stood just inside the doorway, tugging at Elyseba, who'd come into the room far enough to hurl the long bread basket. The satisfaction curving her mouth said much as her eyes searched the room nonstop for another target, a second basket ready to throw.

"Out!" Xena yelled sharply. "Both of you, out!" Adrik yanked the basket from the woman's fingers, threw it in the corner, and pulled her back into the night.

The distraction had cost her. The second warrior had used the opportunity to get within striking range, and now he snarled and went to one knee as the skinny man abandoned his stealth and came running up behind her, dagger high over his head. She turned, caught his belt, then yanked hard. He went flying, landing with a thump and a groan atop his friend, the inept swordsman. The dagger flipped end for end and buried itself in the wall, near the door.

The clutch of five men were all together and all down; Gornius was fighting to haul the trident out of the floor, but the net had him in such a tangle, he couldn't get a grip on anything. Pixus edged up onto hands and knees and began to crawl cautiously across the floor. Xena growled, low in her throat, scooped up the skinny man by the knees and swung him in a half circle. The baker winced as the back of the thin man's head cracked into Pixus's temple. The warrior dropped one atop the other, stepped back so she could survey the entire room, and set her fists on her hips.

"Some of you can hear me," she said sharply. "Anyone moves, any single one of you, and you *all* hurt for it. Got me?" Silence. "Someone say yes," she warned. "Say it now, or I'll hurt you anyway." She bared her teeth. *"Bad."*

"Yes," Gornius snarled from inside the net.

"You'll be very sorry you interfered here," Pixus began.

"Shut up!" Silence immediately rushed into the room. Xena broke it finally, pitching her voice to carry beyond the bakery. "Adrik! Both of you—in here!"

Adrik was pale and he looked nervously around before entering the room. Elyseba's face was fixed, her chin high and defiant. "I thought you two were gonna stay away from this," Xena said.

"I tried," the baker's son replied sullenly. "I turned to say something to her, and she wasn't there. By the time I saw her, she was almost all the way here."

"Where is Kratos?" the woman broke in, and her voice was trembling. "Our house was too dangerous for him to-night; I know he would come here to sleep. I couldn't just leave him—" She bit her lip, swallowed, and spoke more normally. "I thought you needed help."

"That was brave of you, but dangerous," Xena replied softly. "And Kratos isn't here, he's at the palace, with Gabrielle and Helarion." She caught Adrik's eye, and gestured with her head toward the baker, who leaned against the hatch, eyes closed. The younger man stared at his father blankly for a long moment, then hurried over to wrap arms around him. Ukloss sighed faintly and leaned into his son.

"Oh." Elyseba seemed to finally realize how close to danger she had come; she sagged. The warrior caught her just before she hit the floor. "I'm sorry," Elyseba said. "I thought—"

"I can see what you thought. It's all right, you weren't hurt. Here," she added and helped the woman over to where Adrik and his father stood. "Adrik, hang on to them both."

"Warrior," the baker finally murmured. "Thank you. Are the others safe?" He hesitated as she held up a hand for silence, and sent her eyes toward the band of thugs against the far wall. She nodded once then, and he let out a held breath in a relieved gust. "I—thank you. But—what do we do with *them*?"

"Good question," Xena replied. Her eyes stayed on the clutch of men; none of them seemed interested in trying to escape at the moment. "The guard—but we don't know who'd come. And the market jail—that's out, too." She moved across the chamber, toward the door: the horses were stirring—someone was coming.

Coming fast, she realized, but taking care to be quiet about it. A moment later, Kratos slipped into the bakery; he was breathing hard and sweat beaded his high, young forehead. His eyes lit on Pixus and the sullen men scattered around him, and his jaw dropped. He looked from one to another of them, then spun partway around, startled, as the warrior came up next to him. "Is—is it all right here?" he asked at last.

"Fine," Xena assured him. "Come over here, with me," she added, and as they turned, she murmured against his ear, "Don't say anything out loud you don't want them to know, okay?" He nodded briefly, then stopped cold and stared again—but this time only to the least moment. Then he was gone, across the room, his face buried in his mother's shoulder and his arms around her. Elyseba hugged him fiercely, then put him away from her a little so she could sign something. His hands moved rapidly and his face lit up. *Knows his father is safe,* Xena decided. The boy laid a hand briefly against his mother's cheek, then came back and gestured for the warrior. She turned her back to the litter of beaten men and murmured, "What's the word at the palace?"

"We got in, Gabrielle talked to the Queen, everything is fine. The King's coming here with a few men, just before the sun comes up, so they can fix everything," he said rapidly. "I ate with the Queen!" he added in pleased astonishment. "Really good stuff, but the bread wasn't as good as Ukloss's. And my cousin and Gabrielle stayed to talk, but I wanted to make sure my mother was all right . . ." His voice faded as he tried to recall the rest of his message. "Oh. And some of the guards got caught; Agrinon was leading them."

"Oh? That's good." It gave her direction, too. She turned, caught Adrik's eye, and gestured for him to join her. "Adrik, go and get one of the carts, bring it back here. I'll have these men wrapped up by the time you return; you and your father can deliver them to the palace dungeons—"

"You won't dare do that!" Pixus interrupted indignantly.

"Want to bet?" she countered. He subsided, grumbling. "You think Brisus is going to keep you out of prison? Not a chance."

"Brisus will—"

"Maybe he'll get to share a cell with you," Xena said flatly. "If you two aren't sharing a pyre." He glowered, and shut his mouth with a snap. "Don't like it?" she added. "Too bad, deal with it. Adrik."

"Xena?"

"Go. Hurry back here." But he was gone before she finished speaking.

Apparently, Pixus wasn't going to be silenced. He was sitting cross-legged on the floor, hands still braced on his knees. "You're gonna lose this one, Xena," he began softly. "It's—what, you, that lippy little blonde who gave my cousin so much trouble—and people like this baker? Against *us*? Lookit your baker, he's *still* shakin' in his sandals!

"You got no idea how many men we got, or even who they are, do you? And the next guys aren't gonna be caught off-guard, know that? You think putting me in a cell's gonna make any difference around here?" He spread his arms, then prudently withdrew them and resettled them on his knees as her eyes narrowed. "There's plenty guards you don't know about, get us out anytime we want."

"Really," she murmured. Behind her, she could hear the baker conversing with Kratos's mother in a worried undertone.

"Yeah, really," he replied sarcastically. "Also, my brother and my cousin Opher know where I went tonight and how long I was gonna be gone. I don't show, you know what they're gonna do?"

She smiled, flexed her hands. "Walk right into me? I'm *really* scared, little man." She folded her arms across her chest and raised her eyebrows at him. "You were asking the wrong person about Mikkeli, you know." Silence. He stared up at her, suddenly at a lack for words, and she grinned mirthlessly. "What—you aren't interested anymore where he is? Well, it doesn't really matter, because you won't be seeing him *or* that cart again."

"You're lying," Pixus replied hopefully.

"Oh? Well. Guess there's no point in talking about it then, huh?" She glanced over her shoulder, caught the baker's eye, and crooked a finger. "Ukloss. You got any rope around here? And Kratos? I need you."

The baker got heavily to his feet and went to rummage in the small storage room he'd offered her as shelter—less than a day ago? She blinked. *Busy day.* The boy came over and leaned close as she went to one knee and spoke against his ear. "Got your breath back?" she asked. He nodded. "Think you could run back to the palace?" He nodded again. "Good. I'd like Adrik and Ukloss to take these men in so they can feel good about doing *something,* but there are a lot of them and only one of Ukloss; something could go wrong. Do you think you can get back in to see the King?" The boy considered this gravely, then nodded once more. "Good. If the King could send a couple armed guards he really trusts, to accompany the cart, tell him Xena would appreciate it. And if you see Gabrielle, tell her to stay out of trouble."

The boy's mouth quirked in amusement. He repeated, "Tell the King to send guards to help Adrik bring in Pixus, and tell Gabrielle not to get in trouble."

Xena smiled warmly and ruffled his dark hair. "Good boy. Stay safe yourself, save your mother the worry."

"Yes, ma'am," Kratos replied gravely, but his eyes were amused. He signed something quickly to his mother, who looked briefly startled, then nodded emphatically, and then he was gone, out the door and into the night. As his footsteps faded, though, Xena heard two startled exclamations—the boy's and a reedy male voice—and several of the horses whickered and moved aside.

The warrior edged cautiously, sidelong, toward the open entryway, but stopped short as the scroll merchant peered around the corner of the door, then stepped into the room, blinking rapidly. "Ukloss, it's entirely too light in here for the hour," he began, then stopped short. Apparently, his eyes adjusted quickly, Xena thought. His pale gaze was fixed on Pixus, who snarled and glared back at him, and he immediately retreated, then jumped convulsively and yelped as the warrior's hand closed around his elbow.

"What're you doing here, merchant?" she asked in a low voice. "No little winged creatures here."

His face was a little too pale, his eyes all pupil, but he managed a weak grin and eyed her sidelong. "Of course there aren't—but there's bread. 'A loaf of bread, a jug of wine, and thou—' " he began in a declamatory voice; a hard smack on the back left him coughing and gasping for air.

"Sorry, but you're not my type—and I don't think I'm yours, either." He blinked at her owlishly, drew a breath to retort, and began coughing once again. She waited impatiently until he was finished, set her fists against her waist, and demanded, "Isn't there one moment in your whole *life* you've been serious?"

"Why bother?" he asked, as if he really wanted to know. "Everyone else is so serious, and if you ask me, that's a large part of the problem in this world: no one wants to laugh. Now, me . . ." Xena bared her teeth in a mirthless grin and he fell prudently silent.

"Yes?" she demanded. "What about you?"

"Um—ah. Well! I came partly for my morning bread, but mostly to pass a message to the baker—or to you, if you were anywhere about. Now! Is that serious enough for you?" He considered this and became very grave indeed. "Message," he repeated. "Two of Brisus's men were arguing just outside my shop, not an hour ago, and the consensus is—"

"The *what*? Talk good Greek!" she hissed.

"It's *all* Greek to me," he replied, the corners of his mouth rising briefly. Hastily, he added, "Brisus is worried because there's a rumor that you and Gabrielle are in Athens, and he hasn't heard from his man in the palace or his man who was supposed to have returned from the country with fresh mutton or something. And now the man he sent here to question the baker hasn't come back, either. The two men were arguing because one is for Brisus no matter what happens, but the other is afraid the King has regained control, and they'll all die."

"Fine. I understand that. *What is Brisus up to?*"

"He's sent out word for all his men to meet under the statue of Nike, this very morning at daybreak. He's planning on a fast raid on the streets around the baker's fountain, to take more hostages—including Gabrielle."

11

"Nike? *What* statue of Nike?" Xena demanded. Her eyes narrowed.

Peder snorted. "Gift to the arts; if you're fortunate, you won't get a good look at it. The eyes don't match and the nose is an odd shape. Sculpted by an ardent amateur with too much wealth, too much free time—and no talent whatsoever. It's just down the street from here, on the edge of a dry fountain—best place they could find to shove it out of the way without offending the rich artist or anyone with taste if you ask me." He waved vaguely in the direction of the fountain. Silence. He eyed her sidelong, expectantly. Xena's eyes narrowed even more.

"That's the stupidest thing anyone's ever told me," she finally said. She flexed her hands. "You're lying to me!"

He opened his own eyes very wide, and the tip of his tongue darted across his lower lip. "Um—ah—why would I do that?"

"I don't know. For amusement?" She brought her hands up and gently clapped them together. Peder bit his lip and shook his head, but his eyes were amused. *The maddening*

man would joke at his own funeral, even if he'd been ren-
dered flat enough to be buried in his own scroll! But Xena
had to admit, at the moment, his obnoxious sense of humor
was less irritating than usual, and his smart-mouthed remarks seemed more the result of habit than actual effort.
And though it might be merely a trick of the light, he
looked paler than normal, his light hair sticking out in
spikes as though he'd shoved his hands through it repeat-
edly. As if in response to her thought, he sighed faintly,
drove both hands through his hair and tugged at it.

"Xena," he said earnestly. "Warrior. Please. *I'm* the one
who told you about these people and their desperate situation in the first place, aren't I? In the market jail, where
we were both housed for the night, in case you forgot about
that minor detail! Did I lie then?"

She considered this, her eyes fixed on him; the silence
stretched. His arms dropped limply to his sides and he swallowed. "All right," she said finally. "You didn't lie. Then.
As far as *I* know."

"Thank you," he replied stiffly, and turned away from
her to find the baker. Xena frowned as her eyes slid across
Pixus and his men, not quite seeing them until one of them
shifted nervously; her gaze sharpened and he went utterly
still. She gave each of them a chill, appraising stare, then
once more let her gaze unfocus as she tried to make sense
of this latest twist in an already convoluted state of affairs.

Something wasn't quite right here. Something to do with
Gabrielle? But Gabrielle was with King Theseus, likely still
in the palace and safe. Reasonably safe, anyway. *I hope she
is—and that she's being careful.* Careful and Gabrielle: oh,
wasn't that a thought! Gabrielle halfway across Athens
from her. *I knew it was a bad notion, splitting up. Even
though we really had no choice.*

There still was no choice: she'd merely waste time heading for the palace, and Ukloss would be unprotected—as would Elyseba. Knowing Gabrielle, she'd be on her way back here, and there were hundreds of streets, avenues, alleys, dead-ends, market byways, and other routes that crisscrossed Athens and led in straight or roundabout fashion to the palace—the chances of crossing her path were slim and none.

And I'm needed here. These were after all the people Brisus and the Protectors had chosen to exploit. She'd removed one threat to them when she and Adrik rescued their kidnapped people; there was no guarantee Brisus hadn't come up with another scheme just in case of such a situation. He thought that way. Once Pixus went missing, other men would certainly come to find out what was wrong, and not with Pixus's oblivious style.

She knew nothing of these so-called Protectors, other than what she'd learned facing Pixus; they sounded like the average thug—something like Kalamos, without Kalamos's good-to-middling weapons skills. If the other Protectors *were* anything like Pixus—all mouth and no action—they wouldn't be much of a threat. Not to anyone except nonfighting people like Elyseba and her family.

Brisus saw enemies everywhere, and always; he planned for them—complex patterns of plans within plans within schemes, within strategies, within tactics.

Brisus wouldn't be catering to the Protectors, either. Whatever they thought they were doing when they brought him in, he'd be the man in charge at this point.

She eased over to the small storage room as the baker came out, odd bits of twine in his hands. He was still too pale, red handprints sharp on both sides of his face. "All I could find, warrior."

"It's enough. I'll watch," she added as she drew a long-bladed, well-honed dagger and balanced it neatly by the point on the tip of one finger. "You tie them." She sent her eyes toward the scroll merchant. "*You* stay put."

"I should get back to my shop . . . ," he began. She bared her teeth briefly and his voice faded.

"Why? You came for bread, remember? Stay put."

"My pleasure," he agreed faintly, and edged into the corner. On the opposite side of the bakery, Pixus stirred and she thought he intended to say something—bellow it, more likely. She flipped the dagger up, caught it, and began cleaning her nails, her eyes moving casually across the pile of felled thugs; the grubby, silk-robed brute subsided with a visible shudder. The baker's lips twitched, but he walked across the room and began binding Pixus's men.

He was barely finished when the horses just outside the doorway became agitated; one whickered. Xena side-stepped across the room, dagger just out of sight behind her back, and the baker froze; she motioned to him for silence, eyed Pixus and his men—several of them looked truly beaten, but Pixus and two of those closest him were eyeing the entry hopefully. The warrior eased outside, dagger at the ready, then stepped immediately back in. "It's Adrik."

"Oh. Good." Ukloss inspected one of Pixus's knots, ignored whatever the man snarled at him in an undertone so low the warrior couldn't catch the words, then backed away. Five steps from the huddle of men, he turned and strode over to the long counter, where several pottery bowls stood covered in clean cloths. Elyseba hadn't moved in some time, not since she had managed a tired smile for Peder earlier; just now her eyes were closed and the warrior thought she might be dozing.

More noise and movement came from just behind Adrik, who froze in the entrance. He turned and leaned out into the night before Xena could stop him, but he was back at once. "It's—they *look* like King's men," he said doubt-fully.

"I sent Kratos for King's guardsmen," Xena assured him. "Maybe for once something around here is what it looks like."

A very short time later, the bakery was cleared and quiet: the cart and its load of low-lifes were gone, creaking stead-ily toward the palace dungeons, Adrik on the seat and five grim-faced, well-armed, mounted guards surrounding it. The fight had gone completely out of the captives, except for Pixus—and after a few moments of snarling and hurling threats at guardsmen who simply stared through him, he swore and gave it up.

The baker was hurrying back and forth, adding flour, raisins, nuts, and herbs to his various batters, shaping loaves, stoking the ovens. The awning over the hatch flapped loose in an occasional breeze; he'd released it as soon as Pixus and his men were gone. Without that much needed ventilation, the shop would have been unbearably warm.

Elyseba had been persuaded by the baker to retire to his storage room, and when Xena walked by a few moments later, the woman was already asleep, covered with a blanket and curled up on a deep pile of straw that probably served the baker as a bed when he had to be here all night, tending to his batters. *Long day for her,* the warrior thought, then crossed the main room to pick up the basket Elyseba had tossed during the fight; she cast her eyes up, threw the basket back atop the stack near the door, and hesitated there to listen a long moment.

The thugs' horses were gone with the cart, as was the enormous pile of confiscated weaponry—one of the guards had taken all of the blades and other bits with a remark to the baker about reparations. *Good. Sell the horses and the gear, give the money to these people.* It seemed more than fair.

The street itself was very quiet just now, the sky still dark. Two doors down from the bakery, fog lurked in the fountain that occupied the center of the street. Xena leaned out and stared toward the fountain; there wasn't anything to see, across the broad square or down it. She narrowed her eyes, stepped into the open, and gazed in the direction Peder had pointed out. The broad avenue was shadow against shadow, but even in broad daylight she couldn't have seen far. At the bakery the previous morning she'd seen the beginning of the labyrinthlike mess herself, and she'd seen a few such places in other parts of big, ancient cities. The street changed all at once from broad and well paved to a welter of skinny alleys overshadowed by tall, looming buildings. Rather than moving directly from one point to another, there were sudden, bewildering shifts of direction as one old street blended into another, where fallen buildings had been removed and the spaces paved over to make new thoroughfares, as new buildings rose where old, cracked streets had been.

Perfect place for an ambush, though: just the kind of thing Brisus would take advantage of. Because beyond the new fountain, buildings crowded in so close there was barely room for two skinny handcarts to pass. A few paces further she'd seen the series of sharp bends the street took in the direction of the shore. A street like that—all doorways, nooks, hidden places—well, Brisus might plan a neat ambush, but she could, too.

Statue of Nike. Something odd, still; she glanced at the opposite wall, where the scroll merchant sat on the floor, knees drawn up and chin settled on them. His eyes were fixed on the distance. Wondering if he'd have a scroll shop left to go back to, possibly.

I wonder if— She waited; the thought wouldn't complete itself. She swore under her breath, shook her head. It would come, eventually. She could only hope it wouldn't be too late.

As if somehow aware of the direction of her thoughts, Peder stirred and got to his feet. "I really should be—"

"Sit," Xena ordered flatly. She gave him the hard look that could silence even Gabrielle and he subsided, but a short breath later, the warrior bounded across the bakery and snatched at his shirt, hauling him to his feet. "Why would two of Brisus's men carry on a loud argument in the middle of the night—where you could conveniently hear it, merchant?"

"I—ah—I—" He stared at her glassily. Xena shook him, shoved him against the wall, held him there, her face mere inches from his, and waited. His shoulders slumped. "I *told* him you wouldn't believe it—"

"Told *who?* Talk to me, scroll merchant!"

Peder gave her an unhappy look, swallowed hard, and nodded. "Your old friend Brisus found out from Mondavius that you and Gabrielle had been talking to me, the night we shared the King's hospitality. And that stupid guard, Agrinon, told Brisus that Gabrielle had gone to my shop, after she left him. So—Brisus came to my shop tonight. With Opher. And a—a large jar of lamp oil. He said if I didn't tell you exactly what I told you that Opher would pour lamp oil throughout my shop and light it." Xena waited; he shook his head. "That's all I know, I swear! I'm not in league with Brisus; why would I be? I'm a scroll merchant!" His mouth twitched unhappily. "I *was* a scroll merchant. I've been gone long enough, Opher's

211

probably already burned my shop and gone back to his wine jug. He was—Brisus was in a mean mood but *he* was sober—''

''He's like that,'' Xena agreed softly. ''Keep talking.''

''But Opher was—well, I wouldn't be surprised if he passed out, dropped my lamp, and went up with the scrolls.''

Silence. ''You could have told me when you walked in the door.''

''I didn't dare! They said there would be someone outside, listening, that if I said the wrong thing, anything at all, he'd go back and tell Opher . . .'' He swallowed. ''And my shop would be a pile of ashes. And I'd be dead.''

''Nah, nothing like that.'' Gabrielle's cheerful voice. Xena half-turned, her hands still wrapped in the scroll merchant's shirt, and raised an eyebrow as Gabrielle hurried into the bakery. ''Ah—Xena, it's okay,'' she added earnestly. ''Peder really didn't do anything to help those rats, except to promise he'd come here, and if you were here, that he'd tell you what they said. Um—I wonder: was that *really* Brisus?''

''*I* didn't see him,'' the warrior replied mildly. ''He says it was Brisus and Opher.'' She let the merchant go. He eased along the wall and tugged his shirt straight. ''What were you doing at the scroll merchant's?'' she asked finally. ''And where's Helarion?''

''At the— Oh, right, at the scroll merchant's. The same thing as earlier in the day,'' Gabrielle said earnestly. ''Making sure Peder was all right. And it's a good thing, too: Helarion and I came up behind the opening at the back of Peder's shop and I could see light, so I figured he was awake and everything was probably all right, but—''

''Gabrielle.'' Xena cleared her throat.

"Ah—right! And then I heard his voice and he didn't sound all right at all, and these other two, they were threatening him, talking about burning down his shop. Well, I couldn't walk away from *that*, could I?" she demanded indignantly. "All those scrolls . . . Well, Peder left. And I figured he'd be okay once he got here, you'd take care of him, right? And this—Brisus—mean-mouthed little guy, pale hair, good fighting gear—he walks off and there's just this soft-looking guy in a really filthy silk robe, I mean, don't these guys *ever* wash?" Xena's mouth quirked impatiently; Gabrielle flashed her a quick smile and went on, rather quickly. "Okay, he's sitting on a stool, swaying back and forth and singing off-key, something about a drunken harpy, and about then, there's Helarion making bratty faces at him from the front doorway—to get his attention, *you* know—and I snuck in and flattened him with a scroll." She considered her choice of words, bit back laughter, and grinned at Peder, who eyed the warrior with alarm and eased farther along the wall. "Not *that* scroll, it was a blank one, missing a hand grip. And we tied him up with his belt and Helarion went back to the palace for a few honest guards, to take nasty, drunk Opher away." She thought this over, nodded sharply. "Oh. And your shop's okay, Peder, because we blew out the little lamp and Helarion took the oil jar so he could leave it somewhere far from a shop full of scrolls."

Gabrielle turned back to Xena. "Oh. And I think he wasn't lying about the other part, either. Because when I came up just now? I thought I saw someone sneaking away from the back wall—just about where that canvas is, over there." Xena sighed heavily and turned away. "Ah—I'm sorry," Gabrielle said softly. "I guess I shoulda said something about him right away, huh? Except I wasn't really sure, and you had Peder off the floor, and—"

"I'm not mad at you, Gabrielle," Xena replied quietly. "You've done fine, so far. It's the situation—only two of us in a city like this . . ."

"I'd call it bad odds for *them*," Gabrielle said.

"So would I. But I can't be inside and outside at the same time."

"That's why you've got me! Did you hear we found Agrinon? And the guy that was keeping the King out of things—weird little guy, called Mesmer, had Theseus in this trance, and Hippolyta—she asked me to call her that, really sweet, she just had a baby, you wouldn't believe how cute—" She stopped short and her eyes went wide. Xena eyed her in mild alarm, then relaxed all at once. *Visions again. Right,* she was obviously thinking. Gabrielle blinked rapidly, shook her head, and went on, bright and determined. "So, we tossed Agrinon and thirteen guys in the King's prison cells, and the King's got a guy asking Agrinon who's the other fourteen dirty guards."

"That's all? Fourteen?"

"Supposedly." Gabrielle shrugged. She held up a hand, index finger turned down, tapped the next finger. "And six or seven in the country—"

"Taken care of."

She smiled. "I knew that. And everyone back safe, like Kratos said?"

"Tired, cold, and hungry, but all right," Xena assured her.

"Good. And you got Pixus and—"

"And eight men."

"And Opher. Okay! So, according to Mesmer, there's only about another ten out here. Of course, one of them is Brisus, but there's Pixus's brother and whatever scum he's got left. Simple!" She finished and tucked all the fingers into a compact little fist. The warrior smiled and flicked the hair from her forehead.

"*Maybe* only ten or so," she warned. "And if one of them is Brisus, that means we could be looking at a complex situation."

"You told me about him—well, a little bit," Gabrielle amended. "I won't underestimate him, okay? But—what are we gonna *do*?" She looked up, took a step back, and spun partway around as Xena bounded for the door. Half a breath later, five armed men entered the baker's hut, their only mark a labyrinthine badge in bright red and blue. At the sight of their leader, the baker blushed and dropped to one knee.

The King was clad in the same good leather-and-bronze armor as his men, and he crossed immediately to the baker. "Rise," he said. "I don't stand on that sort of ceremony, certainly not with people of mine who have been wronged." He patted the man's shoulder.

"That's a good word for it," Xena murmured. "Wronged." Theseus raised one eyebrow, then held out his hands.

"I've heard a good deal about you," he said. "I'm honored to meet you."

"I've heard about you, too," Xena replied, and gripped his forearms. "We'd better get set; I know Brisus and we won't have a lot of time. I have an idea." Theseus gestured, and two of his men went back outside. Gabrielle listened for a moment to the low conversation between her friend and the King, then wandered over to sit next to Peder.

"Hey," she said softly. "Everything's gonna be fine. We'll get you back to your shop, soon as it's safe."

"Safe," he replied gloomily and let his eyes close. Gabrielle eyed him worriedly, then leaned back next to him and settled her shoulders.

Across the room, the King nodded sharply. "It's a good idea, warrior. Get down by that fountain before Brisus does, get into position, and when they show up—"

"*If* they show up," Xena said. "But I think they will. It's the kind of move I'd expect from Brisus."

"If he anticipates you'll second-guess him, though . . ."

"He might. But he'll still think he has the upper hand. How near are we to first light?"

"Another hour—no more than that."

"Fine. Let's get going." She crossed the room and tapped the baker's arm; he jumped, barely stifled a yelp, and turned to face her. "Leave the bread. Get the boy's mother and get somewhere safe."

"Safe," he echoed blankly.

"Safe. The stable where my horse is. That shrine to Hermes. As long as it's someplace safe, I don't care. You don't want Brisus snatching you, and I don't want it either."

"The bread will burn—"

"Your life's worth more," she said forcefully. "The people around here can buy bread elsewhere for one morning, if they have to. The King's selling Pixus's horses for you; you won't lose the coin. Go, now."

He turned back to his ovens, dithering, then pulled himself together and began to damp the coals. Xena turned away, and went over to haul Gabrielle to her feet. She looked down at the scroll merchant, who eyed her warily as he stood up. "You come with us," Xena said finally.

"I'd rather not—"

"I can't be sure you're safe anywhere else."

His mouth moved the way it might if he were ill. "You mean, you still don't trust me."

"That, too. Move."

"It's all right," Gabrielle said as they went out the door together. "I'll stay with you, you'll be fine. And *I* trust you."

"Wonderful," he muttered, then fell silent as Xena hissed a warning.

It took a little time, getting nearly a dozen of them down the pitch-black street and into the tortuous alley that led to the dry fountain, all the while in complete silence. Lights were out of the question and obstacles were everywhere, but finally they emerged into a slightly wider area surrounded by rickety buildings. Xena drew Gabrielle back and breathed against her ear, "King's man says there's a shrine over there, deserted and filled in with rubble, and a deep doorway where you can keep *him* safe. And yourself, okay?"

"Sounds good," Gabrielle breathed back. "We'll do our best." She tugged at Peder's arm and the two eased forward, staying in deep shadow and well away from the fountain at the center of the narrow square.

Silence. Xena eased cautiously around a spill of stone, booted feet feeling her way one slow step at a time. A bird warbled nearby—she froze, then relaxed. Only one of the small owls that occupied ruined places like this, hunting mice. *Real owl; never met anyone who could copy that cry.* Moments later, she found a deep-linteled porch, the solid stone floor littered with trash and rubble, the posts reasonably sturdy even now, the front door barred shut. Through the gaps in the overhead tiles, she could see the least lightening of the sky. *Not a moment too soon.* King Theseus slowed long enough to hold out a hand; she gripped his wrist, felt the tightening of long, hard fingers, and then he was gone, five men at his heels, and none of them making any more noise than the mice that little owl was hunting.

Silence again. Slowly, it was getting light out there: she could make out the rough line of roofs and broken walls against the sky. She glowered at her hands. *I don't like this city any better than I did the first time I saw it. Fighting a battle inside a place like this—I really don't like that.* She eased to one side of the long porch, then back again. No sound, no movement. All at once, she realized, she could make out the profile of the enormous statue perched on the edge of the fountain. Perhaps mounted on Argo, she'd be able to look it in the eye. From what she could see of it just now, she didn't think she'd care to do that.

Soon, Brisus and his men should be sliding into position. Theseus had said he'd wait for her signal; she hoped he meant it. Pale golden light shone on the highest peak of the roof across from her. Xena sent her eyes around the deserted square once more, then froze. Brisus stood at the base of the statue of Nike, a broad grin on his face, long sword in his hand. He moved it, and a familiar, high voice yelled, "Hey, *do* you mind? You know how hard it is to get blood out of this weave?" The warrior cursed under her breath and leaped forward, chakra half drawn.

Brisus laughed and quickly shouted, "Put it back, sweetheart, or my arm gets tired." She froze; he gestured with his free hand. She risked a quick glance: Sun wreathed the uppermost portion of the huge, hideous statue, but in the shadows at its feet lay Gabrielle, trapped beneath the edge of Brisus's sword. The statue itself, Xena noticed, was unbalanced; perhaps the city hadn't cared enough for it to mount it properly. But that could wait; she had her own problems just now. "Put it back," Brisus repeated flatly.

Silence. Then: "Gabrielle?"

"Xena?"

"You all right?"

"Well—I've been in better places!"

"You can't expect to get away with this," Xena murmured as her eyes locked on Brisus's. "You even think about hurting her and there won't be enough of you left for—''

"Save the threats," he interrupted her.

"They aren't threats if I do what I say."

"You lost this one, Xena." Another flash of teeth. "My men have been settled in here, waiting for you, since before I took that drunk Opher up to the scroll merchant's. You never *could* keep up with me in planning, could you?"

"Why would I bother to keep up with you in any way?" she sneered, then looked around, spread her arms in a broad shrug, and let them fall to her sides. "Where's the profit in a place like this, Brisus? You've come way down in the world, little man."

"Not a bit of it; I wasn't doing this well when I was taking coin and insults from Mezentius. You just cleaned the dead wood out of the pile for me, that's all. Mikkeli— I won't miss him."

She smiled grimly. *Doesn't know about the palace yet.* If his men had been here all evening . . . There was the man Gabrielle thought she'd seen, of course; if he'd been outside the bakery, he'd know. Maybe he hadn't talked to Brisus yet. *Maybe anything. Get Gabrielle safe. Now.* "So," she said finally. "What's your plan, Brisus? I mean, if you're gonna kill us both, then I've got nothing to lose, have I?"

His jaw sagged briefly. "She'll be dead right now, right in front of you, Xena!" he snapped.

"Hey, fine with me, if I gotta go, this is at least quick!" Gabrielle assured her, then prudently fell silent as Brisus snarled at her.

"She's got a point," Xena said calmly, then flexed her fingers, raised her right hand, and gestured. The King and three of his men stepped out of shadow, swords at the ready. Brisus stared at them for a long, blank moment, then, rather wildly, at Xena.

"But the palace is—"

"It's changed hands in the past few hours; sorry no one thought to tell *you*." Silence. "So, how many men have you got, Brisus? My count makes it maybe ten. You and ten men against *me* and you'll lose. Bad."

"You're just not gonna make this easy for yourself, are you?" he hissed. She shrugged. Brisus shouted an order, and a swarm of men emerged from the surrounding buildings to confront the King's guards. "Don't do nothin' until I say, any of yas!" he yelled. "You stay there, keep them guys where they are! Opher's boys better be keeping those pulleys and things lined up!"

"Look, it's that pale-haired fool I separated from his dagger belt and his purse!" A familiar voice rang out across the square. Brisus started and nearly swung around; Gabrielle immediately tried to roll away from him, but when the sharp blade pressed against her throat, she froze.

At a gesture, one of Brisus's men swung around, crossbow up. Helarion darted across the open, angling toward the back of the statue. He was a golden-haired blur, but not fast enough: the bowstring twanged, the sound echoing from the surrounding walls, and with a shriek of pain, the boy fell. Brisus risked a quick glance, then turned back to give the warrior an evil smile. "Take you one at a time? Fine with me," he said. "Four of you keep your bows sighted on the King's men; rest of you take *her*. You hold still!" he snarled as Gabrielle tried awkwardly to knock his legs from under him.

Xena glanced from one of Brisus's men to another, flexed her hands, and took one step back onto the low step of the porch. The five men in greasy or tattered leathers followed warily, weapons drawn.

Xena noticed a sudden movement behind Brisus; Peder had eased into the open, and dragged Helarion into a shadowy doorway. The warrior was vaguely aware of him then starting a quiet, sidelong stalk along a still dim with evening shaded wall, but before she could figure out what he was up to, with a howl, one of Brisus's men launched himself at her. She thrust thought of the merchant aside, leaped up, caught hold of one of the cross beams, and lashed out with both feet, catching the first thug square in his red-bearded face; he flew back into the others, and two more went down with him. She leaped across them, caught hold of two others, drove her elbow into one's face, and then, her arm already cocked, punched the other. She backfisted the red-beard again for good measure, and then kicked him so hard he flew across the narrow courtyard and slid into the fountain. Something in the fountain wall creaked ominously and the already uncertain statue shifted the least bit.

One of Brisus's men, a thick giant of a man who'd had to move out of the way as his red-bearded comrade sailed past, stepped toward Xena, chuckling.

"Well, hello there, Xena," he said, placing the head of his weapon, a massive war hammer, on the ground and leaning on the thick oaken shaft.

"Dekaron." Xena grimaced. "It's been a long time."

He tilted his head to the side good-naturedly, a sheaf of blond hair falling across his shoulder. "I've fought alongside you, but I always wondered what it would be like to actually meet you in battle. Guess this is my lucky day."

"Funny thing about luck," Xena said, drawing her sword. "It's got a way of going bad on you when you least expect it."

Dekaron smiled, and for a moment it seemed as if he might be going to say something else. But then he braced himself, and the huge arms came alive with strain. Grunting slightly, he hefted the hammer and began to move toward her.

For a moment, Xena seemed confused; she looked around, started to go one way and then another, and finally stepped back into the shadow of the porch. Sensing a quick victory, Dekaron raised the hammer into position above his right shoulder and prepared to bring it crashing down on Xena's skull. His outlandish frame seemed to fill the entrance to the porch. A shuffling sound came from the shadows, and Dekaron stopped and peered into the darkness, suddenly apprehensive.

Among the early morning birdsong, the war cry sounded almost like the call of some strange hawk or falcon, a terrifying night creature that had arrived to dispel the tranquillity of daybreak. There was a flash of pale thighs, of wild hair, and Xena burst from the darkness of the porch to vault over the giant, her boots barely grazing his war hammer.

She landed easily behind him, the statue of Nike at her back. Dekaron whirled around, roaring in rage and embarrassment. Xena had begun to smile, an expression meant to taunt the big man, but suddenly she had to duck to avoid the ungainly weapon that was whistling toward her head. The hammer shuddered its way into the side of the statue, and Dekaron had to pause and rock the shaft back and forth in order to free the instrument.

Xena noticed that the statue now had a slight list to it.

She darted in with her sword, and slashed Dekaron across the calves. The muscle was thick however, built up over years of toting around its owner's body, and her cut wasn't deep enough. He roared in pain.

He spun around to face her, so Xena promptly dodged to the side and slipped behind him again. Following her movements, letting the quicker warrior dictate the flow of the battle, he raised the hammer again, ready to strike. Seeing her chance, Xena leaped forward and stabbed up, at the point where his arm and shoulder connected. The big man went berserk.

Staggering around the narrow square, waving his hammer and scattering warriors from both sides, Dekaron was seemingly mindless in his pain. Xena's sword still protruded from his side, and Xena still clung to the hilt, riding out the storm and twisting the blade deeper at every opportunity. Finally, his wild movements threw her off, and she landed in a heap halfway across the square. Meanwhile, Dekaron's mad ranting was taking him closer to the tilting statue. With a supreme, almost heroic effort, he wrenched the sword from his side, and in his agony, slammed the hammer once more against Nike's battered side.

"Nooooo!" It burst from two throats at once: Xena's and the scroll merchant's. She leaped over Brisus's fallen and dazed men, drew her chakra, and fired it straight for their pale-haired leader just as the statue wavered again and slowly began to topple. Brisus ducked, then turned to run—too late. The weapon ringed his neck, spinning furiously. He caught at his throat, face red as he fought for life, then staggered and fell to his knees. Gabrielle shrieked in alarm and threw himself sideways just as Peder launched himself straight at the place she'd been. The statue slammed into the ground, throwing up a cloud of rubble, dust, and debris, and the building where Xena had waited for daylight simply collapsed. Brick, stone, and wood rained down on Brisus's fallen men. Brisus himself was attempting to rise, and one shaky hand was dragging the chakra from the stone parapet where it had become embedded when Xena threw herself on him, driving him to his knees again. She ripped the chakra from nerveless fingers and tossed it aside, hauled him over by one shoulder, and drove her fist into his jaw. He went limp.

Silence. Then one of the King's men was at her elbow, his crossbow drawn. "All yours," she said as she got to her feet. "Take good care of him, he was the real leader of this bunch. There's two more down in the fountain—and watch out for that one."

Dekaran lay motionless on the ground, bleeding slightly from his wounds. He was fine, Xena knew; she'd seen him absorb much worse.

"Already taken care of." But he spoke to her back. Xena had scooped up the chakra and was fighting her way across mounds of rubble to the ruins of the statue. One enormous, fat, carved wing, still intact after the fall, blocked her way. "Gabrielle! Gabrielle where are you?"

"I'm here." Her voice sounded weak, strangled.

"Are you all right?" The warrior edged around the wing, down the far side. Gabrielle knelt next to the rubble, a very pale Helarion next to her, one of the King's men tending a very bloody shoulder. Tears ran unchecked down Gabrielle's face and she pointed toward what was left of the statue. "Gabrielle—swear you're all right?"

She nodded, rubbed her cheeks. "Peder's under that. He tried to save me, and he—"

Xena knelt, wrapped an arm around her, and drew her close. "I'm sorry, Gabrielle. I know you liked him, and it was a brave thing he did. Remember what you said, it was fast. He never knew what hit him, and probably didn't even see it coming." Silence. Gabrielle nodded, finally.

"I know. But it's not fair."

"Things aren't fair, sometimes. People get hurt who shouldn't."

"Because of people like Brisus." Gabrielle's hands clenched into fists and she tried to rise, but Xena held her back.

"Don't waste your time on him. He's not worth it. He's going into King Theseus's prison cell for a nice, long stay, and I'm gonna suggest they put him in with the Protectors, especially Pixus.'' She squeezed Gabrielle's shoulders and got to her feet as the King came over. ''Everything under control?'' she asked.

''It is now.'' He looked around. ''It's not easy, keeping a city the size of Athens in good condition; something needs to be done about this at once.''

''I'm sure you'll do a good job,'' Xena assured him. ''The scroll merchant—''

Theseus swallowed; he'd gone rather pale. ''I saw. Once this neighborhood is ready for people again, we'll put in a new statue, in his honor.'' He looked down at the remains of the vast winged Nike, and his nose wrinkled. ''We won't use the same artist.''

''Good.'' She glanced at the sky, then toward Helarion. ''I'm going to take that boy back to his mother and see the baker knows it's safe to come back to his ovens.''

''Maybe we'll meet again,'' Theseus said.

Xena smiled faintly, and extended her arm; he met it halfway. ''Maybe—but not in Athens. No offense, but your city's been bad luck for both of us.'' Her fingers tightened on Gabrielle's shoulder. ''We'll be leaving as soon as we can. Give Hippolyta and your new son our love.''

''I will.'' He watched as Xena persuaded the red-eyed Gabrielle to her feet, as they both helped Helarion up and got him braced between them; then he began working his way around the broken statue to where his guards were bringing a heavily manacled Brisus. Xena turned briefly, met Brisus's eyes, and smiled. Brisus wasn't smiling, and the look in his eyes was murderous; Theseus's men yanked him away.

Gabrielle sighed as they moved into deep shadow; Helarion patted her shoulder and she sighed again but eyed him sidelong. "You are gonna swear to me you won't steal *any*thing, ever again," she said flatly, "or I'm gonna break your head for you!"

He snorted. "You can't . . ."

"Oh, yes, I can," Gabrielle said vigorously. "After what I've been through because of you and *for* you! And look what happened, you almost wound up leading the dead down to Hades for your father—you think it's okay down there? Well—it's not, especially for snotty-mouthed young thieves; you wind up where people like Brisus are, and *they're* the guys making the rules! You're gonna swear, you got me?"

"And how else am I supposed to make my living?" he asked after a moment, in a small voice. Xena edged them through a patch of rubble and into the open. "This is what I'm good at! Why didn't my father save me? Why would he have given me these abilities and then take them away?" The young man shook his head, despondent. "Maybe Hermes isn't my father after all. What kind of father would let this happen?"

Xena awkwardly squeezed the young man's shoulder. "It's not about who your father is, Helarion. It's about you, and who you really are. You're clever, funny . . . and now you know you're brave as well. That's a far better birthright than most people receive." He considered this, then slowly nodded his head. "Good. Go to the King, as soon as your shoulder's healed. He'll remember you. Apply to be one of his messengers, you know the city, the streets, the people—you'll be good at it. Maybe you'll even wind up with a room for yourself and your mother in the palace."

"Messenger . . . ," he said thoughtfully.

"Hey," Gabrielle assured him. "It's in your blood, remember?"

Epilogue

The road south from Athens was dusty, dry, and hot; the sea crashed against harsh pillars of black stone. Xena led Argo along the track, Gabrielle a subdued presence at her side. A dappled gray mare with plain leather tack ambled along behind her.

"You all right?" Xena asked finally, though she knew the answer. *Get her to talk it out.*

"I'm all right. I . . . I miss Peder."

"You'd miss him anyway, even if you'd just left him behind."

"I know." Gabrielle blinked rapidly and managed a smile for her. "I feel like it was my fault."

"You can't take responsibility for what other people do, remember? You can be sorry if they do the wrong thing, but that's different."

"I know." She looked at the sea as a particularly huge wave hit and surf boomed loudly and echoingly from the rocks. She shuddered. "Glad we're on land," she said finally.

"Glad we're out in the open," Xena said. "Glad we don't have anything to do just now, either."

"I *am* glad Cydavia got to meet you, before we left. I mean, with your word *and* the Queen's, Melosa's sure to take her, isn't she?"

"Maybe. I'm not so sure your friend really knows for certain what she wants."

"Well—at least she'll get the opportunity to try it out. Not everyone gets that kind of chance." The mare lipped her hair; Gabrielle eyed it sidelong, freed the hair, and sighed. "I wish I'd been able to find a nice way to tell the Queen this was *not* my idea of a good reward."

"Never know when a horse will come in handy. I just—" Xena froze, eyes fixed on the distance. "Here." She thrust Argo's reins into Gabrielle's hands and ordered, "Wait here."

"Huh?" But the warrior was gone, sprinting down the road, dagger in hand. And now Gabrielle could see, too: a man in pale tatters, staggering up the road, and on the sand behind him, the wreck of a small boat. Something familiar about the way he walked, though— "Oh, no!" Gabrielle exclaimed, and tugging at the two sets of reins, she went down the road after Xena, who had stopped just short of the man.

His face was nearly unrecognizable for blood and bloody bandages, and the deep bronze coloring from too much sun at sea for too many days. "Help!" he cried out faintly as the two came up; he shoved hair out of his eyes. He rocked back on his heels, and his jaw sagged. "Xena? And—oh, no, not *you*!"

"Salmoneous," Xena murmured softly. "What are *you* doing on the Athens road looking like you just walked off a shipwreck?"

"I— Because I did! They got everyone else, but I slipped over the side and got away, so I could get help, I swear it, and they didn't see!"

"They?" The warrior grabbed his arm and shook him, hard. "Who's *they?*"

"The Sea Raiders," Salmoneous whispered. "They've been jumping little coastal villages in the past week or so but now they're after the ships, too."

Xena looked at Gabrielle; Gabrielle gave the weaving man a hard look, then met the warrior's eyes. "No ships," she said firmly.

"No ships," Xena agreed. "Salmoneous, the city of Athens is," she turned and pointed, "that way, maybe three hours' walk." The man sagged even more and moaned.

"Or an hour's easy ride," Gabrielle assured him and held out the gray's reins. Xena blinked; Gabrielle smiled. Salmoneous eyed her sidelong, as if expecting some kind of joke. He finally took the reins, waited as Gabrielle hauled two small bags from the horse's withers, and shoved himself into the saddle with her help, then stiffly and gingerly arranged his generous bulk.

"I *knew* you'd help me get my ship back!" he began enthusiastically. Xena cleared her throat ominously and he clapped a hand over his mouth.

"Athens," she said flatly. "King. That way." She pointed, then turned away. Before he could say anything, she chucked the reins, and Argo began to move off down the road. Gabrielle hurried to catch up, then finally glanced over her shoulder at Salmoneous, who sat on the motionless gray. Both were gazing mournfully after the two women.

"Xena, we really can't leave him here."

"This is still King Theseus's land," Xena replied firmly. "And no ships, remember?"

"No ships—right. So," Gabrielle turned to face the southbound road and lengthened her stride. "How far do you think we'll get before he catches up with us?"

Xena's lips twitched in amusement. "If we travel fast enough, maybe he won't."

Afterword

As many of the on-line fans of the show are aware, I held a contest to randomly choose two people for "walk-on" parts in this book—partly in thanks for the fan support of the books. Also, since so few of us ever get to meet the actors we admire, I thought it might be fun for two of the fans to at least meet Xena and Gabrielle on paper, talk to them, and even interact with them a bit. The winners were the woman represented as Elyseba, and the merchant woman, Cydavia. Thanks to both of you for allowing me to portray you by the descriptions and character traits you suggested to me.

Also thanks to Peder the scroll merchant (Peder Wagtskjold at Dreamhaven Books in Minneapolis, MN), who has had a (print) death threat hanging over his head since the World Fantasy Convention, New Orleans, thanks to That Book: Yes, it was a nasty death, but you *did* ask for it. At least, you can't say you weren't warned . . . Hope the wake is a good one.

The exciting exploits of . . .

The Empty Throne

In a small, remote village, Xena and her protégée, Gabrielle, make a stunning discovery: all of the men in town have disappeared without a trace. What mysterious and malevolent force is at work? Strange magic? Godly might? Xena must uncover the truth before it's *her* turn to disappear . . .

The Huntress and the Sphinx

When Xena and Gabrielle are asked to rescue a group of kidnapped children, Xena realizes that no one is strong enough to defeat the kidnapper. For who can challenge the power and knowledge of the almighty Sphinx?

All-new, original adventures from
Boulevard Books!